SENSATIONAL
SCIENTISTS

SENSATIONAL
SCIENTISTS

The Journeys and Discoveries of
24 Men and Women of Science

Barry Shell

RAINCOAST BOOKS

Vancouver

Sensational Scientists is an updated and expanded version of *Great Canadian Scientists* (Polestar, 1997) by Barry Shell.

Raincoast Books gratefully acknowledges the ongoing support of the Canada Council for the Arts; the British Columbia Arts Council; and the Government of Canada through the Department of Canadian Heritage Book Publishing Industry Development Program (BPIDP).

Raincoast Books
9050 Shaughnessy Street
Vancouver, British Columbia
Canada V6P 6E5
www.raincoast.com

In the United States:
Publishers Group West
1700 Fourth Street
Berkeley, California
USA 94710

LIBRARY AND ARCHIVES CANADA CATALOGUING IN PUBLICATION

Shell, Barry, 1951-
    the journeys and discoveries of 24 men and women of scientists / by Barry Shell.

    Previously published under title: Great Canadian scientists.
    Includes index.
    ISBN 1-55192-727-6

    1. Scientists—Canada—Biography—Juvenile literature.
2. Science—Canada—Juvenile
literature. I. Shell, Barry, 1951- . Great Canadian scientists. II.Title.
Q141.S53 2005   j509'.2'271   C2005-902491-7

LIBRARY OF CONGRESS CATALOGING-IN-PUBLICATION DATA

Shell, Barry.
    the journeys and discoveries of 24 men and women of science / by Barry Shell.
    p. cm.
    Rev. ed. of: Great Canadian Scientists. 1997.
    Includes index.
    1. Scientists—Canada—Biography—Juvenile literature. 2. Discoveries
in science—Juvenile literature. I. Shell, Barry. Great Canadian scientists. II. Title.
Q141.S299 2005   509'.2'271—dc22   2005014404

Illustration and Design by Warren Clark

Printed and bound in Canada.
1 2 3 4 5 6 7 8 9 10

Table of Contents

Acknowledgements

First I'd like to thank the 24 marvellous scientists who agreed to be interviewed for this book. They gave their time freely because of their belief in the importance of conveying a love of science to the next generation. I am indebted to the patient folks at Raincoast, especially Michelle Benjamin and Derek Fairbridge as well as literary agent Carolyn Swayze. Without their expert marketing, editorial, and business talents, this book would never have become a reality.

I must also acknowledge the financial support of Canada's Natural Sciences and Engineering Research Council. They funded some of the biographical research. Much of this book is available on the website www.science.ca through a series of NSERC PromoScience grants.

Thanks to my wife Dorinda Neave and our children Sam and Davina for their patience, love and support during this project.

I especially want to thank all the people over the years who have worked with me on this project: Suzanne Bastedo, Simon Claret, David Clifford, Mark Bentley Cohen, Marvin Entz, Kyle Kirkwood, David Ritter, Gordon Ross, Alina Smolyansky, Jeff Steinbok, Heather Washburn, Ian Wojtowicz, Derek Yip, and Danny Yoo.

All photographs by Barry Shell or provided by the individual scientists, except for images of galaxy NGC 4261 (p. 79) from the Hubble telescope by Holland Ford and Laura Ferrerese (Johns Hopkins University); image of galaxy NGC 4258 (p. 82), by Soren Larsen, Lick Observatory; the photograph of John Polanyi (p. 126) by Brian Willer, Macleans; and the photo of Melanie Laird (p. 183) provided by Barbara Laird.

Barry Shell
Vancouver, March 2005

Introduction

Pursuing Science

Why pursue science as a profession? What is it that inspired the 24 scientists profiled in this book to follow careers in science? It's not money or fame; it's something else. Take a few minutes to look at the quotes at the beginning of each chapter. In their own words, these messages are what each scientist wants you to understand, above anything else. Look at what they say: They talk about doing your best, questioning authority, experimenting, tuning your mind, finding the essence and discovering something new about how our own world and the universe at large work.

How *does* the universe work? Where does it start? Where does it end? What is energy? Where does it come from? The people in this book strive to answer such questions. They want to understand how two brown-eyed parents can have a blue-eyed child, why some copper compounds become superconductors, or what's in the plant some Amazon tribes use to cure depression. It's not enough to know it works; they want to know *why* it works. And it's not even enough to know why it works; they need to know deep down what makes the "why" happen.

To these people, there's much more to life than making money for day-to-day existence. Sure, they want good food, clothes and cars, but that's not enough. The goal these scientists seek is not something that money can buy — at least, not directly.

Science, like a giant edifice, is built of countless bricks of knowledge. Where do the bricks come from? You can't go to Home Depot and buy these building blocks. In fact, they are free. All the knowledge so far created by science is out there for anyone to use, free. It's published in journals or patents, available in libraries or on the web for anyone to read. New scientific research is always made available freely so that other scientists can take the many ideas, theories, facts and observations and build upon them with more research. This is how science works. What's more, scientists must always question existing theories, push their limits and test them. In other words, they must test the bricks to make sure they will support new rows of bricks above them. It's this questioning, this quest for new knowledge that drives the scientists in this book.

What scientists are really after is a feeling — the feeling that they've discovered something new, something that no human being has ever seen, felt, thought or known before, an essential principle of nature. That is why they pursue science. Anyone can apply himself or herself and work hard to make a lot of money in any sort of job, but very few can discover something truly new, such as the notion that four sugar molecules write the genetic code, or that energy is equivalent to mass. These are profound ideas that shape our world. This kind of discovery goes beyond attaining the "good life." It changes life itself. Scientific discoveries change society and culture. They are the essence of knowledge and creation, and they open doors. It is the search for these essential ideas that makes up the currency of science, the building blocks of the edifice, the ultimate goal of the people in this book, the reason to "do" science.

If you want to question what everyone accepts as true, if you are thrilled by discovering something totally new, if you have ever wondered "how" and "why," then read on.

What Is It about Science?

The thing I like about science is the way you can just add A + B and get C in a predictable way, at least most of the time. In a world so confusing, so unfair at times and often so incomprehensible in so many ways, science can be a comfort. I've always liked science. It made sense to me as a kid. I wasn't a superstar in sports, but I won first place at the local science fair. In university I majored in organic chemistry because of all the wonderful glassware I could play with. It was fun mixing up smelly chemicals to see what happened. I enjoyed watching beautiful, pure crystals appear as if by magic from a saturated solution.

Science and technology dominate today's society in many ways. Wherever you live, nearly everything you do, eat, wear, hear or see is brought to you through scientific discoveries. But how much do you know about these modern-day wonders that rule your life? This book can explain a lot of it.

Science is not perfect. While it can answer plenty of questions, there are many areas where science cannot help at all. For example, when it comes to feelings and aspects of life such as personal relationships, politics, morals, ethics, beliefs or metaphysics, science cannot be counted on to solve our problems. In fact, science may create as many problems as it solves. While science has contributed much that helps the world, it also produces things that can cause harm: nuclear bombs, pollution and eugenics are just a few examples. Even so, I cannot help being fascinated by science and the people who do it. The greatest enjoyment in my work has come from those brief moments, while doing research or interviewing a scientist, when I have found myself saying, "That's amazing!" or "So *that's* how it works!"

People sometimes ask me, "Why does it matter? Why should I care about these scientists and what they've done? What practical value is there in science?" Real-world applications are important, but almost all the scientists in this book did not plan their experiments with a view to making something useful. Asking one of these scientists "What's it good for?" would be like asking a great artist the classic question about a masterpiece: "Will it match the sofa?" In a purely practical sense, great science, like great art, isn't good for anything, unless you consider exploring the limits of human genius and creative expression a good thing or you value pushing forth the boundaries of human understanding of the natural world.

Practical applications of science often come long after the scientific discovery itself, which usually has no initial practical value. In 1917, when Albert Einstein first came up with the concept of stimulated emission of light, the basis for lasers, neither he nor anyone else had any idea how it could be used. (At that time, electric light bulbs were still just catching on!) It wasn't until 1960 that Theodore Maiman made a working laser. Even then, people had few ideas about its use, yet today every household contains many lasers in CD players, printers and pointers, to name just a few applications.

Sometimes, just knowing a scientific fact can be a good thing. For instance, it's nice to know there are such things as black holes out there in the universe, even though at this moment such knowledge is of no practical use. The concept of a black hole is enough to inspire thoughts and daydreams on any number of other subjects. Science charges one's imagination with ideas. That's what is so appealing about it.

At its best, science also teaches you to be critical — not "critical" as in judging other people, but in the sense of assessing information to help you to form opinions and reach conclusions about the world around you. It encourages you to question, to examine everything you know, over and over again. The scientists in this book frequently told me how important it was to question science itself. Perhaps this built-in quality of science — the ongoing questioning and criticizing — is what attracted me as a child; it certainly remains appealing to me as an adult. By asking questions, never taking anything for granted and always reviewing your assumptions, you can improve your knowledge and understanding of yourself, of others and of everything around you. To me, that is the essence of the scientific method.

Profiles

It's great to learn new things and form new ideas about how nature works, but to me the people who do science are always at least as interesting as the discoveries they make. It was fun interviewing these 24 scientists. For a few hours I had their full attention while they talked about what they loved: science! Most of them are great teachers and I always came away amazed by something. Interviewing Hubert Reeves, I learned about dark matter and dark energy and that the universe we

feel and see makes up only five percent of what's out there. Incredible!

It was difficult to decide which scientists to approach for this book. I wanted to interview women as well as men. It was also important to represent many different scientific disciplines and, above all, it was essential to find the most famous scientists — Nobel Prize winners, if possible. Some of the interviews were done because certain scientists visited Vancouver, British Columbia, where I live in Canada. Partly by planning and partly by chance, the profiles evolved.

I had noticed over the years that many popular-science books focused only on the science. For this book, I wanted to find out not only how the science was done, but also something about the people behind the science. The interview questions were designed to bring that out as much as possible.

How This Book Is Organized

Throughout the text you will see words in **boldface**, or thick type. That means the word is explained in the glossary at the back of the book. The chapters in this book contain eight sections headed as follows.

Personal Info

This section has all the vital statistics about the scientists: when and where they were born, if they are alive or dead, where they lived, learned and worked, et cetera. When the scientists in this book were interviewed they were asked, "If you had one message to give to the reader, what would it be?" That message can be found in a quote right near the portrait of the scientist at the beginning of each chapter. They were also asked for the name of a favourite piece of music; to get the full effect of this book and a window on the scientist's mind and emotions, try to play a recording of his or her musical selection as you read.

His/Her Story

Here is your chance to share a dramatic moment in the life of the scientist. Feel what it's like to be out on a field trip, to work in a laboratory, to make a huge discovery or to win the Nobel Prize.

The Young Scientist

What were the scientists like as kids? Were they interested in science? Did something happen that made them become scientists? This is where you find out.

The Science

This section contains an explanation of the kind of science they do. Graphics with supporting text bubbles explain their primary research effort or greatest discovery. You will also learn why the work is important.

So You Want to Be a …

If you are thinking of a career in this particular scientific field, what should you expect? In this section the scientist gives personal impressions and advice. You might also learn how much education is required, how many years it takes and how much you might expect to earn, as well as the various possible job paths for that scientific field.

Activity

Here is a chance for you to be a scientist, too. Almost every chapter has a science experiment or an activity you can try. I hope you will discover something about the natural world, just like a real research scientist does.

Mystery

Every scientist in the book was asked, "If you had to think of a problem in your field that the next generation might solve, what would it be?" These are the big mysteries. Maybe some day you will solve one of them through your own research efforts.

Explore Further

At the end of each chapter is a list of suggested reading material, including scientific review papers, books and websites where you can learn more about the science or the scientist. This is where you can get started on your own personal quest to change the world, perhaps by discovering something essential that could alter society and the way we interact with all that is around us — something far beyond what money can buy.

Sid Altman

Molecular Biologist
Discovered catalytic RNA (*ribo*nucleic *a*cid),
for which he won the Nobel Prize in 1989.

His Story

The year is 1970 and it's an unusually warm June day. Sid Altman is worried. He has no job prospects and little to show for a year of work in Francis Crick and Sydney Brenner's laboratory in Cambridge, England. Crick is the co-discoverer of DNA (*d*eoxyribo*n*ucleic *a*cid), the molecule that encodes the genetic information that tells **cells** how to function and grow. It's an incredible honour for Altman to have been invited to this famous laboratory; at the moment, it's probably the best place in the world for genetic research. But Altman has only two weeks left before he must leave, and he has no idea where he will go or what he will do next.

He is working on mutant cells with malfunctioning **t-RNA** (transfer ribonucleic acid), a substance that is part of the system in a cell that decodes instructions in DNA. DNA and RNA are long, twisty, chainlike molecules. (For more information about these, see the profile of Michael Smith on page 145.) For about the thousandth time, Altman picks up a glass plate on which there is a thin layer of gel. But this plate is special: he is trying a new experiment, something no one has ever tried before. If he can just isolate a special type of RNA called "precursor-RNA," it will explain a lot about the process of reading the **genetic code** from a strand of DNA.

After putting a few drops of material prepared from mutant cells onto the gel, Altman places the plate into a strong electric field. This technique, called **electrophoresis**, is a standard method for separating chemical compounds. The electric field causes different compounds to move across the gel at different speeds. Altman waits several hours, then he lays photographic film on top of the gel. Tiny amounts of radioactive **tracer atoms** in the RNA emit **X-rays** that will leave characteristic bands on the film.

With a friend, Altman takes this latest piece of film into the darkroom to develop it. Within minutes the two young scientists both see the same thing. It's just a white splotch on the negative, but it gives Altman one overwhelming thought: "Now

> **Don't worry if things change. Just do what you do best.**
>
> —Sid Altman

PERSONAL INFO

Born
May 7, 1939, Montreal, Quebec

Residence
New Haven, Connecticut

Family Members
Father: Victor Altman
Mother: Ray
Children: A boy and a girl

Character
Modest, quiet, loyal

Favourite Music
Mozart's Clarinet Concerto

Title
Sterling Professor of Molecular, Cellular and Developmental Biology

Office
Biology Department, Yale University, New Haven, Connecticut

Status
Working

Degrees
Bachelor of science (physics), Massachusetts Institute of Technology, 1960
Doctorate (biophysics), University of Colorado, 1967

Awards
Nobel Prize in chemistry (Swedish Royal Academy of Sciences), 1989

Rosenstiel Award for Basic Biomedical Research, 1989
U.S. National Institutes of Health Merit Award, 1989
Yale Science and Engineering Association Award, 1990

Mentor
Leonard Lerman, a professor of molecular biology at the University of Colorado, who got him interested in molecular biology and introduced him to Francis Crick and Sydney Brenner.

I know I can get a job." He has taken the first step in a long series of experiments that will bring him fame and success.

Altman worked for one more year in Crick's lab, then became a biology professor at Yale University. His work over the next two decades led to the discovery of catalytic RNA, and today he is still working on aspects of the same **molecular biology** system.

THE YOUNG SCIENTIST

Sidney Altman grew up in the Notre Dame de Grâce suburb of Montreal. As a boy he loved books. He liked sports and writing, too, but the library was one of his favourite places. He read widely, from novels to books on sports and science. "I read everything I could get my hands on," he remembers.

When he was 12 years old someone gave him a book called *Explaining the Atom,* by Selig Hecht. The book showed Altman science's power to predict things. From then on he was a confirmed scientist. "I wasn't interested in biology at the time. I liked **nuclear physics**," he recalls today.

One Saturday afternoon, when Altman was still in high school, a friend asked, "Why don't you come with me to McGill? I'm going to take the American SAT exams." These Scholastic Aptitude Tests are a required part of any application to study at an American university. Altman had always thought he would stay in Canada and enrol at McGill University in Montreal, but on a whim he wrote the SAT and he and his friend both

He read widely, from novels to books on sports and science. "I read everything I could get my hands on," he remembers.

applied to the Massachusetts Institute of Technology (MIT) near Boston, Massachusetts. As it turned out, Altman got in, but his friend did not.

Altman's family had to scramble to get the money together to send him to this great school, and he wasn't even sure he wanted to go. There was a big debate in the Altman household. But within three weeks at MIT Altman knew he wanted to stay; he was impressed by the high calibre of the students and he really enjoyed living away from home.

He received his bachelor of science (BSc) degree from MIT, then went to the University of Colorado Medical School in Boulder, where he obtained his doctorate (PhD) in molecular biology and met Leonard Lerman, a professor of molecular biology. Lerman was instrumental in helping Altman win a fellowship to work in Crick and Brenner's lab, where Altman began his winning research. After those early discoveries, Altman returned to the United States and became a professor at Yale University.

The Science

Molecular biologists study the thousands of **chemical reactions** that go on inside cells to create and sustain life. Altman specializes in the chemical processes involved in copying information from DNA and using it to make **proteins**, the molecular building blocks of cells. Information is copied from DNA by the molecule RNA. About six different types of RNA are involved in this transcription process.

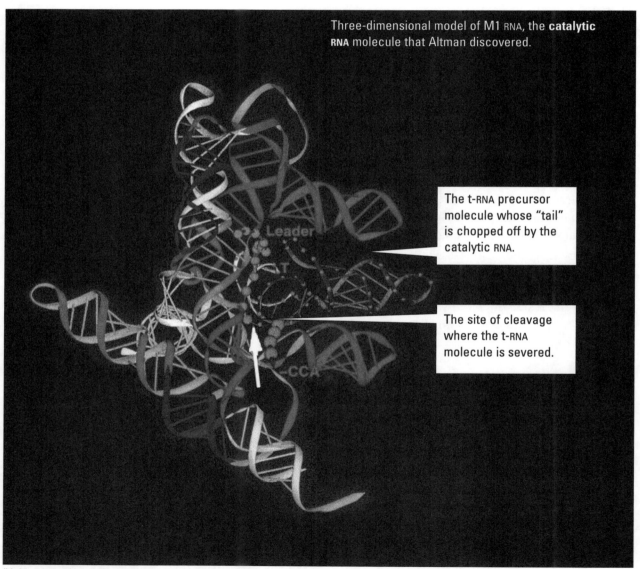

Three-dimensional model of M1 RNA, the **catalytic RNA** molecule that Altman discovered.

The t-RNA precursor molecule whose "tail" is chopped off by the catalytic RNA.

The site of cleavage where the t-RNA molecule is severed.

(Model produced with drawna software by Eric Westhof, Institut de Biologie Moléculaire et Cellulaire, Centre National de la Récherche Scientifique, Strasbourg, France.)

In Crick and Brenner's lab, in about 1970, Altman was investigating part of this complex process. He discovered an **enzyme** called "RNase P" that chops a little "tail" off the end of an intermediate molecule of RNA called "precursor-tRNA." Enzymes are special protein molecules that make chemical reactions go faster, a process called **catalysis**. Enzymes usually do this by holding or bending a molecule in a certain way so that one of its chemical bonds breaks easily. It took about 10 years, but Altman eventually discovered that the enzyme he was studying was not your average enzyme: instead of being a protein like all other enzymes, it was made of two parts — one strand of RNA and one protein. Furthermore, it was the RNA portion that provided the catalysis.

This was a significant discovery, because RNA molecules are much more primitive than protein molecules. Besides offering an explanation for how life might have begun billions of years ago before proteins existed, Altman's discovery also hints at a way to beat a very troublesome primitive life form: the **virus** that causes the common cold. Cold viruses are made of RNA. It may be possible to design catalytic RNA-based vaccines that kill cold viruses by chopping up their RNA.

In recent years Dr. Altman and his research team at Yale University have applied their knowledge of RNA molecular biology to develop a method to inhibit the expression of any **gene** in any organism. They have patented a technique that stops the expression of virus genes in human tissue culture cells. Some day they expect it will work *in vivo* — in people.

The elucidation and understanding of the large role RNA plays in gene expression has expanded greatly since Altman's discovery in the early 1980s. RNA employs a surprising variety of biochemical mechanisms that can result in different protein products coming from the same genetic code. "Tremendous amounts of different kinds of RNAs are now being identified," says Altman. For instance, RNAi (or "interfering RNA") regulates genes in microscopic worms called nematodes, as well as in plants and humans. It can turn genes on or off. These newly discovered powers of RNA are changing our concept of genes. We now know that, with the help of various types of RNA, a single gene can be interpreted in many different ways, leading to expression of various protein products. "It's important, because 20 years ago we predicted this," says Altman. It also helps explain how such a complex organism as a human being can arise from only about 30,000 genes.

It also helps explain how such a complex organism as a human being can arise from only about 30,000 genes.

Careers

So You Want to Be a Molecular Biologist

Career options in molecular biology are expanding rapidly as more and more is learned about the human **genome** and how it affects cellular processes and metabolic pathways. Molecular biologists are relatively well paid. Jobs are available in biotechnology, chemical, pharmaceutical, food, health care, resource, environmental and consulting companies, as well as with government, educational institutions, research institutes and in the forestry and agricultural sectors.

Dr. Altman's advice: "Whatever you do, work hard, and take it seriously. Be prepared for unexpected turns. Do the required work and don't goof off too much." He points out that the goals of teenagers are rarely realized

"Whatever you do, work hard, and take it seriously."

because they evolve as kids learn more. The more education you have, the greater the likelihood you will earn more money. To obtain a job in molecular biology you will need four years of university, followed by about five years of graduate school and a couple of years as a post-doctoral fellow. About ten or twelve years in all.

Altman finds his work interesting and the recognition he has received very satisfying. His main problem is getting enough financial support to do his research. "Everyone has to pay for the war," he says, referring to the tendency of the United States government to spend heavily on its military, "so there is less money available for scientific research."

His final bit of advice to aspiring molecular biologists: "Study chemistry, which I did not do."

Mystery

Altman feels that perhaps the biggest mystery to be solved by the next generation will be the understanding of the human brain.

Explore Further

- Bruce Alberts, et al., *Molecular Biology of the Cell,* fourth edition, Garland Science, 2001.

Pages about Altman on the Nobel Prize website:
nobelprize.org/chemistry/laureates/1989/altman-autobio.html and video interviews,
nobelprize.org/chemistry/laureates/1989/altman-interview.html

ACTIVITY

Objective:

To extract DNA from any living thing.

You need:

- A DNA source (say, 100 millilitres or 1/2 cup of split peas. You can also use an onion, a banana, or even some saliva from your mouth.)
- A large pinch of table salt (less than 1 mL or 1/8 teaspoon)
- A cup of cold water
- A blender
- A strainer
- Some detergent (about 15 mL or 1 tablespoon)
- Enzymes (a pinch of meat tenderizer, pineapple juice, or contact lens cleaning solution)
- Alcohol (isopropyl, ethyl, or 70-95% rubbing alcohol)
- A toothpick

What to do:

1. Put the peas, salt and water into a blender and blend on "high" for 15 seconds. This breaks all the cells.
2. Pour the pea mixture through a strainer into another container, such as a measuring cup.
3. Add liquid detergent and swirl to mix. Let the mixture sit for five or 10 minutes.
4. Pour the mixture into test tubes or other small glass containers, each about one-third full.
5. Add a pinch of enzymes to each test tube/container and stir gently. Be careful! If you stir too hard, you'll break up the DNA, making it harder to see.
6. Tilt your test tube/container and slowly pour rubbing alcohol into it, down the side, so that the alcohol forms a layer on top of the pea mixture. Pour until you have about the same amount of alcohol as pea mixture.
7. DNA will crystallize and form right at the boundary of the alcohol layer and the pea-water layer. You can use a wooden toothpick or some other sort of "hook" to draw the DNA into the alcohol and out of the test tube. It should look like long, wet, clumpy threads.

> **❝** *Know how to judge when to persevere and when to quit. If you're going to do something, do it well. You don't have to be better than everyone else, but you ought to do your personal best.* **❞**
>
> —Willard Boyle

PERSONAL INFO

Born
August 19, 1924, Amherst, Nova Scotia

Residence
Wallace, Nova Scotia

Family Members
Father: Ernest Boyle
Mother: Bernice Dewar
Spouse: Betty, landscape artist and community gallery founder
Children: Robert, Cynthia, David, Pamela

Character
Adventurous, clever, curious

Other Interests
Sailing, skiing

Title
Retired Executive Director of Research

Office
Communication Sciences Division, Bell Laboratories, New Jersey

Status
Semi-retired

Degrees
Bachelor of science, McGill University, 1947
Master of science, McGill, 1948
Doctorate (physics), McGill, 1950

Awards
Ballantyne Medal (Franklin Institute), 1973

Morris Lieberman Award (Institute of Electrical and Electronic Engineers), 1974
Progress Medal (Photographic Society of America)
Breakthrough Award (Device Research Conference, IEEE)
Co-winner, C&C Prize (NEC Foundation, Tokyo), 1999
Edwin H. Land Medal (Optical Society of America), 2001

Mentors
His mother, who home-schooled him till grade 9.
Mr. Bailey, a high-school teacher who taught him confidence.
Lester Germer, a Bell Labs supervisor, who introduced him to culture.

Willard S. Boyle

Condensed Matter Physicist
Co-inventor of the charge coupled device, or CCD.

His Story

Bbbrrring, bbbrrring. It's that darn videophone again. These things will never catch on, thinks Willard Boyle as he squirms in his chair before answering, trying to find a position that is comfortable, but he doesn't put his face in view of the camera. It's too early in the morning to be seen and Boyle knows who's calling — his boss, Jack Morton, head of advanced research at Bell Labs in New Jersey and the father of transistor electronics.

It's about 8:30 a.m., a lovely day in early October 1969. From the window Boyle sees beautiful rolling hills; the leaves have not yet taken on their fall colours. Boyle has a big office at Bell's world-famous think-tank and research centre. Fifteen years of brilliant invention, including the first continuous ruby laser, have elevated him to executive director of device development at Bell Labs. But he still has a boss, a very demanding boss, who calls him every morning on that annoying Bell videophone. Reluctantly, he picks up.

"Boyle?"

"Hello, Jack."

"So what happened yesterday?" came the familiar question.

Boyle shifted a little more in his chair.

"I can't see you, Bill," said Morton.

"Right here, Jack."

"So what'd you guys do yesterday?"

"You know, more of the same. We're still working on those new transistors," said Boyle.

"Look, Bill, the other guys are doing great stuff with magnetic bubbles. It's terrific. What are you semiconductor guys doing? The heck with transistors. Try and come up with something different. I'll call tomorrow." And he hung up.

Boyle thought about it for a while and then called another physicist down the hall, George Smith, to ask him to drop by after lunch. For the rest of the morning Boyle worked on other things.

After lunch, George went to Boyle's office and they brainstormed at the blackboard. They worked on an idea for handling little pockets of charge in a silicon matrix in a way that was similar to the popular notions of moving microscopic

THE YOUNG SCIENTIST

In the late 1920s, when Boyle was about three, his family moved from Nova Scotia to Quebec, where his dad was the resident doctor for a logging community called Chaudiere, about 350 kilometres north of Quebec City. Instead of a car, they got around by dog sled. Boyle received no formal education and was home-schooled by his mother until high school.

One evening, when Boyle was about eight years old, his father asked him to go feed the huskies. The dogs made a lot of noise barking, so they lived in a kennel about 100 metres from the house. Boyle was bundled up in a winter parka, given a bucket of dog food and a small kerosene lantern and sent out into the cold, dark night. There was lots of snow and trees and an absolutely black sky, with no moon or stars. The place had no electricity and no electric lights. "It was terrifying to be in the little circle of light from my kerosene lamp, surrounded by the utter cold, black void," says Boyle. "I had this feeling: I'm a person alone, and if I'm going to get through this, there's only one person that's going to do it and that's me." As it turned out he accomplished his task without incident, but the primal fear he felt that night stayed with him all his life.

Boyle's childhood home near Chaudiere, Quebec.

In grade 9 he went to Lower Canada College, a private school in Montreal. The contrast of coming from the backwoods to join the children of the upper class was jarring, but Boyle did very well, partly because of the many books he had read under his mother's guidance.

After high school Boyle joined the Royal Canadian Navy to fight in World War II, but boats made him seasick, so he applied to the Fleet Air Arm of the navy and was sent to England to learn how to land Spitfire fighter planes on aircraft carriers. Boyle was about 19 years old when he found himself piloting one plane among a small squadron of about three other Spitfires; after weeks of practising landings on an imaginary aircraft carrier painted on a conventional runway, the young pilots were now attempting their first landing on a real ship at sea. Boyle watched from the air as, one after the other, his friends crashed their planes onto the flight deck, or missed the boat completely and ditched in the sea. Fortunately, no one was hurt.

Now it was Boyle's turn. He thought back to that cold, dark night in the woods and said to himself, "Well, you're on your own here again. No one is coming to help you. Let's go for it." He made his turn onto final approach, set up his glide path and headed directly for the large white stripes on the deck. Nobody was more surprised than Boyle when he made a shaky but passable landing. He shut off the engine, raised the cockpit cowling, whipped off his helmet and was wiping the sweat from his brow as he began climbing down when his commanding officer walked up and shouted, "What are you doing, Boyle?"

"I landed it!" yelled Boyle, triumphantly.

"Get back in that cockpit and take off immediately, officer. You do seven more if you want to qualify."

Boyle dutifully completed his pilot training, but the war ended soon after and he never saw active combat. He went on to earn his doctorate in 1950 and three years later he joined Bell Laboratories.

bubbles of **magnetism** around on other kinds of material. They fiddled with some math and drew some sketches on the blackboard showing how this new device could be made. After about an hour and a half Boyle said, "Okay, this looks pretty good."

"We should name it something," said Smith.

"Well, we've got a new device here. It's not a transistor, it's something different," said Boyle.

"It's got charge. And we're moving the charge around by coupling potential wells," said Smith.

"Let's call it a charge coupled device," said Boyle.

"Sure, 'CCD.' That's got a nice ring to it."

Researchers and colleagues pooh-poohed Boyle and Smith's idea, saying it would never work. Remember, at this point it was only a theory, a bunch of equations and diagrams on a blackboard. But the pair decided to take the plans to the shop down the hall to see if the device could be made. Some months later it *was* made, and it worked exactly as expected.

Soon afterwards, Boyle presented a paper about the CCD invention at a conference in New York on "The Future of Integrated Circuits" and, as he says, "All hell broke loose." The phone started to ring with calls from people and companies anxious to learn more. One of the calls was from Boyle's boss, Jack Morton.

"I guess there's probably a future in this semiconductor IC thing after all," said Morton, and that was all the praise Boyle was going to get from him.

In the succeeding years Boyle and Smith went on to win many awards for the device that is at the heart of virtually every camcorder, digital camera and telescope in use today.

The Science

Boyle's branch of science is called **solid state physics** or condensed matter physics, and it involves the behaviour of materials that are solid — things such as crystals, metals and rocks. In particular, he worked on semiconducting materials such as the element silicon.

Boyle's major contributions include the first continuously operating ruby laser, which he invented with Don Nelson in 1962. Ruby was the first material ever made to produce laser light, and ruby lasers are now used for tattoo removal, among other things. Before Boyle's invention, lasers could only give short flashes of light. He was also awarded the first patent (with David Thomas) proposing a semiconductor injection laser. Today, semiconductor lasers are at the heart of all compact disc (CD) players and recorders, but when Boyle patented the idea nobody had even dreamed of CDs. Stereo hi-fi (or high fidelity) records were the new thing.

In 1962 Boyle became director of space science and exploratory studies at Bellcomm, a Bell subsidiary providing technological support for the Apollo space program of the U.S. National Aeronautics and Space Administration. While with NASA, Boyle helped work out where astronauts should land on the moon. In 1964 he returned to Bell Labs and switched from research to the development of electronic devices, particularly integrated circuits, which are now essential building blocks in telecommunications and electronics in general.

Despite all these great achievements, Boyle is

Willard Boyle (left) and George Smith with the first CCD camera at Bell Labs.

best known as co-discoverer of the charge coupled device. Besides their use as image sensors, CCDs can be used as computer memory, electronic filters and signal processors. As imaging devices they have revolutionized astronomy; virtually every large telescope, including the Hubble Space Telescope, uses CCDs because they are about 100 times more sensitive than photographic film and work across a much broader spectrum of **wavelengths** of light. CCDs have created entirely new industries (for example, video cameras and camcorders). To this day, Boyle and Smith continue to receive awards for their invention.

Boyle's major contributions include the first continuously operating ruby laser.

In 1975, Boyle returned to research as executive director of research for Bell Labs' Communications Sciences Division in New Jersey, where he was in charge of four laboratories until his retirement in 1979. Since then he has served on the research council of the Canadian Institute of Advanced Research and the Science Council of the Province of Nova Scotia.

At the heart of many camcorders and digital cameras is a charge coupled device (CCD), typically about a square centimetre in size.

Light in the form of incoming photons enters through the lens of the camera and falls onto the surface of the CCD chip, often passing through a colour filter array. This generates free **electrons** in the silicon of the CCD, more where the light is brighter and fewer where it is less intense. These electrons collect in little packets created by the **geometry** of the silicon and surrounding electrical circuitry, laid out in a two-dimensional grid on the chip. Typical CCD chips have from one to five million such packets of charge, which can also be pictured as buckets on a conveyor belt.

The CCD operates on the principle of charge coupling. The packets of charged electrons can be moved one row at a time by varying the voltage of adjacent rows, thereby creating a potential well that couples two rows and causes the charge to move over.

Imagine buckets on conveyor belts catching falling rain, to represent photons of light. Each bucket (packet) contains a different amount of water (charge), depending on how much rain fell on that part of the array. The buckets are shifted in an orderly fashion to a collecting row, then to a final measuring device at the front. In this way the quantity of water in each bucket is counted. In a typical CCD this can happen very fast: about 30 times per second for every one of millions of "buckets" on the CCD.

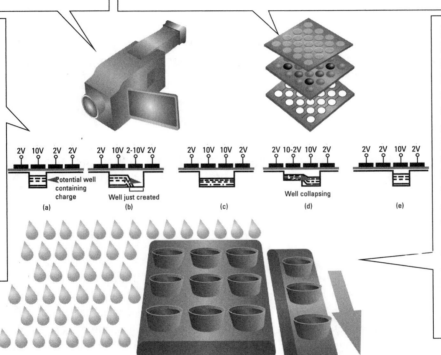

Modern CCDs have colour filters (red, green, blue) arranged in a pattern over the chip so that colour images can be collected. The output of the CCD is a string of numbers that define the intensity and the colour of light over the entire image. A computer or camcorder can store these numbers or use them to recreate the image on any kind of viewing screen or printer.

In recent years, complementary metal oxide semiconductor (**CMOS**) imagers are replacing CCD chips in some imaging devices. These are not based on the CCD principle but are rectangular arrays of individually addressable pixels. CMOS is the dominant technology for all microchip manufacturing, so CMOS image sensors are cheaper to make. In addition, supporting circuitry can be incorporated onto the same device in a single manufacturing process. CMOS sensors also have the advantage of lower power consumption and better infrared sensitivity, or heat imaging, than CCDs. However, for many high-end cameras and camcorders a CCD is still preferred because of its sharper, cleaner images for most photographic applications.

ACTIVITY

Objective:

To measure the presence and properties of invisible infrared **radiation**.

You need:

- An ordinary electric household clothes iron
- A piece of clear glass about 30 centimetres square, for example, from a picture frame
- A sheet of polyethylene, such as a clear plastic bag
- Some heavy-duty aluminum foil
- A weather thermometer, plain or digital
- Something round, such as a basketball, balloon or salad bowl

What to do:

Make a curved, bowl-shaped mirror (a spherical mirror) by shaping some aluminum foil on the round object you've chosen; if it's a bowl, turn it over and shape the foil on the bottom. Try to keep the foil as smooth as possible. It should be about 25 centimetres in diameter.

Turn the iron on high and set it safely at one end of a table. Set up the thermometer about 40 centimetres from the iron, with the bowl-shaped aluminum mirror behind it so that the open part of the bowl faces the iron and the bulb of the thermometer is at the focus of the bowl.

The rays of invisible **infrared light** coming from the iron hit the curved back of the mirror, then reflect and converge on a spot a few centimetres in front of the centre of the mirror. That's where the bulb of the

thermometer or sensor from a digital thermometer should be.

Try the thermometer bulb or sensor in a few different places and watch the temperature reading. You should be able to find a spot that's a bit warmer. That is the focus. Once you set it up, do not touch or move the bulb of the thermometer or the sensor for the duration of the experiment. Do not move the iron, either.

After everything is set up, wait about five or 10 minutes until the temperature of the thermometer is steady. Write down this temperature as the basic warm temperature. Now place something solid in between the iron and the thermometer, for example a cereal box — anything that is opaque to light. Wait about 10 minutes or until the temperature stabilizes. It should be lower by about one or two degrees Centigrade.

Now place a sheet of glass between the iron and the thermometer assembly. Wait again for 10 minutes or until the temperature stops changing.

Now try a sheet of polyethylene plastic, wait 10 minutes and write down the temperature.

Make a table showing the temperature for each of the conditions: nothing, blocked, glass, polyethylene. Which material, glass or plastic, has a higher temperature? (Hint: Polyethylene absorbs infrared light less than glass).

Key point: heat can be transferred by invisible rays called infrared (IR) radiation. Some materials may be transparent to visible light but block IR. Glass is one of these, so a glass greenhouse traps radiant heat or IR radiation. Earth's **atmosphere** also traps IR.

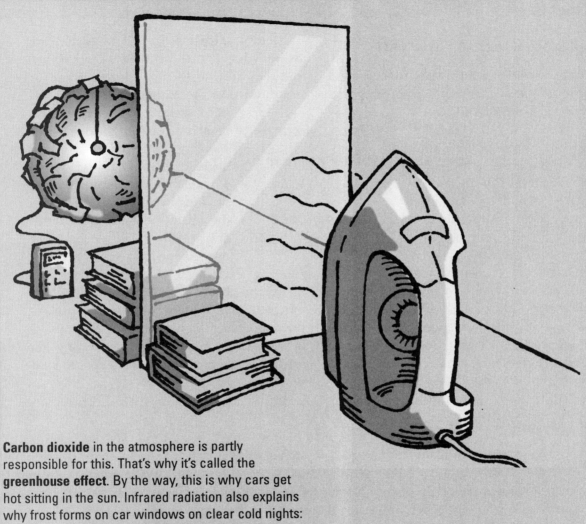

Carbon dioxide in the atmosphere is partly responsible for this. That's why it's called the **greenhouse effect**. By the way, this is why cars get hot sitting in the sun. Infrared radiation also explains why frost forms on car windows on clear cold nights: the radiation of IR from the car windows to the deep cold space of the night sky cools the windows faster than the surrounding air, and so water vapour in the air condenses on the windows as frost.

Careers

So You Want to Be a Physicist

It takes about as many years to become a physicist as any other professional, such as a lawyer or a medical doctor — approximately 10 years of schooling. Many opportunities exist for physicists beyond what we conventionally imagine a physicist would do. A perfect example of this is the analysis of stock markets by theoretical physicists — potentially a way to make a lot of money, too.

It takes about as many years to become a physicist as any other professional.

Physicists can apply their knowledge of mathematics and of how physical systems behave to infer information about stocks, biology, medicine, drug interactions and many other phenomena in the world around us.

Hourly average wages of physicists are typically higher than national average wages, and they are usually also above average for occupations in the natural and applied science sectors. Wages of professionals in the physical sciences have grown at an above-average rate in recent years. Unemployment fell for people working in the physical sciences during the 1990s and early 2000s and is at about two percent right now, so one has a good chance of getting a job as a physicist.

Typical physics careers include specialties in electronics, communications, aerospace, remote sensing, biophysics, nuclear physics, optics, plasma physics, solid state physics, astrophysics, **cosmology** or experimental physics.

Mystery

Boyle expects that many cosmological mysteries will yield their secrets due to the superior imaging power of CCDs, which are now used in virtually every telescope. "We're going to see much greater understanding of the origin of our universe by having the ability to see things that are eight billion light-years away," he says. "The mother of all mysteries is the origin of the universe."

Explore Further

- James R. Janesick, *Scientific Charge-Coupled Devices*, SPIE Press Monograph, vol. PM83, 2001.

Bell Labs website:
www.bell-labs.com/project/feature/archives/ccd/

Bertram Neville Brockhouse

Nuclear Physicist
Won the Nobel Prize in 1994 for designing the triple-axis neutron spectroscope to investigate condensed matter.

His Story

On an ordinary Wednesday morning in October 1994, Bert Brockhouse gets out of bed at his usual time, about 6:45 a.m. As he stretches a bit to loosen the overnight aches of his 76-year-old body, he sees the little red light blinking on the answering machine.

"Who could have called in the middle of the night?" he wonders, as he presses the play button. He listens to a voice announcing that the call is from Stockholm, Sweden: "B. N. Brockhouse and C. G. Shull have been selected as recipients of the 1994 Nobel Prize for physics." Brockhouse is stunned. For a moment he thinks, "Oh, that's interesting," but then he realizes, "I *am* B. N. Brockhouse!" He calls his wife Doris to listen to the tape with him.

The rest of the day is filled with phone calls, telegrams and interviews for Brockhouse, who had been retired. The next year is one of travel, awards, banquets and lectures. Brockhouse is simply beamed out of quiet retirement. In his annual Christmas letter to friends that year, after describing all the festivities in Stockholm, he writes, "If anyone cares, we got a new car in the summer, a Chrysler Neon."

The origins of Brockhouse's Nobel Prize lie back in 1951. Fresh out of the University of Toronto with a doctorate (PhD) in physics, he sat at his desk in a faded, blue-shingled wartime hut at Chalk River, home of the Atomic Energy Project funded by Canada's National Research Council.

Brockhouse gazed out the window at the snow. It was winter, but he felt warm inside the hut. He just sat there, thinking, mulling things over in his mind. The other night he had been at the home of Donald Hurst, his boss and head of the neutron spectrometer section. They had been reading a 1944 paper about **neutrons** — subatomic particles with no electric charge that, together with protons, make up the nucleus of an **atom**. The existence of neutrons had been verified only about 12

❝ *Your mind is your most valuable survival organ. Learn to tune your mind like a radio, filtering out all the noise and other channels, focusing on one thing.* **❞**

—Bertram Brockhouse

PERSONAL INFO

Born
July 15, 1918, Lethbridge, Alberta

Died
October 13, 2003, Hamilton, Ontario

Residence
Ancaster, Ontario

Family Members
Father: Israel Brockhouse
Mother: Mabel Emily Neville
Spouse: Doris Miller
Children: Anne, Gordon, Ian, James, Beth, Charles
Grandchildren: Eight

Character
Modest, honest, absent-minded, frugal, kind, opinionated

Favourite Music
Gilbert and Sullivan, "A Wandering Minstrel I" from The Mikado, and "I Have A Song to Sing Oh" from Yeomen of the Guard

Other Interests
Family, reading, bridge, computers

Status
Deceased

Degrees
Bachelor of arts (physics and math), University of British Columbia, 1974
Doctorate (physics), University of

Buckley Prize (American Physical Society)
Duddell Medal and Prize (British Institute of Physics and Physical Society)
Centennial Medal of Canada
Fellow, Royal Society of Canada
Companion, Order of Canada
Foreign member, Royal Swedish Academy
Fellow, Royal Society of London
Silver Jubilee Medal
Nobel Prize for physics, 1994

Mentor
Donald Hurst, his boss at the Chalk

years before. Not much was known about them. Brockhouse didn't quite understand the theories in the paper, but he felt it had a lot of interesting ideas. He was supposed to be working on something else, but he couldn't stop thinking about the concepts in that paper and how he could do experiments at Chalk River to try out some of the new theories.

He fiddled with some math on his notepad for a while and then went to the coffee room. As he

THE YOUNG SCIENTIST

In the 1920s, Bert Brockhouse's family moved from Lethbridge, Alberta, to Vancouver, British Columbia. They operated a rooming house in the city's West End and Bert had a paper route to help supplement the family income. He liked fishing and went with his buddies to catch shiners, cod and salmon off the pier at English Bay. He fooled around with radios a lot as a teenager, hanging out at radio repair shops and building homemade radios from designs in popular electronics magazines. After high school, instead of going to university, he worked as a radio repairman. Then World War II came along and he used his radio skills as an electronics technician in the Canadian Naval Reserve.

After high school, instead of going to university, he worked as a radio repairman.

When the war ended, Brockhouse went to the University of British Columbia, majoring in math and physics. After marrying Doris, a film cutter at the National Film Board, he finished his doctorate and the newlyweds moved to Chalk River. Brockhouse spent his working life as a researcher at Chalk River perfecting neutron spectroscopes and their applications. He solved problems controlling the source of the neutron beam; limiting it to neutrons of only one energy; getting rid of background radiation from other experiments in the lab; and problems with the sensitivity of the detectors. The resulting triple-axis neutron spectrometer is now used worldwide to investigate crystal structures.

passed the lab that housed the **radioactive nuclear pile**, a controlled nuclear reaction that emitted one of the most powerful sources of neutrons in the world at the time, he wondered whether he could put it to use. In the coffee room he met Hurst. Brockhouse went up to the blackboard and said, "Don, there's something I'd like to show you." He sketched out some equations on the blackboard. The math described a device they could build that would use a neutron beam as a better type of spectrometer, a kind of flashlight that could probe the mysteries of **crystal structures** and other solids such as metals, minerals, gems and rocks.

The Science

Brockhouse conducted experiments in the physics of solids such as metals and crystals. This kind of physics is called solid state physics. As his tool he used the neutron spectrometer that he developed at Chalk River, which allowed him to look right inside the crystalline structure of solids to find out how solid things like rocks and gems are held together.

Imagine shining a beam of light on an object. Your concept of that object is based on the light reflected from it. But at the atomic level, the wave-

The original triple-axis spectrometer (1959). A spectrometer is a device that measures the angle, wavelength and energy of light or other type of radiation, in this case neutron radiation. The panel of 52 rotary switches in the upper centre of the picture could be preset to go through an energy scan of up to 26 points. A feature of Brockhouse's spectrometer was the way he could vary three angles: the direction of the neutron beam, the position of the specimen, and the angle of the detector. Add to this the ability to vary the energy of the incoming neutrons and the sensitivity of the detector and he had a Nobel Prize-winning creation. (Photo courtesy of AECL)

length of the light beam is "too big." The wavelength (or the "size") of the light from a flashlight is about 7,000 Angstroms (one **Angstrom** is roughly the width of a hydrogen atom, or 10^{-10} metre), while the wavelength of a neutron beam is only around one to four Angstroms. In other words, if you could use a beam of neutron "light" you could see details thousands of times finer than you can see with ordinary light. Incidentally, in the same way, the shorter wavelength of X-rays is what gives them the power to penetrate things and reveal inner details that you cannot see with regular light.

According to Brockhouse, "the virtue of neutrons is you can say a great deal about a material by using a neutron beam." You can work out the distance between atoms, the angle of bonds between atoms, the strength and energy of atomic bonds holding the atoms of a solid together, and much more. All these things are very handy and can be applied to working with metal, rocks, gems and other solid materials. But, fundamentally, Brockhouse was just trying to satisfy his natural human curiosity. He wanted to know what things are made of, what rocks look like inside.

How It Works

Detector. The analyzing crystal, similar to the monochromating crystal, can be tuned to pass only neutrons of particular energies. These neutrons then pass through the analyzing crystal on to the detector, which counts them. By knowing the energy, quantity and angle of the neutrons that go into the specimen and then measuring the energy, quantity and angle of the neutrons that come out, physicists can calculate things about the internal structure of the specimen.

Monochromating crystal. "Monochromating" literally means "making one colour." A special crystal of aluminum was used to separate out neutrons of one particular energy or colour. Knowing the exact colour of the beam going in can tell you more about what is inside the material you are investigating. The beam was then aimed and **collimated** (straightened out by going through a series of slits) before being sent on to the target.

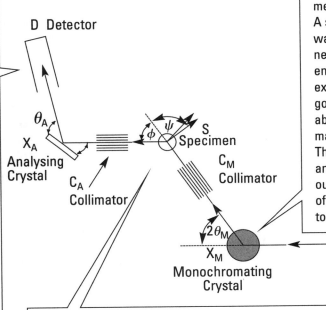

Specimen. The position of the target metal or crystal can be varied on two axes (twirled around sideways or vertically, for instance). The beam of neutrons bounces off the target in different directions that tell something about the atomic structure of the material if they can be detected.

Mystery

Like many retired physicists, Brockhouse liked to explore **metaphysical** ideas — concepts such as spirit, morality, ethics and beliefs. For the last two decades of his life he worked on what he called "The Grand Atlas," a sort of rule book for nature incorporating theories both physical and metaphysical. Brockhouse was a religious man, and his belief in physics theory coexisted with his spiritual beliefs. "Science is an act of faith," he said. Without faith, how can understanding the existence of a neutron help with the larger moral issues in life?

Brockhouse's example of a moral problem is **"Kantian Doom"** — the idea that we are doomed because even though we know that something is bad for us, we do it anyway because everyone else is doing it. Examples might be driving cars, using computers or watching television. Brockhouse believed such problems might require metaphysical solutions, not scientific ones.

Explore Further

- Fritjof Capra, *The Tao of Physics*, fourth edition, Shambhala Books, 2000.

Page about Brockhouse on the Nobel website: www.nobel.se/physics/laureates/1994/ brockhouse-autobio.html
Website for neutron spectroscopy lab in Budapest, Hungary: www.szfki.hu/nspectr/fields.html

ACTIVITY

Objective:

To use a laser to count the number of lines on a compact disc.

You need:

- A laser light source such as a red laser pointer or high school lab laser. Ideally, the wavelength of the laser is known exactly (usually around 665 **nanometres** and written on the laser).
- Any diffraction grating, for example, Mylar "rainbow" wrapping paper, an ordinary audio CD, or a high school diffraction grating of known line number
- A tape measure or ruler
- A table with a simple chemistry equipment stand to mount the laser

What to do:

Set up the laser light source and the target grating (for example, the "rainbow" side of an audio CD) as shown in the diagram opposite. The screen or wall must be perpendicular to the grating on the table. Use a very low angle of incidence for the light source — somewhere around five to 20 degrees. (Keeping a shallow angle lets you ignore angle measurements for the calculations that come later.)

Turn down the lights in the room, switch on the laser and rotate the grating until you get a series of red laser dots on the wall, blackboard, a sheet, or anything perpendicular to the table. You might want to put marks on this screen later when you do the measurements. You may have to rotate the laser in the stand and generally fiddle with things to get it right.

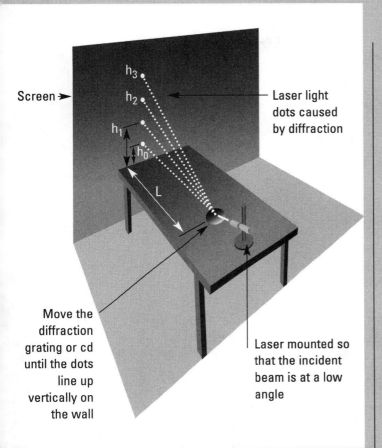

Screen →

h3 •

h2 •

h1 •

h0 •

Laser light
dots caused
by diffraction

L

Move the
diffraction
grating or cd
until the dots
line up
vertically on
the wall

Laser mounted so
that the incident
beam is at a low
angle

The first dot on the wall is called the *specular* dot and is just the direct reflection of the laser beam from the CD. The rest of the dots above it are caused by diffraction, so you start the numbering from the first one of these. The specular dot is the "zero" spot. You might have to adjust the angle of the incoming laser light to get the series of dots to appear. (By the way, you need a laser light source for this experiment because laser light is collimated, which means the light is all nicely straightened out into a solid beam. Note that Brockhouse had to use collimators in his neutron spectrometer. Neither your experiment nor Brockhouse's will work without collimated beams.) After you can see the dots, you need to make a few measurements. First you must establish the baseline, which is the place on the screen that is the same height as the top surface of the CD on the table. Draw the baseline on the wall. Measure the following:

L (the length from the laser spot on the CD to the wall or projection screen.)

h0 (the height from the baseline to the lowest red spot on the wall)

h1 (the height from the baseline to the second red spot on the wall)

h2 (the height from the baseline to the third red spot on the wall)

h3 (the height from the baseline to the fourth red spot on the wall)

And so on for any other dots you want (note: if you only get h0 and h1, that's enough.)

You also need to know either one of these, but not both: λ (lamda, the wavelength of the laser) d (the spacing of the grating)

If you know the number of lines in the diffraction grating (or CD), you can infer the wavelength of the laser light. If you know the wavelength, you can figure out how many lines in the grating. Use the formulas:

$$\lambda = \frac{d\,(h_n^2 - h_0^2)}{2nL^2} \qquad d = \frac{2nL^2\,\lambda}{d\,(h_n^2 - h_0^2)}$$

In Brockhouse's triple-axis spectrometer he could make these measurements in three **dimensions**. He also measured the shift in energy of the neutron beam, which told him more about the vibration of atoms within solids. Using similar techniques, solid state physicists employ beams of radiation to measure physical properties like the spacing of atoms within crystals.

In your experiment, try turning the grating 90 degrees. What happens to the dots on the screen? If it makes you curious about why they form an arc, you might want to find out more about solid state physics.

> **"** *Any high school kid can go out and make fossil discoveries.* **"**
>
> —Robert Carroll

PERSONAL INFO

Born
May 5, 1938, Kalamazoo, Michigan

Residence
Montreal, Quebec

Family Members
Father: John H. Carroll, high school science teacher
Mother: Arvella Mae Wickerham, nurse
Spouse: Anna DiTuri, retired business school teacher
Children: David

Character
Determined, earnest, enthusiastic. Boisterous and lighthearted at times, perhaps bashful as well.

Favourite Music
Puccini's operas *La Bohème* and *Turandot,* much of Brahms, also Fauré's *Requiem*

Other Interests
Singing, hiking and climbing, cross-

Titles
Strathcona Emeritus Professor of Zoology; Curator of Vertebrate Paleontology, Redpath Museum

Office
Redpath Museum, McGill University, Montreal, Quebec

Status
Working

Degrees
Bachelor of science (geology), Michigan State University, 1959
Master of arts (biology), Harvard University, 1961
Doctorate (biology), Harvard, 1963

Awards
Fellow, Royal Society of Canada, 1993

Society of Canada), 2001
Romer-Simpson Medal (Society of Vertebrate Paleontology), 2004

Mentors
His father, who showed him his first fossil and taught him about evolution.
Rolin Baker, director of the museum at Michigan State University where Carroll had summer jobs, who taught him the publish-or-perish rule of academia.
Alfred S. Romer, a Harvard University paleontologist who gave him professional inspiration.
George Simpson, a Harvard professor who taught him the historical aspects of evolution.

Robert L. Carroll

Vertebrate Paleontologist

Recognized and described the oldest known ancestor of all reptiles, birds and mammals, as well as the origins of terrestrial vertebrates and various amphibians such as frogs and salamanders.

His Story

Robert Carroll was relaxing. To an observer it might have appeared that he was working: he was bent over a microscope, pecking away at a fist-sized rock with a tiny pick called a pin vise — a pen-sized tool with a needle-sharp pin clamped into one end. As a graduate student at Harvard in 1961, Carroll's day had been filled with meetings, lectures and seminars and there was nothing he liked more than the exacting yet peaceful chore of exposing fossilized bones. He worked on it for several hours at the end of every day at a desk in the **paleontology** lab, in a pool of light from the microscope. The room was warm and smelled of old stone and varnish. For Carroll, these hours alone with a rock and a pin vise were a kind of meditation.

Sometimes he would listen to music while preparing **fossils**, but he couldn't have distracting daydreams. The work was mentally demanding. Imagine a dentist cleaning teeth: A brief loss of attention could result in a sharp tool slipping and chipping a tooth or cutting a gum. For a paleontologist, such a slip could damage the specimen.

While he worked, Carroll was thinking how each fossil is a unique and highly informative treasure — if it weren't, it wouldn't be worth preparing. He was trying to picture the anatomy of the animal he was holding. What was it like when it was alive millions of years ago? He had to imagine how that related to the broken state of the fossil in his hands. He asked himself, "Where is the surface of the bone likely to continue beneath the surrounding rock? At what angle should I direct the needle so as not to damage the bone I see, or other areas of bone that are still covered?"

The rock he was working on came from Texas. Embedded in the hard, dark shale was a lighter-coloured pattern, a skeleton of a **microsaur**. Carroll was meticulously chipping away the surrounding stone — the matrix — to better identify the bones of the creature. He was trying to figure out whether it was related to the origin of reptiles or of amphibians, the main difference being that amphibians have an early stage during which they live in water. He knew the rock was at least 300 million years old, so this animal had walked the earth 100 million years before dinosaurs appeared. After about a week of chipping and pecking, Carroll was able to see and recognize a number of anatomical features that very clearly distinguished this animal from a reptile.

He was working on this fossil in preparation for a trip to McGill University in Montreal, where he would spend two years studying a collection of fossils discovered in the mid-1800s at Joggins, Nova Scotia, by Sir William Dawson, the first Canadian-born scientist of worldwide reputation. The Joggins find included many groups of primitive amphibians and Dawson believed them to contain the oldest known reptiles, 315 million years old. Carroll wanted to find out whether Dawson's ideas were right.

"With the information I had from the Texas fossil, I was able to recognize the true reptiles of the time, which are actually very similar to some living lizards," says Carroll. He examined the Joggins fossils and picked out reptiles from the numerous animals that lived at that time. This was very important, because the reptiles from Joggins closely match the ancestry of all land animals, including modern lizards, turtles, crocodiles, mammals and birds, as well as the extinct dinosaurs. He eventually discovered that microsaurs, whose name literally means "little lizards," were not lizards or even closely related to reptiles. They were primitive amphibians, but

"With the information I had from the Texas fossil, I was able to recognize the true reptiles of the time, which are actually very similar to some living lizards."

very different from present-day amphibians. As always, Carroll was trying to answer the questions: Where did we come from? How did life evolve?

He studies the anatomy and relationships of Paleozoic and Mesozoic amphibians and reptiles, creatures that lived between 65 and 500 million years ago. He discovered and described the crucial life forms that led to the emergence of vertebrates — animals with backbones — onto land. Recently, he has been integrating paleontology with modern genetics and molecular developmental biology to learn more about how this could have happened.

After graduate school, Carroll began researching fossils of the oldest vertebrates that spent most or all of their life on dry land, in contrast to the earliest amphibians that lived in or very close to the water. Such fossils were part of the Joggins discovery. The fossilized bones of these early terrestrial vertebrates were found inside the stumps of giant lycopods — fernlike trees — rather than in rocks formed in streams, ponds or lakes, where most fossils are found. Carroll showed that the skulls, vertebrae and limbs of these animals were very similar to those of living lizards and that they probably laid their eggs on land. They are the oldest known relatives of all modern reptiles, birds and mammals.

Carroll, with other biologists, also investigated why fish that eventually gave rise to all terrestrial vertebrates originally came onto land. Researchers recognized that the large size (more than a metre long) of early amphibians and their fish ancestor

THE YOUNG SCIENTIST

Like many kids, when Robert Carroll was eight years old, he asked his parents for his very own real dinosaur bone. He was perhaps a bit more serious than most children his age. "I remember saying I wanted either that, or a million dollars to go on an expedition to find one." His father wrote to the chief vertebrate paleontologist at the American Museum of Natural History in New York to explain his son's passion and to ask if there were any spare dinosaur bones not required for research or exhibit. Both father and son were surprised when the left femur (the thigh bone) of an Allosaurus arrived by mail a few weeks later. Allosaurus is a large carnivorous dinosaur and the specimen was from the Morrison formation in Moab, Utah. Years later it would be incorporated into a display in a museum at Michigan State University, but for the young Carroll the fossil bone was a treasure that began a lifelong search for the origins of life on Earth.

Both father and son were surprised when the left femur (the thigh bone) of an Allosaurus arrived by mail a few weeks later.

Carroll was an only child and he grew up on a farm outside Lansing, Michigan. When Robert was five years old, his father brought home a box of fossils from the school where he taught. "I was instantly excited," says Carroll, and he immediately wanted to collect some for himself. He began looking for fossils on the farm by following the horse as it worked the fields. There were not many fossils, but the boy found some. His mom used to take him to gravel pits and there he found more fossils, of plants and marine invertebrates. These he displayed in the family's barn, which he designated the "Mason Museum of Natural History." In his teen years his parents took him on trips to Wyoming and South Dakota, always on fossil-hunting expeditions.

After high school, Carroll went to Michigan State University and earned his bachelor of science (BSc) degree in geology. From there he went to Harvard, where he studied biology and paleontology. After a brief stint in London at the British Museum, he moved to Montreal in 1964 and never returned to live in the United States. He has been the curator of vertebrate paleontology at the Redpath Museum since 1965. One of Canada's oldest museums, the Redpath opened in 1882 to display Sir William Dawson's fossil collections.

Robert Carroll has produced a tremendous amount of work in his lifetime. When asked how he does it, he says, "I never watch TV. I'm reading books and papers all the time — even in bank teller lineups and university meetings." His wife confirms, "His nose is always in a book."

would have enabled them to use the heat of the sun to warm up and stay warm by sunbathing on the shores of ancient oceans. Being warmer, they could be more active, and like modern crocodiles this would make them better at catching fish. To get onto land and back into the water they evolved larger fins, which, over millions of years, gradually evolved into "hands" and feet, very much like those of all later land vertebrates.

Carroll now studies the early history of frogs and **salamanders** and how they evolved from large, clumsy ancient amphibians. One of the most important features of amphibians is the great difference between their aquatic larvae — babies that hatch and live in water — and the adults that live on land. He has been examining the fossilized larvae of ancient amphibians and has shown how one group evolved toward salamanders by specializing their way of feeding in the water and delaying their emergence onto land. A second group had a very different pattern of development: It evolved the capacity to mature very quickly and metamorphose to terrestrial adults, as occurs in frogs.

Carroll is writing a book for general audiences that describes the changes in the anatomy and way of life of these animals over the past 365 million years, explaining how the forces of evolution led to the development of all land animals, including amphibians, reptiles, birds, mammals — and ourselves.

The Science

A vertebrate paleontologist studies the fossilized remains of animals with bones. Robert Carroll says, "Paleontology is a very visual science. Even young children can understand that well-preserved fossils represent once-living plants and animals." Fossils provide the basic evidence for understanding the history of life on Earth. They show that in the past, animals and plants were very different from those living today. And the older the fossils are, the more different they are from modern plants and animals. This gives the investigator an appreciation for both the evolution of life and the overall unity of all living organisms.

The study of paleontology is not just about creatures that died millions of years ago. To understand the nature of fossils one must learn about the anatomy, physiology and genetics of current plants and animals. "To me, this makes paleontology a very unifying profession," says

A paleontologist must be a good draftsperson. When a fossil is found, the bones are usually crushed or disturbed, as shown in the photo of the skull of a Permian microsaur

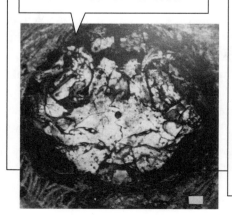

The first step is to draw all the bones as they appear in the rock, then label them. After this, a new drawing is done to reconstruct the skeleton of the original creature based on what we know of the anatomy and physiology of present-day animals. Afterwards, paleontologists can infer details about the animal. This microsaur may have looked like a lizard, but it lived part of its life in the water.

People have been around for a very brief time. This chart, with temperature on the vertical, shows that for most of Earth's history the planet has been more like a tropical greenhouse than an "icehouse." Scientists don't know if we are now in a short period of warming that might end in another ice age in 10,000 years, or if the Earth will gradually warm up to a temperature like that in the age of dinosaurs.

Geological Times (millions of years)

We are here
Past | Future?

Amphibians | Dinosaurs

Warm
Cool

GREENHOUSE | ICEHOUSE | GREENHOUSE | ICEHOUSE

400 | 200 | 0 | +100

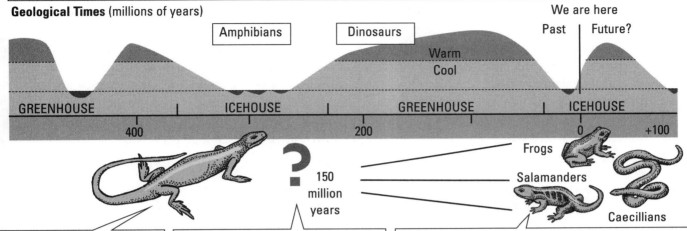

? 150 million years

Frogs
Salamanders
Caecillians

Around 300 million years ago many animals lived on Earth, and countless fossils exist from that period. *Hylonomus lyelli,* shown here, is the oldest known reptile (315 million years).

A mysterious gap in the fossil record of approximately 100 million years exists between any archaic amphibians and the first appearance of fossils of advanced frogs, salamanders and caecilians.

Robert Carroll and his colleagues found the key to the ancestry of frogs and salamanders in fossils of the larval stages of two related families of archaic amphibians with external gills like salamanders, but skulls with very large openings, like those of both frogs and salamanders. Caecilians may have arisen from very elongated microsaurs.

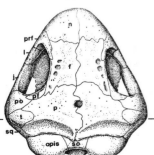

Fossil of a larva of a 300-million-year-old amphibian close to the ancestry of salamanders. Note the external gills labeled "ex-gills" in the drawing of the same creature (above). Also shown: a pin vise used by paleontologists to expose fossilized bones from rock.

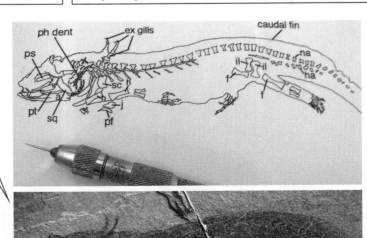

Carroll. Paleontology also requires knowledge of rocks and geology to work out the age of fossils and the nature of the environment in which they lived. This includes knowledge of major changes in Earth's climate and the shifting positions of the continents and the oceans. Ultimately, paleontology provides evidence of our own human ancestry prior to the emergence of written history, and it shows the factors that may explain our evolution from primitive, ape-like animals.

Sometimes Carroll gets very excited when he is chipping away the matrix of a fossil, uncovering something never seen before. Preparation may seem a mechanical chore, but it's the way paleontologists scientifically test their hypotheses. Exposing fossilized bones may help determine the mechanics of a joint, or relationships the animal had with other living things in its environment. It shows the ways of life of extinct animals. Other scientists use telescopes, **gene** sequencing or rockets to Mars, all of which involve mechanical contrivances. Paleontologists use sharp needles.

Time Scales

An understanding of paleontology cannot come without an appreciation for the scale of geological time compared with historical or human time. Compare these approximate times:

Grade school:	12 years
A human lifetime:	80 years
A country's existence (U.S.A.):	200 years
A religion (Christianity):	2,000 years
All recorded human history:	6,000 years

Historical time above/Geological time below

Existence of humans like us (using tools, art):	50,000 years
Humans diverge from apes:	6,000,000 years ago
Disappearance of dinosaurs	65,000,000 years ago
Vertebrates crawl onto the land:	365,000,000 years ago
Multicellular animals appear:	530,000,000 years ago
Origin of life on Earth:	3,500,000,000 years ago
Formation of Earth:	4,600,000,000 years ago
Origin of the universe:	13,000,000,000 years ago

To put this into perspective, the entire extent of all recorded human history (6,000 years) is little more than one one-thousandth of one percent of the time since the first creatures with backbones crawled out of the sea (365 million years ago).

Careers

So You Want to Be a Paleontologist

Besides chipping away at fossils and identifying them, paleontologists must spend a fair bit of time in the field, looking for fossils. Once found, they must be carefully removed from the site, transported and then prepared. This may require a great deal of research into the biology of the creature and the time period when it lived. Carroll says, "What I like best about vertebrate paleontology is that it provides an excuse for research in almost any aspect of biology." During his four-decade career he has come to know something about every group of vertebrates, and he is now becoming interested in the nature of micro-organisms and how they originated.

"What I like best about vertebrate paleontology is that it provides an excuse for research in almost any aspect of biology."

"I sometimes think of paleontology as being an extension of history, just going on for much longer periods of time and involving a diversity of other organisms besides humans," he says. However, paleontology is really a science because it investigates the natural world, a world that would be out there whether or not there were humans. Science is based on observations, followed by hypotheses to explain those observations. Scientific data may be the positions of stars, or the sequence of the genetic code. For paleontologists, data come in the form of fossils that record changes in the structure of bones and the natural history of life on Earth.

"What sometimes disappoints me, as a career scientist, is that many scientists become so committed to a particular area of research, or a particular way of doing science — either their techniques or their concepts — that they become isolated from other related problems, other periods of time, or other ways of learning about the world around us," says Carroll. As a result, he feels, some scientists are unable to advance either knowledge or understanding as much as they could. Science simply becomes another job, rather than a continuing quest.

Careers in paleontology include being a government paleontologist, a university professor, laboratory scientist, chemical, petrochemical, pharmaceutical or pulp and paper industry staff scientist, petroleum/mining consultant, or a private consulting scientist.

ACTIVITY

Objective:

To collect some fossils.

You need:

- Book about fossils
- Chisel or rock hammer
- Carry bag

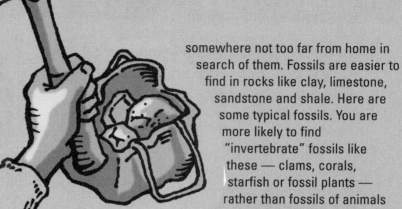

What to do:

First, take a trip to the local library or bookstore and get a book on fossils for your local area so that you will know what they look like and where to look. Fossils do not occur everywhere on the surface of the Earth, but they are common enough that you can probably travel somewhere not too far from home in search of them. Fossils are easier to find in rocks like clay, limestone, sandstone and shale. Here are some typical fossils. You are more likely to find "invertebrate" fossils like these — clams, corals, starfish or fossil plants — rather than fossils of animals with bones, known as vertebrates. Once you find a few fossils you can begin to gather information about what they were like during life and how they are related to plants and animals living today. Try finding pictures of your fossils in library books or on the web.

Mystery

The standard theory of evolution does not explain some things: how generic change occurs, or how specific genetic changes result in specific differences in structure or function. For instance, we still don't know general things such as how life began or how animals and plants originated. We don't know where feathers on birds came from, nor how hair originated on mammals. Only in the last 10 or 20 years, with advances in molecular genetics, have we begun to understand how genes themselves have evolved. Carroll hopes a new generation of molecular developmental paleontologists will, we hope, answer questions about the origins of feathers and hair. They may also find a molecular genetic basis for why we have five digits on our hands and feet. Another paleontological mystery: where did turtles come from? Nobody knows.

Explore Further

- Robert Carroll, *Vertebrate Paleontology and Evolution*, W. H. Freeman & Co., 1987.
- Robert Carroll, *Patterns and Processes of Vertebrate Evolution*, Cambridge University Press, 1997.
- "Palaeontology, The Evolutionary History of Amphibians," *Amphibian Biology*, vol. 4, Surrey Beatty & Sons, 2000.
- *Canadian Journal of Earth Sciences*, vol. 40, April 2003.

The Tree of Life web project: tolweb.org/tree/phylogeny.html

Harold Scott "Donald" MacDonald Coxeter

Mathematician and Geometer
Greatest classical geometer of the 20th century.

His Story

The aroma of antiseptic and crisp sheets mingles with the sooty smell of a small coal-burning fireplace at the end of the infirmary room. Two thirteen-year-old boys are in side-by-side beds, recovering from the flu in their private school's sickroom.

"Coxeter, how do you imagine time travel would work?" asks John Petrie, one of the boys.

"You mean as in H. G. Wells?" says Donald Coxeter, the other boy. H. G. Wells' classic science fiction book, *The Time Machine*, is a popular topic of conversation. Both boys believe time travel will eventually be possible. After a few seconds, Coxeter says, "I suppose one might find it necessary to pass into the fourth dimension." That is the moment when he began forming ideas about hyperdimensional geometries.

Both boys were very bright. They started using the books and games by their beds to play around with ideas of higher dimensional space — spaces and **dimensions** that go beyond the ordinary three dimensions of natural space as we see it. These early musings lead Coxeter to later discoveries about regular **polytopes**, geometric shapes that extend into the **fourth dimension** and far beyond.

> **❝ *I'm a Platonist — a follower of Plato — who believes that one didn't invent these sorts of things, that one discovers them. In a sense, all these mathematical facts are right there waiting to be discovered.* ❞**
>
> —H. S. M. Coxeter

PERSONAL INFO

Born
February 2, 1907, London, England

Died
March 31, 2003, Toronto, Ontario

Family Members
Father: Harold S. Coxeter
Mother: Lucy Gee
Spouse: Hendrina Johanna "Rien" Brouwer
Children: Edgar, Susan
Grandchildren: Six
Great-grandchildren: Six

Character
Obstinate, optimistic

Favourite Music
Bruckner's Ninth Symphony (Third Movement), Te Deum

Other Interests
Art of Escher, novels of Ethel Voynich, plays of George Bernard Shaw

Status
Deceased

Degrees
Bachelor of Arts, Cambridge University, 1929
Doctorate, Cambridge, 1931

Awards
H. M. Tory Medal (Royal Society of Canada), 1950
Fellow, Royal Society of Canada
Fellow, Royal Society of London
Fields Institute/CRM Prize, 1995
Companion, Order of Canada, 1997
Sylvester Medal (Royal Society of London)

Mentor
Professor H. F. Baker at Cambridge University, England.

THE YOUNG SCIENTIST

Soon after he recovered from the flu, Coxeter wrote a school essay on the idea of projecting geometric shapes into higher dimensions. Impressed by his son's geometrical talents and wishing to help the boy's mind develop, his father took him to visit **Bertrand Russell**, the brilliant English philosopher, educator and peace activist. Russell helped the Coxeters find an excellent math tutor who worked with Coxeter, enabling him to enter Cambridge University.

Coxeter was known as H. S. M. Coxeter, though friends and relatives called him Donald. Here's the explanation: At birth he was given the name MacDonald Scott Coxeter, which led to his being called Donald for short. But a god-parent suggested that his father's name should be added, so Harold was added at the front. Then somebody noticed that H. M. S. Coxeter sounded like the name of a ship. They finally changed the names around to Harold Scott MacDonald Coxeter.

At 19, in 1926, before Coxeter had a university degree, he discovered a new regular **polyhedron**, a shape having six **hexagonal** faces at each **vertex**. He went on to study the

At birth he was given the name MacDonald Scott Coxeter, which led to his being called Donald for short.

mathematics of **kaleidoscopes**, which are instruments that use mirrors and bits of glass to create an endlessly changing pattern of repeating reflections. By 1933 he had counted and specified the **n-dimensional** kaleidoscopes ("n-dimensions" means one-dimensional, two-dimensional, three-dimensional, et cetera, up to any number [n] dimensions). This branch of mathematics determines how shapes will behave and how many symmetries they generate when repeatedly reflected in a kaleidoscope.

In 1936 Coxeter received a completely unexpected invitation from Sam Beatty at the University of Toronto, offering him an assistant professorship there. Coxeter's father, foreseeing World War II, advised his son to accept the offer. As Coxeter said, "Rien and I were married and we sailed off to begin our life together in the safe country of Canada."

Coxeter lived to the age of 96, working and lecturing right until his death. He attributed his long life to a strict vegetarian diet and he did 50 push-ups every day. He said, "I am never bored."

The Science

Geometry is a branch of mathematics that deals with points, lines, angles, surfaces and solids. One of Coxeter's major contributions to geometry was in the area of **dimensional analogy**, the process of stretching geometrical shapes into higher dimensions. He is also famous for "Coxeter groups," the inversive distance between two disjoint circles (or spheres).

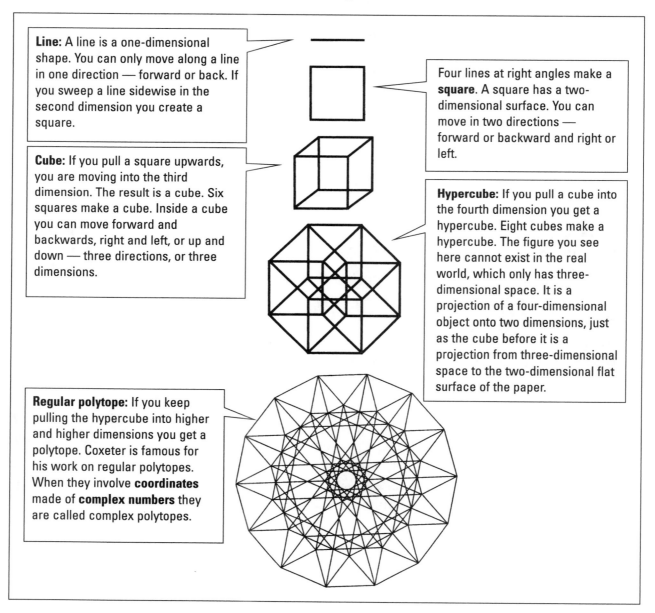

Line: A line is a one-dimensional shape. You can only move along a line in one direction — forward or back. If you sweep a line sidewise in the second dimension you create a square.

Cube: If you pull a square upwards, you are moving into the third dimension. The result is a cube. Six squares make a cube. Inside a cube you can move forward and backwards, right and left, or up and down — three directions, or three dimensions.

Regular polytope: If you keep pulling the hypercube into higher and higher dimensions you get a polytope. Coxeter is famous for his work on regular polytopes. When they involve **coordinates** made of **complex numbers** they are called complex polytopes.

Four lines at right angles make a **square**. A square has a two-dimensional surface. You can move in two directions — forward or backward and right or left.

Hypercube: If you pull a cube into the fourth dimension you get a hypercube. Eight cubes make a hypercube. The figure you see here cannot exist in the real world, which only has three-dimensional space. It is a projection of a four-dimensional object onto two dimensions, just as the cube before it is a projection from three-dimensional space to the two-dimensional flat surface of the paper.

Careers

So You Want to Be a Geometer

Coxeter loved his work and once said of his career, "I am extremely fortunate for being paid for what I would have done anyway." His advice to young people thinking about a career in mathematics: "If you are keen on mathematics, you have to love it, dream about it all the time."

Careers that involve mathematics with a specialty in geometry include architecture, cryptography (secret codes), crystallography, networks, map making, ballistics, astronomy, engineering, physics, computer visualization and computer gaming — any work that involves the visualization or manipulation of things or ideas in multiple dimensions.

Mystery

Coxeter always hoped that somebody would come up with a better proof for the four-colour-map problem, which simply says that if you have any map in two dimensions and the countries are any shape, you need only four colours for the countries so that two countries of the same colour never touch each other. Though it can be demonstrated easily with some paper and coloured pencils, nobody has ever proved (or disproved) this idea with pure geometry and math. A controversial computer proof was completed in the 1970s that claims to prove the four-colour-map problem. The computer tested millions of different maps, but to Coxeter this proof was not satisfying because it is too huge and complicated to be checked by a human being. In recent years, mathematicians have reduced the number of computer-generated maps but this new proof still requires the use of a computer and is impractical for humans to check alone.

Coxeter never felt the computer proof of the four-colour-map theorem was elegant. Such a proof would be easily understood and would use only mathematical or geometrical ideas presented in a logical way with nothing more than a pencil and paper. So, to Coxeter and many other mathematicians, the four-colour-map theorem is still an open problem.

Explore Further

- Martin Aigner and Gunter M. Ziegler, *Proofs from The Book*, Springer-Verlag Telos, 2000.
- W. W. R. Ball and H. S. M. Coxeter, *Mathematical Recreations and Essays*, 13th edition, Dover, 1987.
- H. S. M. Coxeter, *The Beauty of Geometry: Twelve Essays*, Dover, 1999.
- H. S. M. Coxeter, *Introduction to Geometry*, second edition, Wiley, 1989.
- H. S. M. Coxeter, *Non-Euclidean Geometry*, sixth edition, Math. Assoc. Amer., 1998.
- Siobhan Roberts, *King of Infinite Space: The Story of Donald Coxeter, the Man Who Saved Geometry*, Penguin, 2006.
- Robin Wilson, *Four Colors Suffice: How the Map Problem Was Solved*, Princeton University Press, 2003.

Biography at Wolfram Research:
mathworld.wolfram.com/news/2003-04-02_coxeter/

ACTIVITY

Objective:

To make **rhombus** tiles and use them to create various geometric designs.

You need:

- Cardboard or construction paper
- A straightedge or ruler
- A protractor to measure angles
- Scissors or a utility knife

What to do:

A rhombus is a squashed square. Try making some rhombus tiles. Make two diamond-shaped rhombuses, each having four sides of equal length. One rhombus has two angles of 36 degrees and two of 144 degrees. The other one has two angles of 72 degrees and two angles of 108 degrees. It's very important that you use the protractor to measure these exact angles when you draw your rhombus shapes, or else they won't fit together properly to make patterns. You can use this pattern below as a guide. Just draw it onto some coloured paper.

Measure and draw several dozen of these rhombus shapes, or photocopy the pattern below onto coloured paper. Cut out the shapes. Then move them around on a table to make patterns and shapes or glue them in various designs to another sheet of paper.

A rhombus is a two-dimensional or 2-D shape. You can make shapes that look like three-dimensional (3-D) cubes projected onto the 2-D surface of the paper. Try to make 3-D cube projections from these 2-D rhomboids. How many different ones can you make? What other shapes can you make?

Roger Penrose, the brilliant English mathematician and physicist, has shown how these shapes can be used to make an aperiodic tiling of the plane. That means you can tile a flat area with these shapes in a pattern that never repeats. Here's what one looks like. Try it.

If you enjoy this and it gets you thinking and dreaming about shapes and numbers, consider this: multiples of the same 36-degree angle make up all the angles in the two shapes! That is, 36 x 2 = 72; 36 x 3 = 108; 36 x 4 = 144 — all the angles we started out with! If you think this is cool, you may have a future in math and geometry.

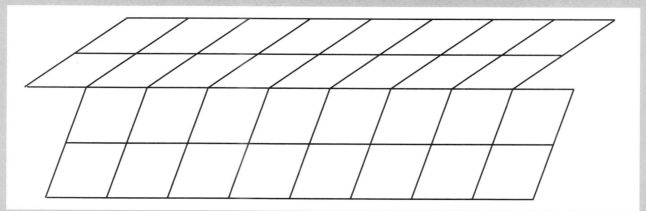

Roger Willis Daley

Meteorologist

Principal constructor of the computerized weather forecasting system now used worldwide.

His Story

It's 1966. Roger Daley is working at the United States Air Force base in Goose Bay, Labrador, on apprenticeship for the Canadian Weather Service. Daley is lonely, spending a lot of time by himself in his humble room in the barracks. It's cold and there's not much to do. The smell of jet fuel is everywhere and the Delta Dagger Interceptors and KC-135 tankers that refuel B-52 bombers in flight roar overhead at all hours of the day and night.

Daley decides to try an experiment. Working alone in his room at night, he makes up little blue cards for all the American pilots to fill out while flying missions in the area. The pilots have to write down things like dates, times, temperatures, altitudes, wind directions, wind velocities and their own general impression of the "bumpiness" of the flight. To Daley, the air is like an ocean of flowing currents and bubbles of different gasses constantly jostling about. It's a fluid like water, but much thinner.

When the cards start coming in, he spends a lot of time poring over maps spread out on his bed late at night, entering the information from the cards onto the maps to get a picture of this ocean of air around him — the atmosphere. Partly out of curiosity and partly just to have something to do, he takes the information and works out some mathematical formulas that relate the complicated interactions of winds, temperatures, altitudes and other factors that create **atmospheric turbulence**, the "bumpy" feeling you get in airplanes sometimes.

The pilots are very interested and cooperative because they "live" in this ocean of air, and knowing the patterns of upper-level turbulence along the Labrador coast will help them fly more safely. They start hanging around Daley's room and talking about the air in which they fly. He realizes he loves this research and, though he never publishes these results, he decides to go back to university to get a degree in meteorology, the science of weather. But the government of Canada had paid for Daley's training as a **weather forecaster** and in return he had to go wherever the government sent him. That's how he ended up in Goose Bay, and he had to work as a weather forecaster for two years.

 *Don't worry if you have not made a choice of career. It can come any time from grade school to graduate school.*

–Roger Daley

PERSONAL INFO

Born
January 25, 1943, London, England

Died
August 29, 2001, Monterey, California

Family Members
Father: Eric Daley
Mother: Mary Daley
Spouse: Lucia Tudor
Children: Kate, Charlie

Character
Curious, hard-working

Favourite Music
Handel's Water Music

Other Interests
History, family, travel

Status
Deceased

Degrees
Bachelor of science (honours, physics), University of British Columbia, 1964
Master of science, McGill University, 1966
Doctorate (meteorology), McGill, 1968

Awards
Fellow, Royal Society of Canada, 1993
Outstanding Scientist (U.S. National Center for Atmospheric Research), 1994
Fellow, American Meteorological Society, 1997
Jules Charney Medal (American Meteorological Society), 2001

Mentor
Professor Robert Stewart.

Then he attended McGill University in Montreal to get a doctorate (PhD) in meteorology. After that he spent some time in Copenhagen, Denmark, doing more research on the mathematics of wind patterns. From 1972 to 1978 he worked at the Canadian Meteorological Centre in Montreal. While there, he headed a research group that developed mathematical techniques called spectral transforms, using them to create computer programs that could predict the weather for about three days ahead. Launched in 1976, it was the first operational global computer weather-modelling system in the world. These numerical descriptions of the atmosphere (or variations of them) form the basis of virtually all forecasting and long-term climate **simulations** in use everywhere in the world to this day, including at the United States Navy's Fleet Numerical Meteorological and Oceanographic Center (FNMOC) in Monterey, California.

In 1978 Daley took on the job of senior scientist at the U.S. National Center for Atmospheric Research in Boulder, Colorado, perhaps the world's leading atmospheric research centre. There he worked on numerous outstanding and difficult problems in global weather modelling, using mathematics and computers. In 1985 he went back to Canada to become chief scientist at the Canadian Climate Centre in Downsview,

Ontario, where he worked for 10 years. In 1991 he wrote a book on atmospheric data analysis, which is considered by many to be *the* classic book on atmospheric modelling. Daley's last project in Canada involved the estimation of atmospheric wind fields based on satellite measurements of minor atmospheric chemical constituents; in other words, he was using information from satellites to track winds in the upper atmosphere.

Throughout his life, Daley was in great demand all over the world and contributed to weather forecasting projects in France, Sweden and China. He was a member of the Intergovernmental Panel on Climate Change (IPCC), the group of scientists who in 1991 issued a cautious warning about **global warming** as a result of rising **carbon dioxide** emissions from the use of fossil fuels.

In 1995 Daley accepted a position in Monterey, California, at the Marine Meteorology Division of the U.S. Naval Research Laboratory, to help develop an advanced shipboard forecasting system for United States Navy ships. The system, called the Navy Atmospheric Variational Data Assimilation System, or NAVDAS, became operational at Monterey for testing purposes around 1998, but Daley died of a heart attack in 2001 before he could see it implemented fleetwide.

THE YOUNG SCIENTIST

Daley's family moved to Canada while he was young, and he grew up in West Vancouver with the Coast Mountains as his backyard. He climbed and skied and at one point his family lived on a small island just offshore from West Vancouver, so he spent a lot of time by the sea and in the family boat. His best subject in high school was history, but he was always good at mathematics. He never wanted to be a research scientist. He wanted to do something useful that related to "normal" life. In grade 12 he had no intention of studying science.

The Science

Meteorology is the study of Earth's atmosphere and weather. If you ever listen to a weather forecast, chances are that you are enjoying the results of Roger Daley's research. Among many other accomplishments, he developed a mathematical technique called **spherical harmonic expansion** that is now used worldwide in computerized global atmospheric simulation **models** to predict the weather.

Just as people make small plastic or wooden models of cars or airplanes, **meteorologists** make models of how the temperature, wind, rain and other things in the atmosphere change over time and space. Instead of plastic and wood, meteorologists use numbers and equations inside a computer to model the real atmosphere. It's very similar to a car-racing video game. The simulated cars and the feeling of racing them can be very detailed and intense, but it's not a real car in a real race. In fact, it's just a bunch of mathematical calculations done by the computer and displayed on a screen. Yet by playing the game a person can get an idea of what it would be like to drive a real race car. In the same way, the atmospheric models used by meteorologists are not real, but they give an idea of what the real atmosphere might be like under certain conditions. Daley's models are used every day to collect weather data and predict the weather all over the world. Good weather forecasts are essen-

If you ever listen to a weather forecast, chances are that you are enjoying the results of Roger Daley's research.

tial for agriculture and all forms of transportation, among many other human endeavours.

Daley's models are also used in studies of global warming — the conjecture that burning coal, oil and gas might generate a large enough increase in carbon dioxide over the next 100 years to cause a greenhouse effect, warming the planet by a few degrees Centigrade. Ice caps would melt and the ocean would rise, drastically changing the world as we know it. Although he served on the IPCC, Daley remained somewhat skeptical about the potential for global warming. He felt there were too many unknown variables and many questions that had not been considered. He was surprised by the amount of public attention the IPCC report generated when it warned about global warming, and he felt it was an overreaction. He was cynical about the many world governments who made a big show of reducing greenhouse emissions while, for economic reasons, they had no intention of ever doing so. He was also critical of the huge number of pseudo-scientists who suddenly became "experts" on global warming after the release of the IPCC report. For this reason, Daley resigned from the IPCC and dissociated himself from global-warming research.

He said, in his very well-educated opinion as the scientist who created global atmospheric modelling: "Our systems cannot predict weather much beyond four days, so attempting to predict global changes 100 years from now seems questionable at best."

Real Earth
Earth's weather is a very complex system affected by ocean currents, temperature, pressure, wind and many other factors.

Weather satellite
Several hundred weather and remote sensing satellites currently orbit Earth, detecting many of the factors that create weather. They send this information back to base stations that relay it to weather computers.

Supercomputer
A supercomputer in a central location records and interprets information from satellites and other sources, updating itself continuously as more and more data come in.

Model Earth
The weather computer constructs a model of Earth based on very complicated mathematical formulas. This model is updated all the time and is used to generate maps that are sent to weather forecasters. They use these maps to help predict the weather.

*The process of combining data in the model with data from real-world observations is called **data assimilation**, and this was Daley's specialty. According to his colleagues in Monterey, he was equally productive and comfortable writing low-level computer code components of weather-modelling systems or working out the abstract matrix algebra of data assimilation theory.*

Careers

So You Want to Be a Meteorologist

Daley decided to become a weather forecaster because, he said, "I wanted to do something practical with my education, something that would help people in ordinary life." The physics of weather seemed more practical to him than nuclear physics, for instance.

Daley liked to remind people, "Scientists don't say 'I.'" Science is a group effort. Ideas evolve and are always based on the thinking of those who came before. Every scientist has colleagues, and virtually all scientific papers have multiple authors. When referring to the global forecasting system he worked on, Daley always used to say, "We did this," or "We implemented that." Yet in his obituary, one of his colleagues at the U.S. Naval Research Laboratory said, "Having Roger on your science team is like having Michael Jordan on your high school basketball team."

Daley felt that for a career in the natural sciences one ought to make an extra effort to get a good foundation in mathematics, because mathematics opens many doorways to countless research and job opportunities.

Mystery

Daley hoped future generations would develop a huge computer system that would be able to model all the **geophysical** systems in the world. (Geophysical systems are the forces and motions that affect Earth's air, lakes and oceans and even continents through earthquakes and volcanoes.) Among other things, such a system would allow us to accurately predict trends in global warming and the formation of **ozone holes**, gaps in the upper atmosphere that appear seasonally over the North and South Polar ice caps.

Explore Further

• Roger Daley, *Atmospheric Data Analysis*, Cambridge University Press, 1991.

Daley Memorial web page:
www.nrlmry.navy.mil/daley.htm
Environment Canada radar and satellite images:
weatheroffice.ec.gc.ca/radar/index_e.html
weatheroffice.ec.gc.ca/satellite/index_e.html
U.S. National Weather Service:
www.nws.noaa.gov- click on tabs for satellite and radar images
Weather Underground:
www.wunderground.com has international weather maps and data

ACTIVITY

Objective:

To simulate how meteorologists track storm clouds.

You need:

- A cup of black coffee (preferably a clear glass cup)
- A little bit of milk or cream
- A ruler
- A watch or stopwatch

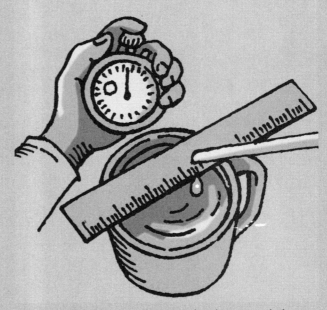

What to do:

In this experiment you will track a drop of white milk as it moves in a cup of very gently stirred black coffee. Imagine that the coffee represents the motion of air in the atmosphere. The drop of milk in the coffee represents a trace gas. By following the motion of the milk, knowing where you dropped it, and using a stopwatch to measure the passage of time, you can determine the **velocity** or speed of the moving coffee.

It's important to stir the coffee very, very slowly. Before you drop in the milk from the end of a stir stick, lay a ruler across the top of the cup and measure the exact distance in centimetres from the centre of the cup to the spot where the drop will fall. This is the radius (r). Before you let the drop of milk fall, get ready with the stopwatch so you can time exactly how long it takes to go all the way around the cup and back to where it started.

When the experiment is over you should have two numbers: r, the radius of the circle, and t, the time it takes to go around the circle one time. You can use the formula $2(\pi)r$ to get the distance the milk travels in one trip around the cup — one rotation. (π is a mathematical constant that is roughly 3.14159, so $2(\pi)$ is about 6.28.) If the radius you measure is two centimetres, then the distance the drop travels in one rotation would be 6.28 x 2 = 12.56cm.) The speed of the slowly moving mixture is the distance divided by the time, so divide the distance the milk travels (say 12.56 centimetres) by the time (say, five seconds) to get 2.51 cm/sec. Now try your own measurements and calculations. How good are your velocity measurements when the milk and coffee become well mixed?

This is how meteorologists work out the speed of moving clouds, winds and storms in the upper atmosphere. They have satellites that can "see" certain naturally occurring gasses in the atmosphere. One such gas is natural gas, or methane, that sometimes seeps from bogs. Meteorologists use the satellites to track this **methane** as it moves about in the atmosphere, just as you tracked the milk in the cup of coffee. If they can calculate how fast the methane is moving, they can figure out wind speeds in the upper atmosphere exactly the same way you calculated the speed of the moving coffee in the experiment. Knowing these wind speeds is very important for jet pilots because, depending on the wind speed and direction, a plane could arrive late or early at its destination.

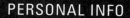 *Somewhere out there is a theory that would explain my empirical observations, and this theory has yet to be discovered. Mathematics thrives on such mysteries.*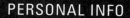

—Henri Darmon

PERSONAL INFO

Born
October 22, 1965, Paris, France

Residence
Montreal, Quebec

Family Members
Spouse: Galia Dafni, mathematician at Concordia University in Montreal
Daughter: Maia

Character
Persistent, obsessive, modest

Favourite Music
Jazz, French singers such as Brassens, Vigneault

Other Interests
Reading novels (particularly science fiction), skiing, swimming

Title
Professor

Office
Department of Mathematics, McGill University, Montreal, Quebec

Status
Working

Degrees
Bachelor of science (mathematics and computer sciences), McGill University, 1987
Doctorate (mathematics), Harvard University, 1991

Awards
Alfred P. Sloan Research Award, 1996
Le Prix de mathématiques André-Aisenstadt, 1997
Coxeter-James Prize (Canadian Mathematical Society), 1998

Fellow, Royal Society of Canada, 2003

Mentors
Jim Lambek, who taught that mathematics is an alive and "happening" subject, with lots remaining to discover.
John McKay, who taught the attraction of things not at all understood, the use of experimental mathematics, and Galois theory.
Jean Pierre Serre, for his elegant mathematical taste and expression and his crystal-clear explanations.
Andrew Wiles, for his style, obsession and creative methods, plus his feel for the doable and his good mathematics instinct.

Henri Darmon

Pure and Applied Mathematician
One of the world's leading number theorists, working on "Hilbert's 12th problem," a famous mathematics mystery.

His Story

Henri Darmon and his girlfriend, Galia, were driving back to Princeton, New Jersey, on a warm Sunday in June after a holiday at Cape Cod. The 20-something couple had been together for two years. They had met in 1991 when Darmon arrived at Princeton University to work as a mathematics instructor and researcher; Galia was studying mathematics as well, finishing her doctorate (PhD).

As mathematicians often do, Henri and Galia whiled away the miles by musing about some of the big puzzles nobody could solve. "So what about Fermat's last theorem?" asked Galia. "Do you think anyone will ever prove it?" She was referring to a seemingly simple problem that Darmon knew a lot about. His own research on **elliptic curves** might someday be involved in a mathematical proof. Over the centuries, millions of people had tried to solve French mathematician Pierre de Fermat's last theorem, which he had scribbled in the margin of a book in 1637, but nobody could do it.

A mathematical theorem is a truth derived from fundamental principles. Fermat's last theorem relates to another classic phenomenon called the **Pythagorean theorem**, which says: for the sides of a right triangle, the sum of the squares of the two short sides equals the square of the long side. The figure opposite demonstrates this idea, which was actually discovered by the Babylonians (the ancient civilization that existed in what is now called Iraq) around 2000 B.C. They used it to figure out the relative value of farm fields for tax purposes, but it is attributed to the famous Greek mathematician Pythagoras, who studied it in great detail.

Usually the theorem is stated algebraically: $a^2 + b^2 = c^2$, where c is the hypotenuse (long side) and a and b are the short sides of the triangle. Lots of numbers satisfy this rule starting with 3, 4 and 5 (replace the b with 3, the a with 4 and the c with 5; then

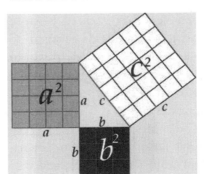

Pythagorean Theorem

you get $3^2 = 9$, $4^2 = 16$ and $5^2 = 25$, and since $9 + 16 = 25$, it all works out). Other Pythagorean sets of numbers are 5, 12 and 13 or 7, 24 and 25. Actually, there are infinitely many.

The branch of mathematics concerning such ideas is called "**number theory**" and it's Henri Darmon's specialty.

Fermat wondered if the Pythagorean rule would work for $a^3 + b^3 = c^3$ or $a^4 + b^4 = c^4$ and he found out that it didn't. But then he wrote, "It is impossible to separate any power except a square into 2 powers with the same exponent. I have discovered a truly marvellous proof of this, which however the margin is not large enough to contain." To put it another way, he was saying the equation $a^n + b^n = c^n$ would never work if n was anything other than 2. And he could prove this. In his life Fermat wrote down many such theorems, but unfortunately he died before he could prove this one on paper. In June 1993, 328 years after his death, this was the only one of Fermat's theorems that had not yet been proved. That is why it's called Fermat's last theorem.

Over the years vast sums of money, at times equivalent to more than US$2 million, had been put forth as the prize for the first person to prove Fermat's last theorem, so when Henri and Galia talked about it, they were serious. Whoever figured it out would literally become rich and famous. Fermat's "marvellous" proof, if it was correct, must have been very complicated because none of the old-fashioned methods seemed to work. Darmon knew that the solution would probably use something he was working on, elliptic curves, and this is what he told Galia. "I have a feeling that Fermat will be settled soon," he said. "Maybe within 10 years."

Back in 1955 two Japanese mathematicians, Yutaka Taniyama and Goro Shimura, claimed that elliptic curves were related to another mathematical object called **modular forms** in a profound and surprising way. No one had ever thought this connection between modular forms — functions involving imaginary numbers that result in amazing symmetrical patterns — could have anything to do with elliptic curves, which are standard formulas like $y^2 = ax^3 + bx^2 + cx + d$.

Taniyama and Shimura could not prove their claim. Mathematicians call something like this a **conjecture** until a proof is found. Interest in the Shimura-Taniyama conjecture had recently increased because in the mid-1980s two other mathe-

Modular Form

maticians (Frey and Ribet) showed that if it were ever proven, a solution to Fermat's last theorem would automatically result. But because the problem seemed so hard, people didn't even know where to begin.

"I don't think anyone will get Shimura-Taniyama in my lifetime, Galia," said Henri, as he pulled into a parking spot near their apartment in Princeton. He thought it was much harder than Fermat's last theorem. "I bet Fermat will be solved first," he said.

The next morning was a Monday and Darmon was in his office at the university. It was a big room in a tower building, with windows looking out over the rural town of Princeton. Just as Darmon was getting down to work, Peter Sarnak burst into the room. Sarnak was a charismatic and assertive mathematics professor at Princeton. He said, "You know Wiles has got it. He's going to prove Fermat."

"What?" said Darmon, shocked. He knew Andrew Wiles, another Princeton mathematics professor and one of Peter's best friends. Wiles was attending a mathematics conference at the Newton Institute in Cambridge, England.

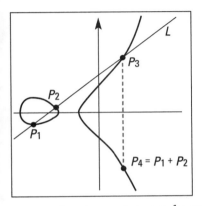

Elliptic curves are not ellipses, though they were originally used hundreds of years ago to help calculate the perimeter of an ellipse. The rational points on an elliptic curve (that is, points that are whole numbers, or ratios of whole numbers) have interesting properties. Any two points can be used to find a third. Number theorists love elliptic curves because they answer many questions about equations and their solutions.

Darmon was stunned. Could it be true? "How is he going to do it?" he asked.

Sarnak said, "He's going to prove Shimura-Taniyama."

Darmon was now doubly amazed. Not only would Fermat's last theorem be solved, but so would the Shimura-Taniyama conjecture. "Do you have the manuscript?" he asked Sarnak, figuring he'd need to see the proof to believe it.

"No, I'm sworn to secrecy. I shouldn't even be telling you, Henri." Sarnak spoke with a charming South African accent. He said, "Andrew is giving three lectures to build up to it, and he won't be showing the Fermat proof until his final lecture on Wednesday, so *please* keep this to yourself. When Andrew gets back, just ask him for a copy."

Wiles' proof turned out to be 200 pages long and was so complicated that only a few mathematicians on Earth could fully appreciate it. "In the end, it was not so much that he did it," says Darmon, "rather it was *how* he did it." By bringing together two apparently unrelated areas of mathematics (modular forms and elliptic curves), Wiles

THE YOUNG SCIENTIST

Henri Darmon was born in Paris, but when he was three his family moved to Quebec City in Canada. His father had a position at Laval University, teaching business administration. When Henri was 11 the family moved to Montreal, where his father began teaching at McGill University. As a teenager Henri liked to travel, and while he was on the road he enjoyed obsessing over hard mathematics problems. He would sometimes work all summer on one problem while he travelled. He still does it: "I some-times get my best ideas on buses and trains."

The summer he was 17, Darmon took a trip to Morocco. He had recently discovered calculus, the mathematics for describing continuous change, and that summer he set himself the personal challenge of finding the anti-derivative of $sinx/x$ as he travelled. This combination of calculus and geometry looked simple enough, but he spent all summer on this and never found the answer. The reason: there *is* no simple solution.

had done something much greater than proving one simple theorem. He had performed a kind of *grand unification* of mathematical thinking. It was a symbolic victory.

"Wiles changed what I thought was doable and psychologically moved me to go in directions where I wasn't sure I would get an answer," says Darmon. In the same way, Wiles has inspired millions of other mathematicians to discover many new mathematical relationships in recent years.

The Science

Henri Darmon is a mathematician specializing in number theory. Many scientists feel that mathematics is the purest of all the sciences, and most mathematicians will agree that number theory is the purest form of mathematics. Unlike other sciences, mathematics requires no laboratory experiments or observations of the natural world. It rests on its own internal consistency and logic, requiring nothing more than the intellect of the human mind. As one mathematician observed, it's the only job for which you can lie down on a sofa, close your eyes and get to work.

What are number theorists doing when they close their eyes? They imagine how numbers relate to each other. They see patterns. They invent formulas and equations that capture these patterns and amplify them. Have you ever wondered about the curious features of the nine-times table (9, 18, 27, 36, 45, 54, 63, 72, 81)? Notice that the digits for any of these numbers always add up to 9 (1 + 8 = 9, 2 + 7 = 9, et cetera). Note the symmetry of the series: After you hit 45, the numbers become mirror images of the ones that came before (45/54, 36/63, etc.). This is a very simple example of what number theorists think

The number system starts with the **natural numbers**: 1, 2, 3, 4 and so on. Next, add zero and the negative numbers to get the **integers**. Between each integer are fractions. Mathematicians call these the **rational numbers**. Each bigger group includes the smaller ones. After fractions come numbers that cannot be expressed simply as one number divided by another, like the square root of 2. This includes imaginary numbers, required to explain numbers whose squares are negative. Collectively they are called **irrational** or **algebraic numbers**. Beyond these are more exotic numbers like **pi** (3.14159 ...) or *e* (2.17828 ...), numbers with simple logical relationships — for example, pi is the ratio of a circle's radius to its circumference — but they cannot be expressed as ratios of whole numbers. They go beyond ordinary counting, so mathematicians call them **transcendental numbers**.

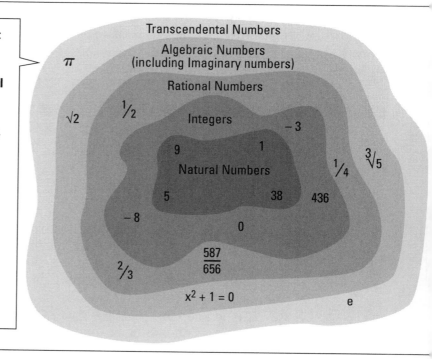

about, but they go much deeper than this. They want to know why the nine-times table behaves like this. (It has to do with our counting system having 10 digits, including zero.) They like to figure out what these patterns and relationships mean.

While they rarely look for practical applications, number theorists have provided many useful tools for all the other sciences. For instance, by picking a counting system that uses two digits (0 and 1) instead of 10, mathematicians developed a way for machines to do mathematics. It's called binary arithmetic and is the basis of all computer language. Usually, number theorists are not looking for ways to use numbers for practical things. They are just fascinated by the amazing natural relationships that can be discovered in the world of numbers.

Like adventurous explorers seeking new terrain, mathematicians are always looking for newer and more fascinating number patterns. Darmon thinks of the world of numbers as a natural wilderness, like the Arctic tundra or the Amazon rainforest. Just as these places on Earth have abundant plant and animal relationships, the number world is a place loaded with connections, patterns, structure and even animals of a sort. But you don't explore it in a boat or a plane. You go there in your mind.

In the 1960s a couple of English mathematicians named B. Birch and H. Swinnerton-Dyer formulated a conjecture based on many complicated counting exercises they had done. Their conjecture, if it were ever proved, would provide a systematic mathematical method (an algorithm) to calculate the set of solutions to elliptic curve equations that describe Abelian fields. In May 2000, to set the stage for a century of mathemat-

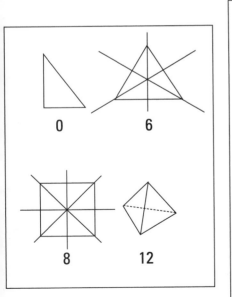

0   6

8   12

Symmetry: Just as biologists catalogue plants, mathematicians categorize numbers. A very simple example would be all the even numbers, but a better tool is the **number field**, a collection of numbers that is preserved under addition, subtraction, multiplication and division and obeys rules involving symmetries like the multiplicative inverse (a x b is the same as b x a).

Number theorists measure the complexity of a number field by the amount of symmetry it possesses. Consider a square and a rectangle. You can rotate a square by any multiple of 90 degrees and flip it around any of its four axes of symmetry for a total of eight possible transformations. But a rectangle, because of its unequal sides, has only four such ways of flipping and rotating. The figure depicts the number of symmetrics below each shape.

Darmon works with a kind of number field that obeys a special kind of symmetry. When two symmetries are applied to an **Abelian field**, they can be applied in any order and the outcome will be the same; like flipping, then rotating, the square above. In a sense, Abelian fields are the simplest class of number systems because they have this "symmetry of symmetries." Mathematicians would like to find equations that describe all the possible Abelian fields and it turns out that elliptic curves can help.

ical problem solving, the Clay Mathematics Institute in Cambridge, Massachusetts, offered a US$1-million prize for the solution to each of seven big problems, including the Birch and Swinnerton-Dyer conjecture.

The Clay Institute was echoing an event that occurred in May 1900, when one of the greatest mathematicians of all time, David Hilbert of Germany, gave a famous lecture in Paris in which he laid out 23 extremely challenging problems for mathematicians of the 20th century. The 12th one was a question about generating Abelian fields. More than 100 years later, Hilbert's 12th problem remains unsolved, but Henri Darmon is making progress toward a solution.

Put simply, Hilbert asked, "How do you get an effective and efficient method for constructing all the Abelian extensions containing a given field?" Years later, commenting on the problem, Hilbert said, "The theory of complex multiplication (of elliptic modular functions), which forms a powerful link between number theory and analysis, is not only the most beautiful part of mathematics but also of all science."

So Henri Darmon's pursuit is noble indeed. If he can find what he's looking for in the mathematical wilderness, according to Hilbert he will affect all of science. He might also become a millionaire. A few years ago Darmon proved a connection between Hilbert's 12th problem and the Birch and Swinnerton-Dyer conjecture. And it all hinges on clever manipulation of elliptic curves.

On the practical side, patterns generated by elliptic curves provide a very efficient way to encode and decode information. Such encryptions are small and fast to calculate, so they are ideal for quick transactions with credit cards, ATMs and online shopping.

Careers

So You Want to Be a Number Theorist

The world in which we live is becoming increasingly mathematical. Mathematics underlies all modern security systems, genetic sequencing, cell phones and other radio signal-processing systems, computer-controlled machines and cars, marketing statistics and political opinion polls, to name just a few examples. A solid knowledge of mathematics can therefore lead to careers in many different areas.

Mathematics can be a superb foundation for any career requiring computer programming. Henri Darmon says, "When mathematics students with no programming knowledge begin computer programming, I find their code is better, much more structured, than code written by students without mathematical discipline."

As far as pure mathematics research is concerned, Darmon points to the many open problems in mathematics, not the least of which are the seven Clay Institute problems. He feels the driving force behind mathematics and science is to discover something

Mystery

Solutions to many mathematics problems are waiting to be discovered. Hilbert's 12th problem, the Birch and Swinnerton-Dyer conjecture and other millennium problems from the Clay Institute remain unsolved.

new. "There's this mystery, this problem or this structure that's *there*. When you probe it, it seems to yield all kinds of fascinating patterns that are also very mysterious. We just want to understand them for their own sake. That's the primary motivation for any scientific pursuit, including mathematics."

According to Darmon, mathematics can be a solitary activity. "When you are thinking about a problem, you tend to do it by yourself. So in some ways mathematics can be lonely, but it can also be very exciting when you have been working on a problem for a long time and you finally have a creative insight that lays the solution out before you. These are very exciting but very private moments." Partly because of the solitary quality of the work, mathematicians like to collaborate. "One of the nice things about mathematics is that there are usually other people working on the same problem, and when that moment comes that you really solve something, that you get a new insight, you can share it with someone."

Most scientists, such as biologists or chemists, conduct experiments in laboratories, but mathematicians traditionally do not do experiments. Today, however, they have computers. Darmon runs software like Maple, Mathematica or Pari to conduct "experiments" on numbers (see Activity section).

To Darmon, one of the qualities that's the most important to succeed in research, even more important than being brilliant, is the sheer ability of sticking to it — not getting discouraged. For some problems in mathematics you *know* there is going to be an answer, and although they can be very hard problems, there's a sense they are doable if you keep plugging away at them. The truly difficult challenge in mathematics, or any aspect of science, is to embark on a search for a solution to a problem that may have no answer. Seeing Wiles solve Fermat's last theorem taught Darmon that it's okay to work on such daunting projects.

Typical mathematics careers include mathematician, statistician, systems analyst, computer programmer, accountant, financial auditor in the fields of finance, insurance or high technology, teacher, investment analyst and financial planner.

Explore Further

- Amir Aczel, *Fermat's Last Theorem*, Delta, 1997.
- Albert Beiler, *Recreations in the Theory of Numbers*, Dover, 1964.

To learn more about elliptic curves, try Ed Eikenberg's website at the University of Maryland: www.math.umd.edu/~eve/cong_num.html

To find out how to win a million dollars doing mathematics, visit the Clay Institute website: www.claymath.org/millennium/

ACTIVITY

Objective:

To "play" with symbolic mathematics software and get a sense of the fascination and power of elliptic curves.

You need:

- Software such as Mathematica (free trial available at mathematica.com) or Maple, or download Pari free from pari.math.u-bordeaux.fr/
- A computer with an internet connection

What to do:

Download Pari from the Mathematics Department of the University of Bordeaux in France. Pari is a free symbolic calculator similar to ones used by number theorists like Henri Darmon. The download includes an excellent user manual and a tutorial to get you started experimenting with numbers. Be sure to look at the tutorial right away; it provides examples of things to type into Pari to immediately discover what it can do. Functions exist for number fields and elliptic curves among many other number theory tools.

Here are a few fun calculations you can do with Pari that illustrate the power and mystery of elliptic curves. Without actually explaining what is going on, Darmon hopes these examples will entice you to learn more.

Exercise 1 (easy)

Calculate on Pari the exponential of pi times the square root of 163 by typing the following into Pari at the command line prompt:

```
exp(Pi*sqrt(163))
```

What do you observe?
Increase the accuracy to 50 digits by typing:
default(realprecision, 50)
and repeat the calculation. The explanation of why this number, while not an integer, is extremely close to one, lies in the theory of complex multiplication.

Exercise 2 (harder)

a) Consider the elliptic curve $y^2 = x^3 - x$, and given a prime number p, let N(p) be the number of pairs of integers (x,y) with x and y between 0 and p-1, such that p divides $y^2 - (x^3-x)$. Calculate the first few values of N(p), for p = 3, 5, 7, 11, 13, 17, 19, 23, 29. What patterns, if any, do you observe? (Note: read the Pari manual to learn how to work with elliptic curves.)

b) A classical theorem of Gauss asserts that an odd prime p can be written as a sum of two squares precisely when 4 divides p-1. Verify this on the first few values of p (= 5, 13, 17, 29) by writing p as $a^2 + b^2$ in each case, with a odd and b even.

c) What relationship do you observe between a and N(p)? This exercise will give you a feeling for one of the aspects of modularity, which asserts that the N(p) can be described in terms of interesting arithmetical data.

Biruté Galdikas

Physical Anthropologist
World's foremost authority on orangutans.

Her Story

Sweat pours down her face. She feels thirsty. Swatting at mosquitoes, Biruté Galdikas balances on a slippery log. The logs are always slippery. "I don't know why, but they always are," she thinks. Then she slips. She tries to avoid touching a thorn vine and a tree with toxic bark as she regains her balance. She stands waist-deep in tea-coloured swamp water in the dark, dank Indonesian **rainforest**, her joggers, socks and jeans soaking wet. Two pairs of socks, one tucked under and one pulled over her jeans, keep out leeches and other unspeakable menaces that thrive in the murky water. She's wearing a khaki, long-sleeved shirt with lots of pockets and a cotton jungle hat she bought at an army surplus store.

Catching her breath as she stands in the swamp, she spots two huge male **orangutans** standing face to face, glaring at each other's massive cheek pads. They're not that close, and she can only glimpse their shadowy forms in the dense foliage, but she can tell they are ready to fight for the chance to mate with the female that Galdikas has been tracking for days. The sounds are horrific: snarling, grunting, loud and frightening. The pair wrestle and tumble, smashing through the brush, trying to bite each other on the head and shoulders. Finally, one flees into the bush. Moving forward to see better, Galdikas snaps a twig, distracting the other one. Suddenly,

he grabs two thick vines, swings down until he hangs only a metre above her head and stares into her eyes, so close that her nostrils tingle from the stale odour of his sweat.

In 34 years of jungle observations, Galdikas has had only a handful of such close encounters, so rare are orangutans' meetings with humans or even with each other. But this fellow's message is clear: "Leave me alone."

Galdikas has learned more than any other human being about what it means to be an orangutan, and what she has found out is that orangutans like to be left alone. An adult male's range is at least 40 square kilometres, and he can spend

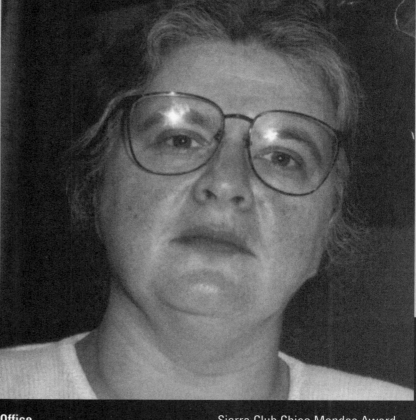

> **❝ I've always wanted to study the one primate who never left the Garden of Eden. I want to know what we left behind. ❞**
>
> —Biruté Galdikas

PERSONAL INFO

Born
May 10, 1946, Wiesbaden, Germany

Residence
Deep Cove, British Columbia; Los Angeles, California; Borneo

Family Members
Spouse: Pak Bohap
Children: Three

Character
Patient, determined, loyal

Favourite Music
Indonesian folk songs

Other Interests
Children, reading, walking, Indonesian culture

Title
Professor of Anthropology

Office
Simon Fraser University, Burnaby, British Columbia

Status
Working

Degrees
Bachelor of arts (psychology, biology), University of British Columbia, University of California at Los Angeles, 1966
Master of arts (anthropology), UCLA, 1969
Doctorate (anthropology), UCLA, 1978

Awards
Guggenheim Fellow, 1983
PETA Humanitarian Award, 1990
Eddie Bauer Hero of the Earth, 1991
Sierra Club Chico Mendes Award, 1992
United Nations Global 500 Award, 1993
Officer, Order of Canada, 1995
Tyler Prize (University of Southern California), 1997

Mentor
Louis Leakey, the world-famous anthropologist who supported Galdikas' research efforts.

weeks loping slowly from tree to tree eating fruits, nuts, insects, leaves and bark without meeting any of his kin.

Biruté Galdikas has devoted her life to studying orangutans. She wanted to know why these great apes did not evolve the way our ancestors did into human beings. Human beings evolved from a different type of ancestral ape that learned how to live in communities. Orangutans never learned this. They have not changed in millions of years because the forests where they live have not changed. They have always had enough food and space to continue their solitary existence.

THE YOUNG SCIENTIST

From the age of five, Biruté Galdikas has wondered where human beings came from. She knew they had evolved from ancient apes but she wanted to know more. When she was 12, she loved to go into the wilder sections of High Park in Toronto. There she would pretend she was a Huron or Iroquois Native slipping through the woods, at one with nature. She spent hours like this, quietly and secretly observing the wild animals in the park.

She spent hours like this, quietly and secretly observing the wild animals in the park.

When she went to university, she combined her love of nature with her curiosity about the great apes by studying psychology and biology. At 22, while she was working on her master of arts (MA) degree in **anthropology** at the University of California in Los Angeles, Galdikas met Dr. Louis Leakey, who was famous for discovering **fossils** of early humans in Africa. Leakey was helping Dian Fossey with her studies of mountain gorillas, and Jane Goodall, who was documenting the behaviour of chimpanzees. Together with the National Geographic Society, Leakey helped Galdikas set up a research camp in **Borneo** to study orangutans. Her husband, Pak Bohap, a Dayak rice farmer in Borneo, is a tribal president and co-director of the orangutan program there.

The Science

Anthropology is the study of human beings, but Galdikas studies physical anthropology, looking to our evolutionary ancestors and relatives, the great apes, to help understand the mysteries of human nature. Galdikas has been working and living in the rainforest for more than 30 years. During this time she became the co-founder of Orangutan Foundation International and other orangutan support groups all over the world. She has written articles for *National Geographic*, *Science* and other journals as well as several books on orangutans.

Structural brachiators:
Orangutans are structural brachiators, which means they are built to swing from branches with their upper limbs, but they have become too heavy to move quickly like this. Adult orangutans are the largest tree-dwelling animals on Earth, averaging about 100 kilograms for males.

Food-collecting:
A mother orangutan collects sweet *habu-habu* bark for her baby. This is one of over 400 types of food orangutans enjoy in the rainforest, and Galdikas has tried many of them herself. One way she has learned to spot orangutans in the dense foliage is to listen for the sound of fruit peels and pits dropping to the ground.

The baby is reaching for the food:
Through the repeated transfer of food between mother and baby, young orangutans learn what kinds of food are good to eat and how to eat them. They watch and imitate. They learn by trial and error. For instance, they might try eating the peel of a fruit and discover that it is too bitter. After making this error once or twice, they don't try it again.

At any given time, about 200 orangutans live in the Orangutan Care Centre and Quarantine Galdikas set up in Kalimantan Tengah, Indonesian Borneo. The centre releases about 30 into the wild every year, but more are always coming in, found as orphans as a result of palm-oil plantation development, which is destroying the tropical rainforest at an alarming rate. Galdikas spends an increasing amount of time in conservation and activism efforts to preserve the wild rainforest where her study animals live. In 1998 she persuaded the Indonesian government to set aside 76,000 hectares as an orangutan reserve. She is currently fighting to halt the expansion of palm-oil plantations in the 400,000-hectare Tanjung Puting National Park. "Even though I'm a scientist, the animals I'm studying are going extinct so I've had to get involved in political activism," says Galdikas. She believes there are only about 6,000 orangutans left in the park.

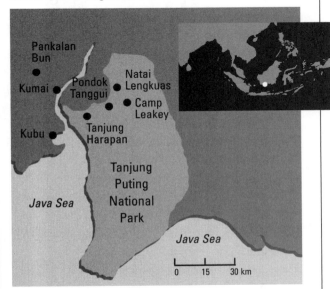

The rainforest:

The tropical rainforest is one of the most stable natural places on the planet Earth. A huge variety of plants and animals thrives there, and nothing has changed for millions of years. This is why the common ancestor for all apes, and humans, may have been somewhat like an orangutan. Orangutans have no serious predators other than humans. Their dietary knowledge of the irregular fruiting patterns of tropical plants indicates how intelligent they are. It also explains their solitary lifestyle and the long interval between births. A big animal needs a lot of foraging territory, without too many competitors around who eat the same kinds of food.

Babies:

Baby orangutans cling to their mother's fur until they are four years old. They are very dependent and remain with the mother for nine years. Females have perhaps four offspring in a lifetime. Orangutan males live solitary lives, looking for other orangutans only to mate. The orangutan's natural lifespan is about 60 to 70 years in the wild. In zoos they normally die at around 35 years of age, but some have lived for up to 56 years in captivity.

Decades of observation have resulted in many new discoveries about orangutans. "We now know they have the longest birth interval of all mammals," says Galdikas. A female will have her first baby at the age of 15 or 16, but then an average of eight years will pass before the second baby comes. This is mostly because of the long period that a young orangutan must remain with its mother to learn how to live in the rainforest. There are many dangers and hundreds of different ways of finding and preparing food.

Galdikas and her team have contributed to veterinary medical knowledge about orangutans, including treatments for malaria, tapeworm parasites and throat-pouch infections.

So You Want to Be a Physical Anthropologist

Galdikas advises anyone interested in a career in physical anthropology or wildlife **ecology** to begin by volunteering. "Get as much volunteer experience as possible," she says. You can ask at veterinary clinics, zoos and animal field hospitals. Opportunities abound, but you have to look for them. Good places to search are newsletters, journals and websites of organizations that work with animals. For instance, the American Society of Primatologists' newsletter would be a good place to look if you are interested in orangutans and other apes or monkeys. Call professors at universities, too. "If you can't do primates you can do chipmunks," says Galdikas, who spent a summer as a teen working at an archaeological dig on an Apache reservation in Arizona. Another year she worked on a dig in Yugoslavia. "Archaeological experience will give you training in different cultures."

A career in physical anthropology could lead to many jobs, such as veterinarian, zookeeper, science reporter, high school or university teacher, field conservationist, as well as government, organization or parks policy developer. It takes five to 12 years to get a degree, depending on whether or not you get a graduate degree.

Galdikas also advises young people to prepare themselves by doing a lot of reading; be aware of opportunities and talk to people. She got the idea of approaching Louis Leakey while talking to her pit partner on a dig in Arizona. Get a university degree — preferably a doctorate or a master's — in biosciences or anthropology and learn a skill that others don't have. For instance, learn DNA gene sequencing, geographical information systems (GIS) mapping, or hormone analysis. "You want something that gives you a new way to analyze things. It's like having a key to open the data in new ways," says Galdikas.

The thing she likes most about her career is the feeling she gets when she discovers new things. "Just being with the animals in their pristine rainforest environment is a thrill, but it's always very difficult and demanding." She also had to learn diplomacy and patience, due to the many long negotiations required to get governments to preserve orangutan habitat.

"The saddest thing about my career is that orangutans are going extinct," says Galdikas, but she feels she has made a difference through her foundations and environmental activism.

> *"Just being with the animals in their pristine rainforest environment is a thrill."*

Mystery

Galdikas would like to know the relationship of males to females in a given range of rainforest habitat. Males come and go. How far do they go when they disappear? How many females do they mate with? How far apart are the females? Over how large an area of rainforest does one single male mate, and how successful are these matings? These are all open questions.

Another thing that bothers Galdikas is the way she sees orangutan behaviour appearing in modern men and women. It's a mystery to her why human beings who are normally social, gregarious creatures, are becoming more individualistic like orangutans. She says, "What I have learned from orangutans is that we humans must not turn our backs on our own biological heritage. Modern society promotes the ideal of the rugged individual. For men you have the Clint Eastwood persona — the Marlborough Man. For women you have single moms raising their kids alone. The ideal Western male rides into town, fights the bad guys, falls in love and then heads off into the sunset. He is strong and solitary just like an orangutan, but he represents an evolutionary dead end. Many of today's problems are a result of abandoning our human biological roots. We must look to our distinctive gregarious human heritage; living and working in family groups and communities if we want to be successful. Otherwise we are just stressed out 'orangutans' in an urban setting."

Explore Further

- Biruté Galdikas and Karl Ammann, *Great Ape Odyssey*, Harry N. Abrams, 2005.
- Biruté Galdikas, *Reflections of Eden*, Back Bay Books, 1996.
- Biruté Galdikas, *Orangutan Odyssey*, Harry N. Abrams, 1999.
- Biruté Galdikas, "Orangutans: Indonesia's People of the Forest," *National Geographic*, p. 444, October 1975.
- Biruté Galdikas, "Living with Orangutans," *National Geographic*, p. 830, June 1980.

Orangutan Foundation International website: www.orangutan.org

NOTE: Many people ask how they can volunteer to help Biruté Galdikas work with orangutans. Volunteers are always welcome, but they must pay their own room and board (about $5 a day) to stay in Tanjung Puting Park. A typical stay is six weeks. Galdikas cannot respond to individual requests. Please contact the Orangutan Foundation International:

Orangutan Foundation International
822 S. Wellesley Avenue
Los Angeles, CA 90049, U.S.A.
Tel: +1 (310) 207-1655; fax: +1 (310) 207-1556
E-mail: ofi@orangutan.org
Web: www.orangutan.org/

ACTIVITY

Objective:

To observe an animal's activities and behaviour scientifically. You will call your chosen subject your "focal" animal.

You need:

- A **focal animal**, whether it's a pet, a human being, or a squirrel to observe in the park
- A notebook
- A pencil
- A watch

What to do:

Observe your focal animal for at least one hour, writing down what time each new activity starts and how long it lasts. Note what the animal does, how it holds things, its posture, utterances, everything. Make two columns: one for the exact time and one for the activity. For instance:

Time	Activity
11:02	Left hand picks up cup
11:02:05	Sips about 5 millilitres

Afterwards, break down the activities into categories like Eating, Moving, or Resting, and add up how much time the animal spent on each. Categories can be divided further. For instance, Eating could show time spent on each type of food. Finally, draw a graph to display your results. Your graph could look like this pie chart, in which each slice represents an activity:

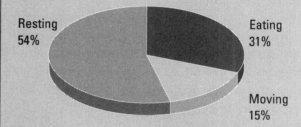

Resting 54%
Eating 31%
Moving 15%

Consider drawing a graph to show the breakdown of food types, with each column representing a type of food.

Gerhard Herzberg

Physicist and Spectroscopist

Won the 1971 Nobel Prize in chemistry for using spectroscopy to discover the internal geometry and energy states in simple molecules, and in particular the structure and characteristics of free radicals.

His Story

Gerhard Herzberg bends over the piles of paper on his big desk. He is overwhelmed. As director of the Pure Physics Department at Canada's National Research Council, the fall of 1959 is a very busy time for him. Jack Shoesmith, his research technician, comes into the sun-filled office and walks up to the tall windows overlooking the Ottawa River. He says, casually, "I have an interesting spectrum to show you."

Herzberg thinks of all the meetings and conferences he has to organize, the paper he is writing, presentations he is preparing and the book he is trying to finish, the third volume of his series, that included *Molecular Spectra and Molecular Structure*. "I don't have time for this," he thinks.

"It's good," says Jack.

Reluctantly, Herzberg gets up from his chair and follows the young technician down a flight of stairs to the lab below. It's a big high-ceilinged room, dimly lit and smelling of ammonia and hot electric wiring. There's a hint of **ozone** in the air, as before a thunderstorm. They walk past the special **spectrograph** that Shoesmith has built — a long steel tube about 50 centimetres high and 3 metres long. Vacuum hoses and electrical wires snake around the base of the apparatus, but the pumps and electricity have been turned off. The big room is quiet except for the murmurs of a small crowd that has gathered in the corner.

Herzberg hurries over to see what they are looking at. A long, thin strip of glass with a seemingly random pattern of vertical lines blackening its surface — a **spectrogram** — lies on a viewing screen. Recognizing it at once, Herzberg picks it up for a closer look. Instantly he shouts, "That's it!" and breaks out laughing. "Eighteen years," he thinks. "I've been looking for you for eighteen years."

What Herzberg held that day was the first spectrogram of a simple chemical called **methylene**, a molecule consisting of a carbon **atom** with two **hydrogen** atoms, one on either side, written CH_2. What was special about this? Methylene is a very unstable molecule, a **free**

> **" You shouldn't do science just to improve wealth — do science for the sake of human culture and knowledge. There must be some purpose in life that is higher than just surviving. "**
>
> —Gerhard Herzberg

PERSONAL INFO

Born
December 25, 1904, Hamburg, Germany

Died
March 4, 1999, Ottawa, Ontario

Family Members
Father: Albin H. Herzberg
Mother: Ella Biber
Spouse: Monika Tenthoff
Children: Paul, Agnes

Character
Jovial, modest

Favourite Music
Mozart's Quartet for Flute, Violin, Viola and Cello

Other Interests
Singing, music, mountain hiking

Status
Deceased

Degrees
Engineering Diploma, Darmstadt Institute of Technology, 1927
Doctorate, Darmstadt Institute of Technology, 1928
Privatdozent (post doctorate), University of Goettingen, 1929
Honorary degrees from Universities of Oxford, Cambridge, Chicago and many others

Awards
H. M. Tory Medal (Royal Society of Canada), 1953
Joy Kissen Mookerjee Gold Medal (Indian Association for the Cultivation of Science), 1954
Gold Medal (Canadian Association of Physicists), 1957
Medal of the Society for Applied Spectroscopy, 1959
Frederic Ives Medal (Optical Society of America), 1964
Willard Gibbs Medal (American Chemical Society), 1969
Faraday Medal (Chemical Society of London), 1970
Royal Medal (Royal Society of London), 1971
Linus Pauling Medal (American Chemical Society), 1971
Nobel Prize in chemistry (Swedish Royal Academy of Sciences), 1971
Chemical Institute of Canada Medal, 1972
Earle K. Plyler Prize (American Physical Society), 1985
Jan Marcus Marci Memorial Medal (Czechoslovak Spectroscopy Society), 1987
Minor Planet 3316-1984 CN1 officially named "Herzberg," 1987

Mentor
Hans Rau, his thesis adviser at Darmstadt Institute of Technology in Germany, who inspired Herzberg to find his own problem to study, then supported his early studies of molecular spectroscopy and sent him to meet Erwin Schrödinger, the brilliant Viennese physicist.

radical — a transition molecule created briefly in a chemical reaction when molecules come together and transform themselves into something new. Free radicals last only for the length of time it takes for their constituent atoms to rearrange themselves with other molecules into new molecules — a few millionths of a second — so it's very difficult to obtain a spectrum of such fleeting entities. Herzberg was delighted because the spectrum of the CH_2 free radical was a key to proving many outstanding theories concerning the internal structure and energy states of molecules. That particular spectrum that Herzberg identified in 1959 eventually resulted in his winning a Nobel Prize in 1971.

THE YOUNG SCIENTIST

As a 12-year-old in Hamburg, Germany, Herzberg and a friend named Alfred Schulz constructed a homemade telescope. They patiently ground the glass lenses and set them in handmade mounts in a metal tube. On clear nights they used to take the streetcar to the city park and set up the telescope to look at the moon and planets.

In 1933, Herzberg was working as a lecturer at the university in Darmstadt, Germany, when the Nazis introduced a law banning men with Jewish wives from teaching at universities. Since Herzberg had married a Jewish woman in 1929 — Luise Oettinger, a spectroscopist who collaborated with Herzberg on some of his early experiments — he began making plans to leave Germany near the end of 1933. Earlier that year he had worked with a visiting **physical chemist** named John Spinks, from the University of Saskatchewan. Spinks helped Herzberg get a job at the university in Saskatoon. It was very difficult for German scientists to find work outside Germany; thousands of them were leaving to escape the Nazis and they were all looking for jobs at the same time. When Herzberg and his wife left Germany in 1935, the Nazis let them take only the equivalent of $2.50 each, as well as their personal belongings. Fortunately, before he left, Herzberg was able to buy some excellent German spectroscopic equipment to take with him to Saskatoon. At the time you couldn't buy such equipment in Canada.

Leaving Germany was very painful for the Herzbergs and they had no idea what they would find in Saskatoon. But Saskatchewan turned out to be a good experience for them, although it was very different from Germany. During the 10 years they lived there, Herzberg taught physics and wrote his famous book *Molecular Spectra*. His children were born in Saskatoon.

After moving to Chicago for a few years, Herzberg accepted a position with Canada's National Research Council in Ottawa and was director of physics there from 1949 to 1969. During this time he made his Nobel Prize-winning discoveries in molecular spectroscopy. He worked at the National Research Council as a distinguished research scientist until his death at the age of 94 on March 4, 1999.

The Science

Herzberg was a physicist, but his discoveries are important to chemists because they involve the internal **geometry** and energy states of molecules. Remember: When Herzberg was born, the concept of an **electron** was just catching on. When he graduated from university, people had yet to discover how atoms combined to form molecules. It was all new theory. Very little had been proven.

To try to prove all these exciting ideas, Herzberg became a pioneer in the field of molecular **spectroscopy**, the study of how atoms and molecules emit or absorb light. By analyzing spectrograms — a sort of photograph of the way a molecule emits and absorbs light — he was able to tell a lot about molecules. For example, by measuring the distance between the lines on a spectrogram and counting how many lines there were, he was able to apply some mathematical formulas that described the energy levels and probable locations of the electrons in the molecule. This was very useful to chemists, because the new knowledge helped them to imagine new ways to combine chemicals to create new substances.

Once the spectrum of a molecule is known, astronomers can also use it. They can characterize the composition of distant stars and nebulae by training spectrographs on them through telescopes. This is handy if you are interested in knowing what stars are made of. It's a way to learn what is out there, millions of light years away, without having to make the impossibly long trip to visit a place and take samples. This is one thing that really interested Herzberg, because it tied in with his childhood love of astronomy.

A spectrogram is created with a machine called a spectrograph. It takes a beam of light created by burning the chemical you wish to investigate. The light is focused by a lens, then passed through a **prism** and spread out into its component parts, like a rainbow. But this rainbow is very precise and appears as dark and light vertical lines that you can measure.

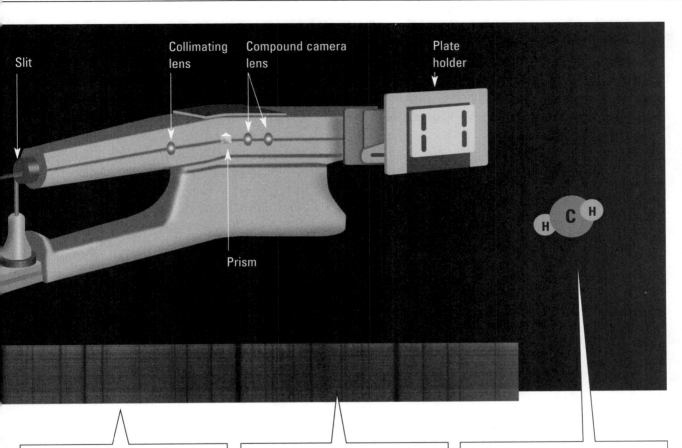

Slit

Collimating lens

Compound camera lens

Plate holder

Prism

H C H

A spectrogram is a long piece of plate glass coated with photographic chemicals. After they have been exposed in a spectrograph and developed, the plates have dark, vertical lines. By measuring the spacing and thickness of the lines, physicists can apply mathematical formulas and determine some of the energy states of the molecules whose light produced the spectrogram.

The distance between the larger lines in the spectrum is proportional to the molecule's "vibrational" energy. The small groups of lines clustered around the major lines represent the "rotational" energy of the molecule. These lines and their mathematical relationships are called **Balmer lines,** for the Swiss high school teacher who figured them out in 1885.

Methylene (CH_2) is a free radical, which means it has an extra pair of electrons that it tries to share with another molecule. These extra electrons make the free radical very reactive, meaning it will combine quickly, usually within a few millionths of a second, with some other molecule.

Careers

So You Want to Be a Physicist

When Herzberg finished high school at the age of 19, he dearly wanted to become an astronomer. At that time there was a vocational office in Hamburg where young people could go for career guidance. Herzberg went there and asked a counsellor, "How do I become an astronomer?" His request was sent all the way up to the director of the top observatory in Hamburg, but the answer was disappointing: he was told he would need to be independently wealthy to support himself as an astronomer. There was no way of making a living as an astronomer. Instead he was advised to go to university and study physics.

He still had no way to pay for a university education, but he wrote a letter to one of the biggest shipbuilding companies at the time, Hugo Stinnes Lines, and was lucky enough to get a scholarship. That was enough for him to live on while he attended university, launching him on a lifelong career as a physicist.

Mystery

Strange as it may seem, in his later years Herzberg liked to remind people that they should not do science for the purpose of doing something useful. "That's not why I did it," he said. "Scientists wonder how certain things work, so they try more and more to find out how and why. Whether or not their work will lead to something useful, they don't care, because they don't know, and for that matter, they're not that interested. If you develop science only with the idea to do something useful, then your chances of discovering something useful are *less* than if you apply your mind to finding something essential." According to Herzberg, a true scientist looks to uncover the mysteries of nature for the sole purpose of advancing human knowledge. The usefulness of this knowledge becomes self-evident *after* it is discovered. Prime examples of this are X-rays and lasers, both of which were discovered by physicists who had no idea how useful their discoveries would later become.

Explore Further

- Gerhard Herzberg, *Atomic Spectra and Atomic Structure*, Dover, 1944.
- J. Michael Hollas, *Basic Atomic and Molecular Spectroscopy*, Wiley-RSC, 2002.
- Boris Stoicheff, *Gerhard Herzberg: An Illustrious Life in Science*, McGill-Queen's University Press, 2003.

Website about spectroscopy:
http://imagine.gsfc.nasa.gov/docs/teachers/lessons/xray_spectra/background-spectroscopy.html

ACTIVITY

Objective:

To demonstrate the conservation of angular momentum, a basic principle of physics.

You need:

- A revolving chair or stool

Background:

Angular momentum can be thought of as the energy of turning. When a car is turning, you feel angular momentum as a pulling force to the outside. It's why you lean into a turn.

What to do:

Sit in the revolving chair or stool. Now, holding your arms stretched out to each side and your feet sticking straight out in front of you, spin yourself around, or have someone else spin you. As you spin, quickly bring your arms and legs in. You should notice a change in your rate of rotation. Is it faster or slower? This change you feel is caused by the conservation of angular momentum, a basic principle of physics. When you tighten the circle of turning, the energy of turning has to go somewhere and it ends up making you turn faster. Figure skaters use this, too, when they bring their arms in to spin faster and faster.

Conservation of energy is a law of nature according to modern science. The energy of turning, which is present in all spinning molecules and atoms, must go somewhere when things change, as they do in a chemical reaction or in burning, heating or freezing. Among other things, Herzberg showed exactly how the lines in a spectrogram represent the conservation of angular momentum in a molecule as its spinning electrons move between different quantum levels of energy. Certain lines in a spectrogram show the different energy levels that a molecule can have, and they also fit into a clever mathematical system called **quantum mechanics**, a theory that underlies most of modern physics. Quantum mechanics says that many things in nature happen in discrete (separate) steps called quantum levels.

> **" *If you really enjoy your work you never need a holiday.* "**
>
> —Werner Israel

PERSONAL INFO

Born
October 4, 1931, Berlin, Germany

Residence
Victoria, British Columbia

Family Members
Father: Arthur Israel
Mother: Marie Kappauf
Spouse: Inge Margulies
Children: Mark, Pia
Grandchild: Allison

Character
Self-deprecating, enthusiastic, obsessive, absent-minded. Has a wry sense of humour.

Favourite Music
Arthur Schnabel's recordings of Beethoven's piano sonatas

Other Interests
Has a huge music collection, collects second-hand books, enjoys swimming, jogging, hiking.

Title
Emeritus Professor (Physics)

Office
Department of Physics, University of Victoria, Victoria, British Columbia

Status
Semi-retired, teaching two courses

Degrees
Bachelor of science (physics and mathematics), University of Cape Town, 1951
Master of science (mathematics), University of Cape Town, 1954
Doctorate (mathematics), Trinity College, 1960

Awards
Fellow, Royal Society of Canada, 1972
Medal of Achievement in Physics (Canadian Association of Physicists), 1981

Research Prize in Science and Engineering (University of Alberta), 1983
Izaak Walton Killam Memorial Prize, 1984
Fellow, Royal Society of London, 1986
Officer, Order of Canada, 1994
Medal in Mathematical Physics (Canadian Association of Physicists), 1995

Mentor
John Lighton Synge, the great Irish mathematician at Trinity College in Dublin, Ireland, who taught him a style of reasoning and how to draw pictures to understand relativity theory.

Werner Israel

Cosmologist

Wrote the first logically precise theory
for the simplicity of black holes (1967).

His Story

Werner Israel relaxes into the barber chair, daydreaming. He's thinking about his pending retirement and move to Victoria, British Columbia, while the hair stylist throws a protective cape over his chest and fastens it behind his neck. A 20-something woman, she's been cutting his hair for about two years. The shop is in an Edmonton strip mall on 87th Avenue, not far from the University of Alberta where Israel works. He's just gazing out the window when she draws him out of his thoughts by saying, "So what do you actually teach?"

Israel teaches **cosmology**, but he doesn't answer right away. A few weeks earlier he had been interviewed for a television show, and the interviewer had mistakenly prepared all sorts of questions about makeup and cosmetics. He doesn't want that to happen again, so he decides to first tell the hairdresser about the difference between cosmology and cosmetology; cosmology has nothing to do with lipstick or eye shadow. He launches into some basic ideas, about how the universe could have come from nothing, about the **big bang theory** — the idea that a false vacuum state could be the source of the enormous amount of energy that must have come from nowhere to create everything in an instant, and how cosmologists can accurately predict the relative amounts of elements manufactured in that moment of creation.

The hair stylist cuts his hair, listening attentively.

Israel then describes his own research into **black holes**, how they are these incredibly massive objects with so much gravity that anything near them falls in, even light. He gets carried away as he explains some of his theories about what happens if you fall into a black hole, and he doesn't even notice that the haircut is over. "I'm terribly sorry if I've been boring you with all this physics," he says, apologetically.

"Oh no, that was absolutely awesome, what you were telling me about cosmosis," she says.

Israel quietly pays the usual $12 and his customary tip and walks out into the springtime sunshine, wondering about the meaning of this interesting new word the stylist has invented. At least he wasn't a cosmetologist this time.

THE YOUNG SCIENTIST

When Werner Israel was about nine years old, both his parents became very ill and had to be hospitalized. Werner and his brother ended up living in the Cape Jewish Orphanage in Cape Town, South Africa, for four years. But they were not unhappy years. Israel remembers how one day, after his father began to feel better, he showed up with a set of encyclopedia books he had obtained from a peddler in exchange for an old suit. His father had been astute in recognizing his son's talents, for the young Israel spent many hours poring over those books.

Israel became fascinated by stars and cosmology as a boy, but he had to teach himself some mathematics to understand what he was reading. He remembers sitting on the beach in Cape Town when he was 12, studying *Calculus Made Easy* by Silvanus P. Thompson, and he has never forgotten the epigraph on its first page: "What one fool can do, another can."

By the late 1950s, Israel was working at the Dublin Institute in Ireland as a research scholar. When his term was almost up, he began looking for a job and discovered an assistant professorship available in Edmonton, Canada. He had no idea at the time where Edmonton was, but he knew it was where mathematician Max Wyman worked. Wyman's papers on the theory of **relativity** were well known to Israel. So in 1958 Israel and his wife, Inge, moved to Edmonton, where they stayed for almost 40 years.

> *"What one fool can do, another can."*

The Science

Cosmology is the study of stars and other heavenly bodies. Cosmologists are physicists who ask, How was the universe created? When will it end? How big is the universe? Israel is particularly famous for some of his theories about black holes.

A black hole is not really a hole. It's a region of space that has so much mass concentrated in it that nothing can escape its gravitational pull. Black holes are thought to be formed when very old stars collapse in upon themselves. Scientists believe that black holes have such strong gravity that they act like gigantic vacuum cleaners, sucking in any matter that comes too close. Whether it is a comet, a planet or a cloud of gas, that matter is crushed to infinite density and disappears forever. The gravity is so intense that it slows down time and stretches out space. Not even light can escape from a black hole, so it's impossible to see one. That's why the American physicist John Wheeler named them "black holes" in 1968, even though the first person to think of the idea was British amateur astronomer John Mitchell in 1783.

Despite all this, Werner Israel believed that a black hole was actually a very simple thing. Until he published this theory in 1967, it was thought that the only truly simple things in nature were elementary particles such as **electrons** or **neutrons**. An electron only has three properties: mass, spin and charge. Virtually everything in nature is much more complicated and cannot be described so easily. Rocks have jagged cracks. Planets have rugged mountains. Stars have complex magnetic fields. Israel used mathematical techniques to show that black holes are the simplest big objects in the universe. Like an electron, they can be described completely by their mass, spin and charge alone. "The surface of a black hole is as smooth as a soap bubble," says Israel. But you'd never be able to see this, since light is not reflected by a black hole.

"Einstein's theory is OK for everything until you get very deep inside a black hole."

Israel is currently working on several projects involving the internal geometric structure of black holes. He wants to know what goes on inside a black hole. To answer this question he hopes eventually to use **superstring theory** — the idea that instead of using tiny, point-like particles to describe matter as we have done up to now, perhaps things can be broken down into tiny, line-like "superstrings." Israel says, "Einstein's theory is okay for everything until you get very deep inside a black hole." You need another approach, because relativity theory does not handle infinity very well, and a lot of things become infinite inside a black hole.

For example, Israel is trying to figure out what happens when a black hole evaporates. What becomes of all the information stored inside it? Is it totally randomized and lost when the black hole turns into a huge amount of radiant heat? Or is this **radiation** only apparently random, and are there subtle correlations stored within it that contain the "lost" information? This is what most string theorists believe today. But Israel can't understand how this information can rise from the depths of the black hole to its evaporating surface without violating causality, that is, travelling faster than light from the future to the past.

If you could watch from the outside as an object falls into a black hole, it would seem to you that it never gets there. The closer the object approaches the hole's **event horizon**, the slower it seems to travel. You can think of the event horizon as the surface of the black hole, but it's not solid. To you, the object would appear to stop, seemingly forever suspended at the event horizon. It would begin to turn orange, then red, then fade fairly rapidly from view. Though the object is gone, you never saw where or how it disappeared.

If you yourself fell into a black hole you would not even notice the event horizon. From there on, everything goes only one way: in. You could not send out messages for help. However, you could still receive messages from outside so, to you, everything would seem okay. You would never know when you had crossed the event horizon — except that the increasing gravity would draw your body longer and longer, squeezing you in from the sides. You wouldn't last long, which is too bad, because the properties of time and space are so altered in a black hole that some scientists think time travel might be possible. Or you might be able to travel to a parallel universe through a **wormhole** — holes in the fabric of space and time. The only problem is: how do you survive the tremendous gravity?

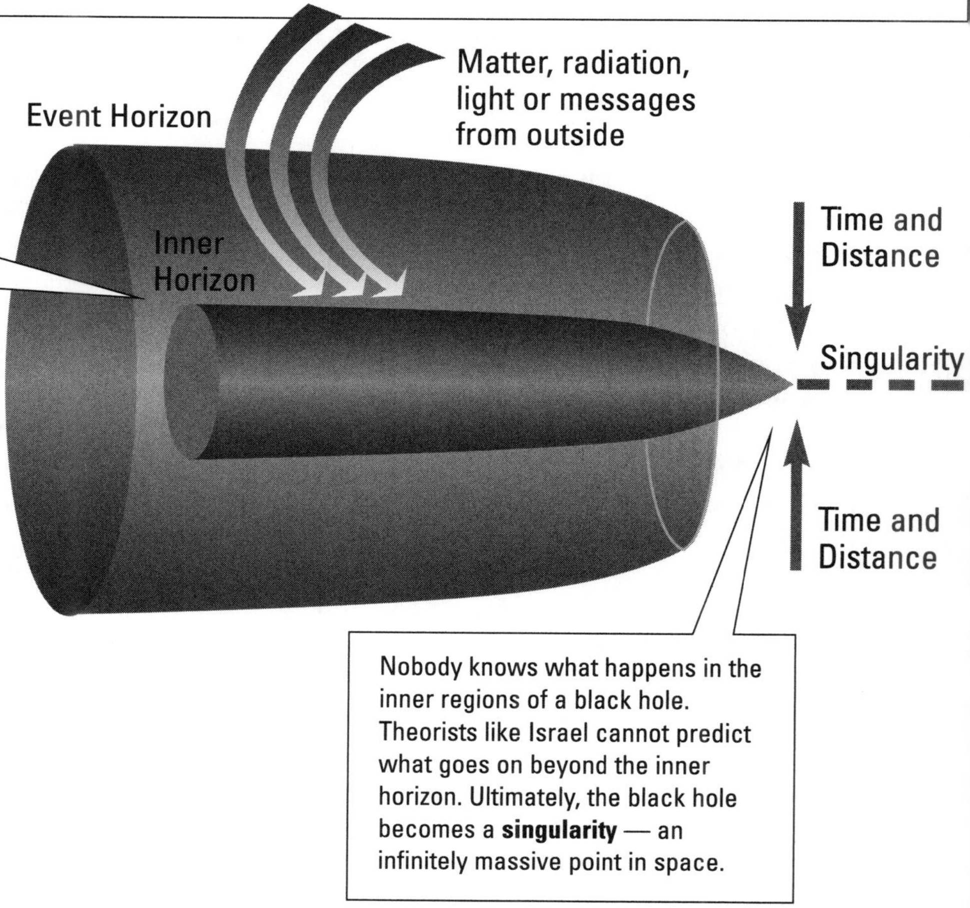

Event Horizon

Matter, radiation, light or messages from outside

Inner Horizon

As you fall deeper into a black hole you would come to the **inner horizon**. This is the point beyond which you cannot even see out. As you reach the inner horizon, all events in the universe that had ever happened throughout all of time would seem to accelerate and appear to you in a fraction of a second.

Time and Distance

Singularity

Time and Distance

Nobody knows what happens in the inner regions of a black hole. Theorists like Israel cannot predict what goes on beyond the inner horizon. Ultimately, the black hole becomes a **singularity** — an infinitely massive point in space.

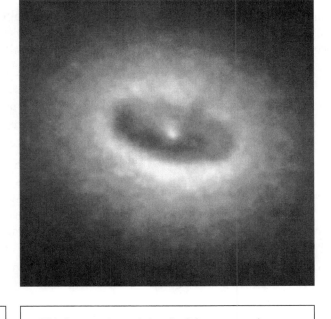

The fuzzy blob in the centre is a ground-based photo of the giant elliptical galaxy called NGC 4261, as it appears through a telescope in ordinary light. (Since there are billions of galaxies, most have numbers rather than names. NGC stands for the New General Catalog of galaxies, which was started by astronomers in the 1860s.) NGC 4261 is one of the 12 brightest galaxies in the Virgo cluster, located 45 million **light-years** away from Earth. It contains hundreds of billions of stars. A superimposed radio image shows a pair of giant opposed jets shooting out of the galaxy, spanning a distance of 88,000 light-years.

This is an enlarged detail of the same galaxy, taken by the Hubble Space Telescope. The improved quality of the image shows that the centre of the fuzzy blob has a giant disc with a 300-light-year ring of cold gas and dust around a bright central core that is probably feeding matter into a black hole, where gravity compresses and heats the material. Hot gas rushes from the vicinity of the black hole, creating the radio jets. These jets provide strong evidence for a black hole in the centre of NGC 4261. The Hubble Space Telescope has now provided fairly convincing evidence that black holes probably exist at the centre of many galaxies, including ours.

So You Want to Be a Cosmologist

"There is no great demand for cosmological eggheads in industry and commerce," says Israel, but the analytical and computing skills of such physicists are highly valued and properly rewarded by big business. He explains, "In the 1980s and '90s, when university jobs were particularly hard to find, many cosmology graduates became financial analysts for banks or took jobs in the chemical industry." The banks in particular were happy to pay salaries of US$150,000 plus housing and other benefits to attract smart physicists. At the other end of the scale, Israel was making about $5,000 per course per term as a part-time university lecturer in the 1990s. For many years, a cartoon hung on the wall of his office showing a man and a woman talking at a cocktail party. The man is saying, "My biggest mistake was going into cosmology for the money."

According to the 2001 Occupational Employment Statistics Survey conducted by the U.S. Department of Labor's Bureau of Labor Statistics, physicists rank as the 15th-highest-paid profession in the United States, with annual average salaries of $83,750 a year.

Typical physics careers include specialties in electronics, communications, aerospace, remote sensing, biophysics, nuclear physics, optical physics, plasma physics, solid state physics, astrophysics, cosmology or experimental physics.

To become a research-level physicist or astrophysicist takes four years (bachelor of science degree, honours) plus one to two years for a master of science (MSc) degree and two more years for a doctorate (PhD), then two more as a post-doctoral fellow for a total of ten years before applying for a permanent teaching position. The very lucky ones may get a pure research position. Says Israel, "It is a long, hard road, and none but the very dedicated should attempt it."

To prepare for a career as a cosmologist, he suggests reading popular books on science. "One can never know too much mathematics," he says. "Of course, it is not enough just to read passively. One must actually work at it — fight the text!"

Asked what it feels like to be a cosmologist, Israel says, "When you have caught this bug, it is impossible to shake off." There is a lot of hard slogging, many disappointments when the result of several weeks' work goes into the wastebasket, and disputes with seemingly uncomprehending colleagues who, however, sometimes turn out to be right. But the moments of insight more than make up for all of that. And if one happens to be lucky enough to stumble upon a major discovery, "Well, I imagine that can only be compared to getting high on a mind-altering drug, but without the downside."

Mystery

Perhaps the biggest puzzle facing cosmologists is the problem of the cosmological constant, or "dark energy" as it is known today. In 1917, just after Albert Einstein had finished his theory of gravity, which he called general relativity, the distant stars and galaxies were still believed to be at rest (on average). Einstein was disturbed by the thought that a universe starting out at rest would get pulled together by gravity and should soon collapse, which certainly wasn't happening. To fix the theory, he needed an extra term in his equations — the cosmological constant — to provide a repulsive force that would counterbalance gravity and hold the universe at rest.

Then, in 1929, the American astronomer Edwin Hubble discovered that the universe was not at rest but actually expanding. There was no longer any possibility of a quick collapse. Gravity could perhaps slow this expansion, but there was certainly no need for a repulsive force. Einstein then dropped the cosmological constant, calling it the biggest blunder of his career.

"It wasn't," says Israel, "There were one or two others which vie for that distinction."

But in 1998 cosmologists got an even bigger surprise. Astronomers found that the expansion was not slowing down. It was speeding up. Something must be there, some kind of dark energy producing a repulsive force stronger than gravity but completely invisible and undetectable to human observers. What's more, it works only over very long intergalactic distances, not ordinary astronomical distances such as between the Earth and the sun. So it appears that Einstein's "greatest blunder" was not such a dumb idea after all.

According to Israel, there are really two great mysteries. First, what exactly is dark energy? And secondly, why is its density (that is, the cosmological constant) just about the same as the average *present* density of matter? According to Einstein, this value should have stayed constant since the beginning of the universe. But the density of matter has decreased by 120 orders of magnitude over the same period — that's 10 times 10, 120 times! Is it just a fantastic coincidence that the densities of dark energy and present-day matter are the same, or is there something else going on? Cosmologists call this the cosmic coincidence problem. "I think it will take a young Einstein to solve these mysteries," says Israel, "and, of course, one always hopes that one's current grad student will be that person!"

Explore Further

- Heather Couper, et al., *Black Holes*, Dorling Kindersley Publishing, 1996.
- Werner Israel, "Imploding Stars, Shifting Continents, and the Inconstancy of Matter," *Foundations of Physics*, vol. 26, no. 5, May 1996.
- Edwin F. Taylor and John Archibald Wheeler, *Exploring Black Holes: Introduction to General Relativity*, Addison Wesley, 2000.

Cambridge University website on black holes: www.damtp.cam.ac.uk/user/gr/public/bh_intro.html

Michigan Technological University website on black holes, which has movies of imaginary trips to black holes: antwrp.gsfc.nasa.gov/htmltest/rjn_bht.html

ACTIVITY

Objective:

To calculate the mass of a typical black hole.

You need:

- A calculator

Background:

Consider this: if gas and stars can be observed orbiting a black hole at a velocity of v kilometres per second, and if the orbiting objects are at a distance of r light-years from the black hole, then the mass of the black hole in units of **solar masses** (M) can be calculated with the formula $M = 75 \times v^2 \times r$

What to do:

In a nearby active spiral galaxy (NGC 4258), 21 million light-years away from Earth, there is an object called a **maser** — sort of a giant natural microwave laser — that can be observed orbiting something at the centre of the galaxy that is probably a black hole. The maser is 0.3 light-years from the black hole (r) and is orbiting it at a speed of 900 kilometres per second (v). Plug these values into the above equation, multiply it all together, and discover the approximate size (in solar masses) of the black hole. (The answer is about 18 million solar masses. So that is 18 million times more massive than our sun.)

You can learn more about this system on the web with a simple Google search of "ngc 4258".
There is a giant galaxy called M87 in the centre of the Virgo cluster, 65 million light-years from Earth. Similar observations and calculations show a black hole at the centre of M87 with a mass of two billion suns!

NGC 4258 spiral galaxy

Doreen Kimura

Behavioural Psychologist

World expert on sex differences in the brain.
Wrote the book *Sex & Cognition*, which argues that there truly is
a difference between male and female brains.

Her Story

The room is dimly lit, quiet and small. There are no windows. The ventilation system is the only sound in the psychology building at the University of Western Ontario in London, Ontario.

A young male university student sits at a table, ready for the test, while a female graduate student gets her stopwatch ready on the other side of the table. She gives him a sheet of paper that has rows and rows of little pictures on it and starts the stopwatch. The fellow taking the test is getting $10 to sit for a half hour checking off pictures that match. (See example test question on page 86.) As soon as he finishes one page, she puts another one in front of him, until two minutes are up. Then she gives him other, similar tests. When he finishes, other students, both male and female, come into the room and do the test, again for two minutes each.

The test subjects have been randomly chosen so that they represent a cross section of the total student population, coming from different backgrounds, with a range of ages, heights, weights, etc. Later, after about 100 people have been tested, the graduate student organizes the results to see how many rows of pictures males matched correctly compared with how many rows females got right. This takes many hours of careful calculation and tabulation of the test results, including a statistical analysis. Some days later, Doreen Kimura comes to take a look at the results. Right away she can see they are onto something.

84

> **"** *Don't take too seriously the advice of people who supposedly know better than you do. As long as you are finding out things we didn't know before, you are doing something right.* **"**
>
> —Doreen Kimura

PERSONAL INFO

Born
February 15, 1933, Winnipeg, Manitoba

Residence
Vancouver, British Columbia

Family Members
Father: William J. Hogg
Mother: Sophia N. Hogg
Daughter: Charlotte

Character
Independent, non-conformist, self-assured

Favourite Music
Blue Rodeo, R & B, Rolling Stones, Beethoven, Bach, Mozart

Other Interests
Political activism

Title
Visiting Professor

Office
Department of Psychology, Simon Fraser University, Burnaby,

Status
Working

Degrees
Bachelor of arts (psychology), McGill University, 1956
Master of arts (experimental psychology), McGill, 1957
Doctorate (physiological psychology), McGill, 1961

Awards
Distinguished Contributions to Canadian Psychology as a Science award (Canadian Psychology Association), 1985
Outstanding Scientific Achievement award (Canadian Association for Women in Science), 1986
Fellow, American Psychological

Fellow, Royal Society of Canada
John Dewan Award (Ontario Mental Health Foundation), 1992
Sterling Prize in support of controversy (Simon Fraser University), 2000
Furedy Academic Freedom Award (Society for Academic Freedom and Scholarship), 2002
Donald O. Hebb Distinguished Contributions Award from the Canadian Society for Brain, Behaviour and Cognitive Sciences, 2005

Mentors
Donald O. Hebb and Brenda Milner, McGill psychology professors who taught her to think of behaviour in terms of the nervous system

THE YOUNG SCIENTIST

Kimura grew up and went to school in Neudorf, a small town near the Qu'Appelle Valley in southern Saskatchewan. Facilities for studying science were almost non-existent at the schools she attended, so Kimura was initially interested in writing, languages and algebra. Before finishing high school, she dropped out to teach in one-room rural schoolhouses, first in Saskatchewan and then northern Manitoba. She was 17. While in Manitoba she saw an ad in a teachers' magazine for an admission scholarship to McGill University in Montreal. She applied for the scholarship just for the fun of it, and got it!

At McGill she became interested in psychology as a result of having Donald O. Hebb as her introductory psychology course professor. Hebb was the famous neurologist who identified brain structures he called **cell assemblies**, or what are now called Hebb synapses. His theory guided experiments that foreshadowed neural network theory, now an important tool for artificial-intelligence research. After Kimura obtained her doctorate (PhD) in physiological psychology — the study of how the brain's biology affects behaviour and experience —

"You just have to go ahead and find things out for yourself. This is the mark of a good scientist."

she spent two years as a post-doctoral fellow at the Montreal Neurological Institute before working at the University of California, Los Angeles Medical Center and the Zurich Kantonsspital in Switzerland. She became a professor in psychology at the University of Western Ontario in 1967 and worked there for 30 years. She also has a small consulting business that sells **neuropsychological tests** she developed. In 1998 she moved to Vancouver and took up a position in the Department of Psychology at Simon Fraser University.

Kimura is founding president of the Society for Academic Freedom and Scholarship, and she is concerned about new attitudes in the university research environment. For instance, certain areas of scientific inquiry are now frowned upon because some people might take offence at the way research may describe the abilities of certain groups (such as seniors or women). She also does not like the emphasis on collaborative research. "Both these trends kill the creative freedom of the individual. You just have to go ahead and find things out for yourself. This is the mark of a good scientist," says Kimura.

The Science

Behavioural psychologists study the workings of the human brain to understand how people differ from each other. One method is to give people psychological tests.

Kimura currently studies how male and female brains process information differently — their **cognitive functions**. She also looks at how natural chemicals in our bodies, called **hormones**, relate to different cognitive patterns in men and women, in much the same way that other hormone studies have discovered different physical asymmetries in men and women. For example, researchers have found that, on average, men have larger right tes-

Mental Rotation Test: In this test, you must match the object on the left with two in the group on the right. On average, men can pick out matching rotated objects like these faster than women; women are better at matching objects when they have to pick them out of an array of objects.

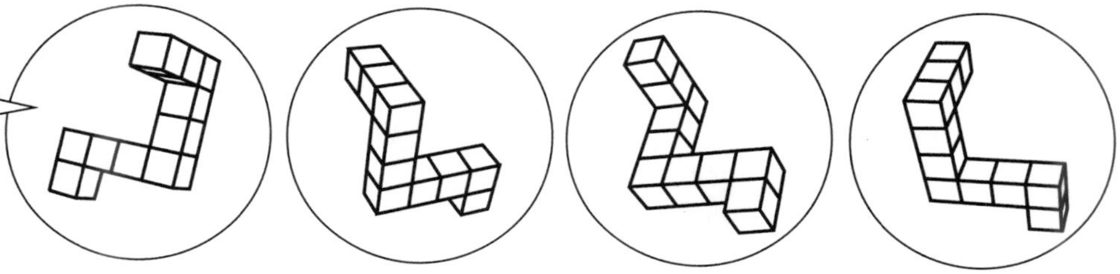

Aphasias, or speech disorders, can occur when people's brains are damaged by some kind of accident or disease. In women, aphasias occur more often when the brain damage is in the front of the brain. In men, these disorders occur when the damage is in the back of the brain.

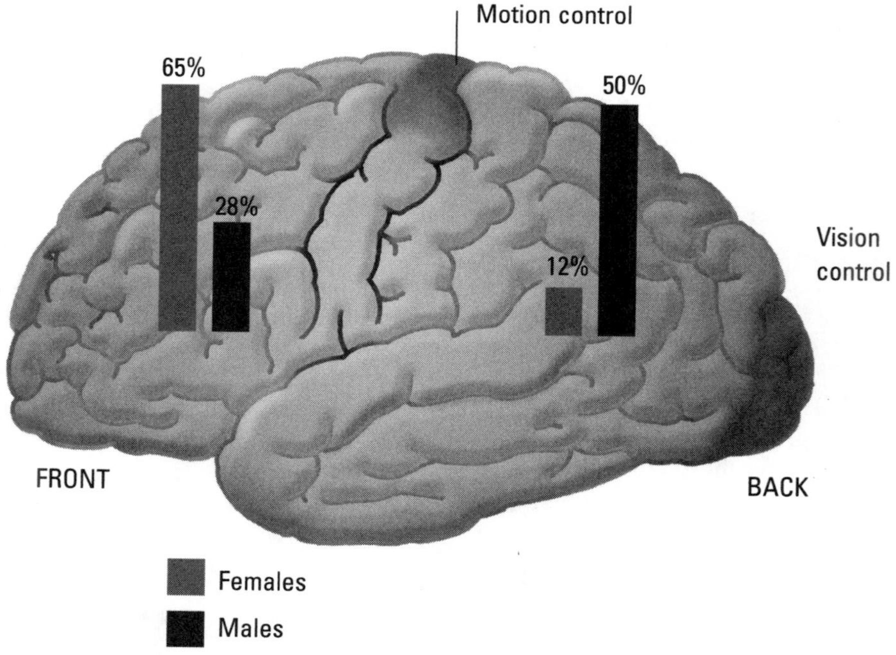

Motion control

65%

28%

50%

12%

Vision control

FRONT

BACK

Females

Males

ticles and women have larger left breasts. Kimura's research has shown that, on average, men outperform women on a variety of spatial tasks, especially when an object must be identified in an altered orientation, or after certain imaginary manipulations such as folding. Men also excel at tests of mathematical reasoning, with the differences between sexes most remarkable when it comes to the most brilliant mathematicians. Women, in contrast, are generally better able to recall the spatial layout of an array of objects, to scan arrays quickly to find matching objects and to recall words, whether word lists or meaningful paragraphs. These sex differences usually begin at an early age and last a lifetime. They also occur across cultures.

Kimura is investigating why women have an advantage over men in the recall of verbal material. She has shown that this advantage applies to words such as "idea," which convey abstract concepts, as well as to words like "potato," which name real things. Strangely, she finds that, on average, women are not better at recalling nonsense words such as "borgin," a preliminary finding she is pursuing.

Kimura experiments purely for the purpose of increasing human knowledge about the differences between men and women with no particular practical application in mind. However, in an environment where it can be politically dangerous to question popular notions of the equality of men and women, her research is perceived by some to be very controversial. Kimura believes it's natural for men and women to choose different careers, preferring jobs that best fit their innate talents.

According to Kimura, the larger number of men in fields of mathematics, computing, engineering, and physics is a fact of life. She criticizes recent initiatives to increase the representation of women in these disciplines. She says, "Engaging in coercive social engineering to balance the sex ratios may actually be the worst kind of discrimination. It also serves to entice some people into fields they will neither excel in nor enjoy."

Kimura counts the number of finger ridges between two specific points on a person's fingerprint. People with high ridge counts on the left hand are better at "feminine" tasks such as the visual matching tests above. On average, any **sample group** of people will have more ridges on their right hands. But Kimura has found that, on average, sample groups of women and groups of homosexual men have a higher incidence of individuals with more ridges on their left hands. Some people consider findings such as Kimura's to be controversial: They would like to believe that there are no differences between men and women, or heterosexuals and homosexuals, or that these differences are not biological, but learned. Kimura has spent a lifetime conducting experiments that indicate there are statistically significant biological differences between men and women. In recent years she has de-emphasized the finger ridge studies, though she claims they still hold up to scientific scrutiny.

So You Want to Be a Behavioural Psychologist

Assuming that a university education is in your future, Kimura does not recommend making career decisions as early as high school. She says, "I think the best method is to take a variety of courses in the first year or two of university, so that you can find out what you like and what you are good at." If you end up in life working on things you enjoy and do well, she says, that's as good as it gets. If you are interested in neuropsychology, you will need to take an introductory biology course and some further courses in physiology and neuroscience.

People who become psychologists often work in a clinical or academic setting. Neuropsychologists in hospitals assess patients with brain damage from accidents, diseases or birth defects. The precise description of a person's abilities can help in planning his or her course of rehabilitation, for example, or to predict when she or he can go back to work. Neurological testing also helps to diagnose brain disorders and to decide whether surgery or some other therapy is required.

People who choose to become university professors or college instructors probably will do research similar to the work described in this chapter. They will teach courses to students, as well as conduct seminars with graduate students.

All psychologists at a professional level must obtain a graduate degree, usually a doctorate. If they enter clinical fields, this will usually include a process of training and examination to become licensed or registered in the province or state where they work. The time from obtaining a bachelor's degree to completion of a doctorate is variable but will be a minimum of four years, often longer. A PhD program requires research and the writing of a thesis (a book-length document) based on original research.

Kimura's career began with an undergraduate honours program in psychology at McGill University, which she did not enter until the third year of a four-year program. She then obtained a master of arts (MA) degree on an aspect of brain asymmetry. Her PhD research at the Montreal Neurological Institute involved the role of the temporal lobes of the brain in speech perception and in memory.

Like many young people, Kimura entered the field of psychology because she wanted to do something that would help people. "But once I started to do research I was far more interested in how things actually worked, so although I did some clinical assessment and enjoyed it, it became secondary to the research questions," she says. She subsequently served as clinical supervisor at the University of Western Ontario, both as neuropsychologist at the University Hospital, where she studied neurological patients, and in the university's Department of Psychology, guiding the training of graduate students in clinical neuropsychology. The university position was her main job.

Her research helped improve the diagnosis of disorders after brain damage. Several tests she devised became widely used in clinical neuropsychology, so she ended up helping people after all. Kimura says, "It is often the case that what we consider 'pure' research may become just as useful in helping people as activities specifically designed to help. This is one of the strongest reasons for supporting research that is not intended to be applied for any useful purpose, but is guided only by a search for truth."

In an average day as a psychology professor Kimura prepares lectures for classes, conducts research at the university on "ordinary" people and at the hospital on neurological patients. She looks at data obtained from research and analyzes it to discover what might be happening — for example, how the level of certain sex hormones in an individual relates to his or her spatial perception ability. She also spends time writing up experimental findings for presentation at conferences and for publication in journals. Much of the research is conducted by graduate students, so as their supervisor Kimura needs to meet and confer with them over every step, and in this way the students receive training in academic research and writing.

The bottom line to Kimura: "A super day is one in which we discover something new from our findings. Looking at data is what I like most about my career. What I like least is the time spent preparing lectures, because this eats into research time."

Mystery

Kimura offered no mystery for future generations to solve, saying that it's the unpredictability of science that makes it interesting.

Explore Further

- Doreen Kimura, *Dissenting Opinions*, 3 Wolves Press, 2002.
- Doreen Kimura, *Sex & Cognition*, MIT Press, 2000.
- Doreen Kimura, "Sex Differences in the Brain," *Scientific American*, May 2002.

Kimura's homepage: www.sfu.ca/~dkimura

ACTIVITY

Objective:

To study hand movements during conversation in men and women and to explain why they may be different.

You need:

- A notebook and pencil
- A watch
- A human subject

What to do:

Find someone you can see clearly for five minutes while they are talking. They don't need to be talking to you; they could be in a restaurant or a bus, or they could be with you but talking to someone else. They should have nothing in their hands, since the idea is to record their hand movements while they talk.

Make a table to record your data. The table has three columns: one for each hand, and one for both hands. It has two rows, so that you can record how many times people touch themselves and how many times they move their hands in the air. Touching their own hair or chest or brushing lint off their own clothes would be marked as self-touching in your table. Tapping a hand on a table or waving hands in the air would be marked as free movement.

After watching several different people, count the totals of hand movements for each individual. Did you record more right-hand or left-hand movements? While people are talking they use speech centres on the left side of the brain. Which side of the brain controls the movements of the right hand? Your experiment might help answer this question. If you pool your observations with dozens of others at your school, you may have enough data to calculate a left- and right-hand-movement average for men and an average for women. Scientists like Kimura study thousands of people to get better average results. Even then, it's important to realize that the results are true only for the set of people who were tested; for instance, college-age students, North Americans, people who were observed in the 2000s, et cetera. In your experiment, which sex did you find uses their right hand the most while talking? Why do you think this is? How could you use this information and how might it affect people?

	Left hand	Right hand	Both hands
Self-touching			
Free movement			

Charles J. Krebs

Zoologist, Animal Ecologist

Famous for writing *Ecology: The Experimental Analysis of Distribution and Abundance* (now in its fifth edition), a textbook used worldwide to teach ecology, and for his work on "the Fence Effect."

His Story

Charley Krebs sits at the back of the sled, tired and happy to be pulled along by the noisy snowmobile. Its high-pitched whine breaks the serenity of the frozen lake in Canada's North. But Krebs loves it, the crisp cold, the wide-open whiteness. The wind sprays snow in his face as the snowmobile plows through another drift.

Krebs thinks about the morning as the sled swooshes along over bumps and cracks in the ice. With him are four **ecology** students from the University of British Columbia, two riding in front of him on the sled loaded with research equipment, two up front on the snowmobile. They are returning from a six-hour session of tagging **snowshoe hares** on a remote island in Kluane Lake in the southwest Yukon Territory. Working in teams, they have just finished checking live-hare traps placed throughout the island. They have removed many hares from the traps, taken notes on weight, sex and health and clipped ID tags on their ears before letting them go. They have piles of notebooks to show for their work.

Krebs is satisfied. He's thinking about how all this new information will fit into a paper he's working on, when suddenly the student driving the snowmobile yells, "Hold on, guys!" and revs the engine to jump across a crack in the ice. It's early May 1980. The lake is starting to break up with the spring thaw and they have crossed a few cracks already. The snowmobile makes it across, but it opens the crack too much. Before they know it, the sled, the equipment and three people are sinking fast in icy water. It doesn't help that they're all wearing winter parkas and heavy snow boots. Krebs treads water with one hand and holds the bundle of notebooks up with the other, yelling, "Save the data! Save the data!"

They did save the data in the notebooks, and themselves, fortunately. But his students never let Krebs forget that day. Data are hard to collect when you are a **wildlife biologist** like Krebs. He doesn't work in a laboratory. His lab is the great outdoors. Since animal life cycles take years, you need decades of observation and data collection to understand a particular animal.

One of Krebs' students tells a similar story.

> **❝ We should be conservative in the ways we deal with natural systems. ❞**
>
> —Charles Krebs

PERSONAL INFO

Born
September 17, 1936, St. Louis, Missouri

Residence
Mayne Island, British Columbia

Family Members
Father: Lawrence Krebs
Mother: Jeanette Krebs
Spouse: Alice J. Kenney
Children: John, Elsie

Character
Patient, efficient, direct, organized, fair, confident, intimidating, even-keeled, fun. Makes lots of wisecracks.

Favourite Music
Beethoven's Sixth Symphony (Second Movement)

Other Interests
Photography, classical music, skiing, hiking

Title
Emeritus Professor of Zoology

Office
Department of Zoology, University of British Columbia, Vancouver,

Status
Retired, but working as much as ever

Degrees
Bachelor of science (biology), University of Minnesota, 1957
Master of arts (animal ecology), University of British Columbia, 1959
Doctorate (animal ecology) UBC, 1962

Awards
Terrestrial Publication of the Year award (Wildlife Society), 1965
Fellow, Royal Society of Canada, 1979
Killam Senior Fellowship, 1985
President's Medal (University of Helsinki), 1986

Sir Frederick McMaster Senior Fellowship (Commonwealth Scientific and Industrial Research Organisation), 1992
C. Hart Merriam Award (American Society of Mammalogists), 1994
Fry Medal (Canadian Society of Zoologists), 1996
Terrestrial Publication of the Year award (Wildlife Society), 1996
Fellow, Australian Academy of Science, 2002
Eminent Ecologist Award (Ecological Society of America), 2002

Mentor
Dennis Chitty, professor at UBC and world expert on lemming cycles.

Once, with a different group of students, Krebs became trapped on an island in Kluane Lake. They had been flown in for the annual hare-counting and tagging session, but weather conditions became so bad that no plane could return to pick them up when they were done. The stormy weather went on and on. After they had been there two weeks longer than planned, the food ran out and the students suggested they eat some of the hares. Krebs refused, because the hares were his experimental subjects. The students were frustrated. They had all these traps and there were plenty of animals. Were they going to starve to death for the benefit of science? After a few more days, when people were getting really ravenous, Krebs finally relented and said they could catch and eat hares — but only if they didn't have ear tags.

 ## THE YOUNG SCIENTIST

Charles "Charley" Krebs grew up in a small Illinois town near St. Louis, across the state line in Missouri. He remembers as a kid fishing for catfish in local rivers with his grandfather. Charley admired his grandfather and his tales of natural adventures and wildlife. In particular Krebs was drawn to the Canadian Arctic. At eight years of age he wanted to be a forest ranger. Even then, he was reading books about basic ecology and the science of wild animals. He was fascinated by the big mysteries of the North — for instance, did **lemmings** really commit mass suicide by jumping off cliffs?

All through his high school years, Krebs had an unusual summer job. He worked for a St. Louis fur-trading company harvesting seals in the **Bering Sea**. Each summer he travelled by train for three days to Seattle, then by boat for seven days up the west coast of Canada to the northern islands. Krebs was curious about all the wildlife on the islands.

After getting his bachelor of science (BSc) degree, Krebs moved to Vancouver to study at the University of British Columbia with Dennis Chitty, who was (and still is) the world expert on lemmings. Krebs obtained a master of arts (MA) and a doctorate (PhD) in zoology, then after a two-year fellowship at Berkeley, California, he went back east to teach zoology at Indiana University. In 1970 Krebs returned to Vancouver and he has been there ever since as a professor of zoology at UBC.

In 2002 Krebs retired from teaching and began spending part of the winter working with the Rodent Research Group at the Commonwealth Scientific and Industrial Research Organisation in Canberra, Australia, to help them figure out why house mice in Australia reach very high populations at irregular intervals and cause extensive damage to grain crops. He also continues to work on snowshoe hares and other animals of the boreal forest in southwestern Yukon, Canada.

Krebs' textbook, *Ecology*, is the standard teaching text for ecology courses worldwide. His interests have become a family affair. His wife is a research associate in ecology at UBC and often goes on field trips with him. His son works for the B. C. Ministry of the Environment, and his daughter is an expert on birds.

The Science

Zoology is the study of animals. Krebs is an ecologist, a person who studies natural systems of plants and animals. His specialty is animal ecology, a combination of physiology — the study of the workings of an animal's body — genetics, evolution and behaviour. One way animal ecologists conduct experiments is to mark off a section of wild country with a grid; the markers might be stakes in the ground, string or coloured ribbons. By keeping logs of the numbers and behaviour of

The Fence Effect, also known as the Krebs Effect, is here demonstrated on Westham Island in Delta, British Columbia, with voles, a type of small rodent. A **population explosion** has occurred on the left side, the fenced-in area, and the voles have eaten everything except the thistles. After the population explosion there's a **population crash**, in which almost all the voles die. What interested Krebs is that these population explosions and crashes occur in lemmings and other wild animals in nature.

This graph shows the population explosion and crash caused by the fence. The grey line is for voles in a similar but unfenced area. The black line shows the number of voles over time in the fenced area.

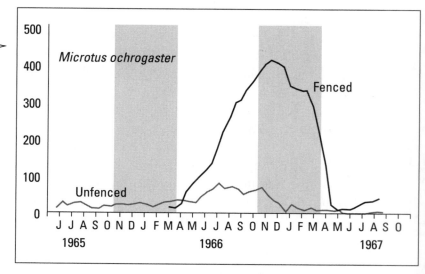

animals in different sections of the grid, animal ecologists uncover facts about animals that help us understand more about the mysteries of nature.

Krebs is still trying to unravel the mystery of lemmings and other small northern mammals whose populations rise slowly and then fall sud-denly, for no apparent reason, every four to 10 years. Hudson's Bay Company fur-trading records show these fluctuations stretch back for hundreds of years. By accident, Krebs discovered something that might help explain what's been happening. In 1965 he tried a simple experiment in an Indiana pasture: He fenced in an area of grassland the size

Over the years Krebs has systematically eliminated possible reasons for the Fence Effect. Food is not a factor: you can supply the fenced-in area with unlimited food and the explosion-and-crash cycle is still observed. Predators are not the answer: You can make the fence low enough to let predators in but high enough to keep the voles from escaping; the Fence Effect still happens. The fence is never a deterrent for birds of prey like hawks, yet you still see the Fence Effect. Krebs now believes that the effect might be due to **social behaviour** among the voles and animals like them. For instance, male voles would naturally migrate — that is, move to other areas — but the fence stops them. Also, as living conditions become more crowded within the fence, aggressive voles can't leave or be kicked out, so they have more impact on other voles. According to Krebs, with voles the final crash seems to be caused by an increased tendency for mothers to kill all the babies in neighbouring mothers' nests.

Lemmings are small rodents that look like guinea pigs. They live throughout the world in northern latitudes. Every four years, their population increases up to 500 times and then crashes to almost nothing. Even after 50 years of research, experts still don't know exactly why populations of lemmings in the North seem to disappear like this. But one thing is for sure: they do not jump off cliffs.

of a soccer field to see what would happen to the population of **voles** living inside the fence. Voles are like mice, but they have shorter legs and heavier bodies. The fence extended down into the soil for several centimetres to stop tunnelling.

Amazingly, within a year he found that the population of voles had increased by about five times, much more than it would have had the field been left unfenced. The population changes that resulted were called the **Fence Effect**. It is now also called the Krebs Effect, since Krebs was the first to study animals this way. He has spent his working life trying to explain the Krebs Effect. He says, "You just put a fence up. You don't do anything to the animals. So what is the fence doing?" In nature you find that populations of animal species on islands are much higher than similar populations on the mainland. Is this an example of a natural Krebs Effect?

Krebs says you have to learn a lot of details about the natural history of any animal you are trying to understand. He is driven by pure curiosity, a desire to learn more and more about the wonders of the natural world. His findings could ultimately be used to help manage wildlife or to design better, more sensitive methods for using natural resources.

Krebs' largest research project spans 20 years, studying the 10-year population cycle of snowshoe hares and their predators in the Yukon, in collaboration with eight other scientists from three Canadian universities. The group has discovered that the snowshoe hare is the dominant herbivore in the Yukon boreal forest and that the changing size of its population is caused by predation by **lynx**, coyotes, great-horned owls and goshawks. Nearly 90 percent die because a predator kills them; almost no snowshoe hares die of starvation or disease.

In 1999 Krebs was one of 31 biologists who took part in the Swedish "Tundra Northwest" project, sailing on the Canadian icebreaker *Louis St. Laurent*. The group visited 17 sites during three months in the Canadian Arctic Archipelago, from Baffin Island to the north Yukon and as far as the north magnetic pole on Ellef Ringnes Island. The data collected on the expedition demonstrated food chain interactions between the plants, herbivores and predators of the Arctic.

Krebs says, "Ecology has become concentrated on two of the world's most serious problems: conservation of endangered species and the impact of climate change on ecosystems. Both of these problems have been ignored since September 11, 2001 [when the attack on the World Trade Center in New York turned nations' attention to global terrorism], and yet both are more serious in the long run than the problem of terrorism." Ecologists work hard to find out how human impacts affect threatened species and how we can design parks and protected areas to conserve our natural heritage. Like many ecologists, Krebs has an almost religious drive to conserve the natural world for future generations.

He is driven by pure curiosity, a desire to learn more and more about the wonders of the natural world.

Careers

So You Want to Be an Ecologist

A wildlife ecologist never has a typical day. A university professor will spend several hours a week lecturing, many hours talking to students, several hours going to research seminars and many hours reading and writing scientific papers. Krebs typically spends about three months of each year in the field doing physical work: live-trapping hares and other animals, measuring trees and vegetation and doing other field work.

The thing he likes most about being an ecologist is the freedom to explore important intellectual issues and questions whenever he likes, for as long as he wants. He says, "In short, I have the ability to think on my own schedule." What he dislikes is dealing with uninformed bureaucracies, both in universities and governments.

Wildlife ecologists can work for universities, the government or private consulting companies. Many mining and forestry companies contract out their environmental studies to private consulting firms. If you want the freedom to work on anything you like, then a university career will offer the best opportunities, but if you want to make money you would be better off working for an ecological consulting company.

To become a wildlife ecologist you will need at least a BSc degree (four years) and preferably an MSc (two or three more years). The best jobs with the most freedom require a PhD (three to five more years). Most ecologists are 27 to 30 years old before they complete their training.

The typical salary range in Canada for an ecologist with a bachelor's degree is about $30,000 to $35,000 a year. A master's degree raises that to $40,000 to $45,000, and an ecologist with a PhD can expect to earn $40,000 to $60,000. "No one should become a wildlife ecologist if they desire to be wealthy," says Krebs.

To succeed as an ecologist you will need good skills in all the natural sciences from mathematics to chemistry, physics and, of course, biology, as well as computer skills. You must also learn how to write effectively.

Mystery

Krebs still has not entirely figured out the mystery of the Fence Effect. One thing he would like to know is the following: The Fence Effect only happens if you put up a fence. If you don't fence an area, you won't necessarily see a population explosion and crash in that area. Yet you *always* see it if you fence in an area. Krebs wonders, How big does a fenced-in area have to be before the Fence Effect disappears?

Explore Further

- Charles Krebs, *Ecology: The Experimental Analysis of Distribution and Abundance*, fifth edition, Benjamin Cummings, 2001.
- Charles Krebs, S. Boutin and R. Boonstra (editors), *Ecosystem Dynamics of the Boreal Forest: The Kluane Project*, University of Oxford Press, 2001.

ACTIVITY

Activity 1

Objective:

To learn about voles' territory by mapping their runs.

You need:

- Four small pegs
- Four metres of string
- A notebook and pencil

What to do:

Go to any large, grassy field, such as those outside most airports, and put your nose to the ground. Part the grass and inch along, separating it in a straight line for at least 10 metres or until you find a vole runway. This will be an unmistakable tubular path about two or three centimetres wide, like the inside of a toilet paper roll. If you don't find one on the first try, try again, maybe in a different field. These runways branch in all directions; they look like curving tubes at the bottoms of the grass stems, right near where the stems join the roots. When you find them, mark off a small area with string and pegs, about one square metre. In your notebook, try to draw a map of the vole runs in this little section of the field.

Activity 2

Objective:

To learn about snowshoe hares by following their tracks.

You need:

- A trip to the countryside
- A notebook and pencil

What to do:

If you live somewhere that has a snowy winter, you probably can find a spruce forest nearby. In the winter, go cross-country skiing or hiking in the forest, looking for snowshoe hare tracks. You should be able to find some without too much trouble. They look like this:

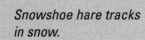

Snowshoe hare tracks in snow.

Once you learn to spot the tracks, follow a set and try to determine what the hare is eating. You can examine its fecal droppings or look for bits of food the hare dropped while eating. Is there lots of food? Where is it located? Where do snowshoe hares like to hang out? How do they avoid predators such as lynx and other wildcats? Try to write down answers to all these questions in your notebook based on what you observe.

If you are ambitious and you want to get a feeling for what professional animal ecologists do, try picking a place in the woods and every winter go back. Count the number of hare tracks that cross 100 metres of your path in that same part of the woods at the same time of year. Write this in your notebook every year. After about 10 years you should see a cycle begin to emerge.

Snowshoe hare in summer.

Snowshoe hare in winter.

> **The most important thing: Never shut off your options. You never know what the next year is going to bring. If you leave your options open, then when something happens you know, 'That's where I want to go.' And you do it! Never box yourself in.**
>
> —Julia Levy

PERSONAL INFO

Born
May 15, 1934, Singapore

Residence
Vancouver, British Columbia

Family Members
Father: Guillaume Albert Coppens
Mother: Dorothy Frances
Spouse: Edwin Levy
Children: Two
Grandchildren: Four

Character
Determined, impatient, shy

Favourite Music
Vivaldi's flute concertos

Other Interests
Opera, gardening, family and kids, tennis, cooking, writing fiction, a cedar cabin on Sonora Island

Title
Executive Chair of the Scientific Advisory Board of QLT

Office
QLT Incorporated, Vancouver

Status
Semi-retired

Degrees
Bachelor of arts (experimental pathology), University of British Columbia, 1955
Doctorate (microbiology), University College, 1958

Awards
Fellow, Royal Society of Canada, 1980
Gold Medal for Medical Research (British Columbia Science Council), 1982
Killam Senior Research Prize, 1986
Officer, Order of Canada, 2001

Future of Vision Award (Foundation Fighting Blindness), 2001
Women of Distinction award (YWCA), 2001
Friesen-Rygiel Prize, 2002
Canadian Society of Pharmaceutical Sciences, 2002
Helen Keller Award for Contributions to Vision, 2003

Mentor
Her mother, Dorothy, who in the 1940s had to support the family while Levy's father was in a Japanese prisoner-of-war concentration camp.

Julia Levy

Microbiologist and Immunologist

Co-discovered photodynamic anti-cancer and ophthalmology drugs, co-founder of the company QLT Incorporated.

Her Story

In 1986 Julia Levy was giving a talk to some doctors in Waterloo, Ontario about her work on new light-activated drugs. A few years before, she had formed a spinoff company called Quadra Logic Technologies (now QLT Inc.) to commercialize her university research. The doctors were trying these drugs on **cancer** patients and they were very upset because Johnson & Johnson, another drug company, was closing down their **Photofrin** research program. Photofrin was one of the new photodynamic drugs, and it appeared to be effective against cancer. Many people were being helped by this technology, but soon they would not be able to get the drug. "It was a very upsetting experience for me," says Levy, who until that point had worked on these drugs only in a laboratory. "For the first time, I became aware that we were talking about real patients being treated for real cancer."

That night, on the plane flying back to Vancouver, Levy began thinking: We're in the business of **photodynamic therapy**. We should get into this at the first level and we should perhaps start making Photofrin, at least for Canadian investigators. She sat pondering this all the way home and became very excited. When she got off the plane she immediately called her business partner, Jim Miller, and said, "We've got to do something." She just wanted to help cancer sufferers. "Let's make the product. We know how to make it." But Miller surprised her. "We'll take over the company," he said, meaning the Johnson & Johnson subsidiary that was making Photofrin. They made a deal with the pharmaceutical company American Cyanamid, raised $15 million and took over the subsidiary. It was a major turning point for QLT and for Levy.

"Being in business — in commercial science — focuses your science," says Levy. "The big difference between university and commercial science is not the quality of the research; it's your awareness that as you move a drug forward towards getting it into a patient it's going to cost you a fortune." Getting a new drug treatment perfected costs about 10 times as much as inventing it in the first place, and therefore you cannot afford to make mistakes. Maybe that's why it suits Levy's personality. She likes to do things right the first time and she hates retracing her steps in any way. She says, "You can't afford too many goofs when a single experiment costs $50,000."

In April 1993 the Canadian government approved Photofrin for the treatment of bladder cancer. It can also be used to treat cancers of the skin, lung, stomach and cervix. In 1995 QLT received approval to treat esophageal cancer in Canada and the United States, and it obtained very broad approval in Japan to treat a wide variety of cancers.

Throughout the 1990s QLT embarked on many new research programs to treat other diseases using photodynamic therapies. It looked at **autoimmune diseases** such as **arthritis, psoriasis** (a skin disease) and **multiple sclerosis.** "It's way beyond cancer," says Levy, excited about the potential to cure other diseases with this new drug.

By far QLT's biggest success is Visudyne, a photodynamic drug for the treatment of the eye disease called **macular degeneration.** Based on the active ingredient in Photofrin (a **benzoporphyrin derivative** that goes through a chemical change when exposed to a particular **wavelength** of light), Visudyne is QLT's biggest **biotechnology** product in terms of sales (about a half billion U.S. dollars in 2004). It is the most lucrative drug product ever launched in the history of eye medi-

"You can't do it just with luck, but luck helps."

cine. "We got lucky," says Levy. "You can't do it just with luck, but luck helps."

The chain of "lucky" events begins in the late 1980s, around the time Levy was investigating how to cure cancer with photodynamic therapy. Her mother began losing her vision from age-related macular degeneration (AMD). Levy had never heard of AMD, so she decided to read up on it. She discovered that, worldwide, about half a million people get the "wet form" of AMD every year — the kind that her mother had. It's the leading cause of blindness in people over the age of 55.

Shortly after learning about AMD, Levy happened to be at a conference on photodynamic therapy where, for the first time, she heard a doctor talking about how the eye was the perfect organ for treatment by photodynamic therapy. Unlike lungs and bladders, where doctors have to thread in a long **fibre optic** cable to treat a tumour with light, with an eye they can simply shine the light directly in. They don't need much fancy equipment. The doctor listed many eye abnormalities and diseases that might be treated by photodynamic drugs. Even at this point, the "light did not go on" for Levy. She knew QLT did not have any money for eye research at that time.

A few months later she was at Harvard University in Cambridge, Massachusetts, to meet scientists who were conducting trials of QLT drugs on patients with skin cancer. Levy had only dropped in to see how things were going, but she met an ophthalmologist there named Ursula

Schmidt, who had been going to the skin cancer research lab to get the empty bags of QLT photodynamic drug out of the garbage bins; she would take them back to her lab and squeeze out the last drops for use in experiments on animals with eye diseases.

"As it turned out, we had just raised some new money in Vancouver and we were looking for research projects," says Levy. By then it was too late for her mom, but Levy decided that QLT should work on a photodynamic drug for eye disease.

Within five years, by 1995, QLT had a drug ready to try on a human patient. Even that first crude drug gave a positive effect. The rapid development of Visudyne was very unusual. Most drugs take more than 10 years of testing before they are considered safe to use on humans. Visudyne went to market faster because it satisfied a great need.

THE YOUNG SCIENTIST

During World War II, a few years after Julia Levy was born in the Asian city-state of Singapore, her father was captured by the Japanese and put into a prisoner-of-war camp. Just before this, her mother had escaped to Canada with Julia and another daughter. After the war her father rejoined his wife and children in Vancouver, but his experiences as a prisoner left him a broken man and he was not able to support the family. This taught Levy to be self-sufficient and that a woman should never get married just to have someone to look after her.

Even as a little girl Levy was interested in biology, though she always felt she would grow up to be a piano teacher. On weekends she would return home from Queen's Hall boarding school in Vancouver and go for walks with her mother in the woods near their house. Their dog would romp along, collecting stray mutts that would stay at their house for several days. Sometimes Julia would take a sieve and a jar on the walks to bring back frogs' eggs; she and her sister would grow tadpoles in wash basins in the basement.

She and her sister would grow tadpoles in wash basins in the basement.

Levy enjoyed mathematics in high school and in grade 11 had a particularly inspiring biology teacher, a woman. After obtaining a bachelor of arts (BA) degree in biology from the University of British Columbia in Vancouver and a doctorate (PhD) in experimental pathology at University College in London, England, Levy became a professor of **microbiology** at UBC. In the 1980s she co-founded QLT.

By 2004 QLT had become a world leader in sales of drugs that treat macular degeneration. It was one of the most successful high-tech companies in Canada. When asked how it feels to create such extraordinary wealth, Dr. Levy says, "Well, when I look at it I think ... *me*?" She gets a look of wonder on her face but quickly adds, "And a lot of other people — you can't do it alone."

The Science

Microbiologists research such areas as bacteria, fungi, viruses, tissues, cells, pharmaceuticals and plant or animal toxins. Julia Levy is a microbiologist and **immunologist**, someone who studies the human **immune system**, the collection of molecules and cells that help the body fight off disease. Together with colleagues from UBC she develops drugs that are unique because they are **photosensitive**, which means that upon being exposed to light they change in some way that makes them toxic to cells. This photodynamic therapy can be used to treat lung cancer and other diseases such as AMD.

AMD affects a very tiny part of the eye called the macula, the "business part of the eye," as Levy calls it. The eye is like a camera, with a lens at the front and a sort of "film" at the back called the retina. The retina's job is to convert light into nerve signals for the brain to turn into images. The macula is just a few square millimetres near

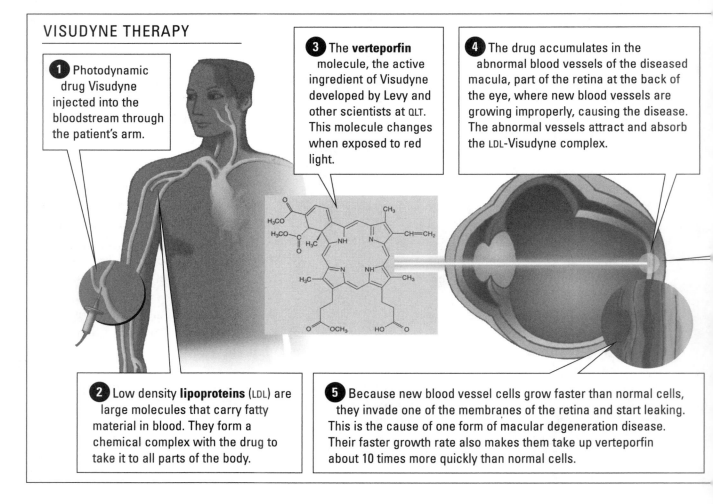

VISUDYNE THERAPY

1 Photodynamic drug Visudyne injected into the bloodstream through the patient's arm.

2 Low density **lipoproteins** (LDL) are large molecules that carry fatty material in blood. They form a chemical complex with the drug to take it to all parts of the body.

3 The **verteporfin** molecule, the active ingredient of Visudyne developed by Levy and other scientists at QLT. This molecule changes when exposed to red light.

4 The drug accumulates in the abnormal blood vessels of the diseased macula, part of the retina at the back of the eye, where new blood vessels are growing improperly, causing the disease. The abnormal vessels attract and absorb the LDL-Visudyne complex.

5 Because new blood vessel cells grow faster than normal cells, they invade one of the membranes of the retina and start leaking. This is the cause of one form of macular degeneration disease. Their faster growth rate also makes them take up verteporfin about 10 times more quickly than normal cells.

A simulation of how the world appears to a person with AMD.

6 About 10 or 15 minutes after the injection, doctors shine cool red laser diode light into the eye for about 90 seconds. The light has a wavelength of 690 **nanometres**, which is the optimum shade of red for activating the verteporfin, creating free oxygen molecules. The oxygen reacts with the abnormal blood vessel cells and effectively "burns" them up.

7 The abnormal vessels are destroyed.

All the science for Visudyne is done in Vancouver, but the active ingredient is made in Edmonton, Alberta, and then modified in Japan to make it soluble. Finally, the product is bottled and labelled in the United States. More of this process will soon be moving to Vancouver.

the middle of the retina, but it has millions and millions of finely tuned light receptor cells — many more per unit area than the rest of the retinal surface. It's the part of the eye where we turn our focus to read and write, to draw or work with our hands, to watch TV, to prepare and eat food or to recognize faces, among many other activities that require the discrimination of fine detail.

In people with AMD, microscopic blood vessels grow abnormally and invade one of the membranes at the back of the retina, where the vessels start leaking. "The macula is the only part of your body where if even one micron (one-millionth of a metre) of it is hurt, your vision is damaged," says Levy. Most other parts of your body can sustain damage in large chunks and work just fine, but not the macula. It's one of the most incredible parts of the body.

For people with AMD, the centre of their vision is blurred or distorted or things appear odd in size or shape. For instance, things that are normally straight, such as doorways or telephone poles, might seem bent or crooked. As the disease gets worse, a blank patch or dark spot forms in the centre of their sight. This makes activities like reading, writing and recognizing small objects or faces very difficult. Nobody knows why AMD occurs, but there seems to be a genetic component; it runs in families. Europeans are more prone to get it than Asians or Africans. It is also related to age; about half of people over 85 have it.

Careers

So You Want to Be an Immunologist

The whole area of clinical biology and biotechnology is expanding rapidly and will become a significant part of our future. Not long ago, if you were a biologist you had only one real option: teaching. Now there are countless career opportunities: clinical research, regulatory work for government and industry, marketing, manufacturing and quality control in biotechnology, chemical, pharmaceutical, food, health care, resource, environmental, forestry, agriculture and consulting companies. There are more courses being taught, as well, in universities and colleges. A strong scientific base with a university degree is now a prerequisite even for the marketing jobs at biotechnology companies and in other high-tech industries. Salaries start at about $30,000 a year and can go up into six figures. However, Levy says, "I've never found money to be a compelling reason to do anything."

Typical training required for a degree in biotechnology is a four-year bachelor's degree, followed by three to five years of post-graduate work leading to a master's or doctorate. Jobs are available with any of these levels of university education. "Above all, you need to have a love of science and a curiosity for the subject," says Levy.

There's no such thing as a typical day for Julia Levy. Some days are spent in meetings with other companies, others reading scientific literature, still others meeting her QLT colleagues to work out business strategies. Levy likes everything about her job except the travelling and talking to investors.

Mystery

Levy says that although researchers know a lot about the biology of cancer cells, how cancer cells develop is still one of the biggest mysteries around.

Explore Further

- Frederick Su, "Photodynamic Therapy: A Maturing Medical Technology," OE Reports, *Journal of the International Society for Optical Engineering*, no. 194, February 2000.
- Hui Sun and Jeremy Nathans, "The Challenge of Macular Degeneration," *Scientific American*, October 2001.

Julia Levy's personal web page at QLT Inc.:
    www.qltinc.com/Qltinc/main/mainpages.cfm?InternetPageID=183

ACTIVITY

Objective:

To understand why Levy and her team use red laser light to activate their photodynamic drugs.

You need:

- A strong flashlight
- A dark room

What to do:

Turn on the flashlight and put your hand over it so that the light shines through the skin between your thumb and first finger. What colour is the light that you see through your hand?

Why it works: Our bodies are mostly transparent to red light. That means red light can pass through our body's tissues. The red laser light at 690-nanometre wavelength that Levy uses to activate photodynamic drugs passes right through skin and flesh. Even **haemoglobin**, the protein that makes blood red, does not absorb red light at that wavelength.

Why do you think red light passes through our bodies? This turns out to be a handy quality, because it means that many diseases can be treated by taking an injection of photodynamic drug, waiting a few hours, then sitting in a room with strong red light.

Walter Lewis

Ethnobotanist

World expert on **airborne** and **allergenic** pollen and famous for discovering and cataloguing medicinal plants in the tropical rainforest.

Memory Elvin-Lewis

Ethnobotanist and Infectious Disease Microbiologist

An expert on evaluating traditional medicines and their use.

Their Story

Holding his half-full gourd of "**chicha**," Walter Lewis smiles, wishing he didn't have to drink another drop. It tastes so sour, like a combination of yogurt, warm beer and mashed potatoes. But the headman — the *apu* of the Achuar Jivura village in the Peruvian **Amazon** jungle — is looking him right in the eye. To refuse this friendship ceremony drink would be an insult to his hosts.

Lewis takes another look at the yellowish liquid in his gourd. He knows that Achuar women make chicha by chewing a kind of **cassava root** and spitting it into a huge bowl. Then they let it stand for a while to **ferment**. The air in the open hut is wet and hot. Lewis feels his shirt stick to the sweat on his back as he turns to glance at his wife, Memory, sitting among the women just outside the men's circle. A smouldering cooking fire gives everything the smell of smoked fish. The forest outside is alive with shrieking jungle birds while inside the hut, pet parrots, monkeys and dogs squawk and bark. A crowd of gawking, naked children surrounds the Lewises. "We are the zoo," thinks Lewis as he takes a final sip of the brew like a good **ethnobotanist**.

The Lewises have travelled to the Peruvian jungle in search of plants that might yield new drugs. They are ethnobotanists and they specialize in communicating with native peoples around the world to learn about their traditional medicines. Mariano, the headman, is telling Walter about the healing powers of a certain plant whose roots are used to help women through the final stages of childbirth.

While Walter is talking to Mariano, Memory

> **" Do what you enjoy and go where your heart takes you. "**
>
> —Walter Lewis

PERSONAL INFO

Born
June 26, 1930, near Ottawa, Ontario

Residence
St. Louis, Missouri

Family Members
Father: John Wilfred Lewis
Mother: Florence
Spouse: Memory Elvin-Lewis
Children: Memoria, Walter Jr.

Character
Congenial, determined

Favourite Music
Andean flute music

Other Interests
Gardening, antiques, family, travel

Titles
Emeritus Professor of Biology, Washington University; Senior Botanist, Missouri Botanical Garden, St. Louis

Office
Biology Department, Washington University, St. Louis, Missouri

Status
Semi-retired, but still working

Degrees
Bachelor of arts (honours), University of British Columbia, 1951
Master of science (botany and biology), UBC, 1954
Doctorate (biology), University of Virginia, 1957
Post-doctoral work at Kew Gardens in London, England, and at the Swedish Academy of Sciences in Stockholm

Awards
Guggenheim Fellowship, 1963
Fellow, Linnean Society of London, 1983
Martin de la Cruz Silver Medal (Mexican Academy of Traditional Medicine), 2000
Janaki-Ammal Medal (Indian Ethnobotany Society), 2004

Mentor
Walter H. Flory, who was his thesis adviser for his doctorate.

> ❝ *Remember to have patience for technology to catch up to you and your discovery.* ❞
>
> —Memory Elvin-Lewis

PERSONAL INFO

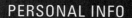

Born
May 20, 1933, Vancouver, British Columbia

Residence
St. Louis, Missouri

Family Members
Father: Richard James Elvin
Mother: May Winnifred Foster
Spouse: Walter Lewis
Children: Memoria; Walter H. Jr.
Grandchildren: Florence, Lilian

Character
Sociable, patient, stolid, forthright

Favourite Music
American folk music

Other Interests
Gardening, antiques, family, travel, gourmet cooking

Title
Professor of Biomedicine in Microbiology and Ethnobotany

Office
Biology Department, Washington University, St. Louis, Missouri

Status
Working

Degrees
Bachelor of arts, University of British Columbia, 1952
Medical Technologist, Pearson Tuberculosis Hospital, Vancouver, 1955
Master of science (medical microbiology), University of Pennsylvania School of Medicine, 1957

Master of science (virology and epidemiology), Baylor School of Medicine, 1960
Doctorate (medical microbiology), University of Leeds, 1966

Awards
Fellow, Linnean Society of London, 1995
Martin de la Cruz Silver Medal (Mexican Academy of Traditional Medicine), 2001

Mentor
Her father, who encouraged her to understand science and medicine.

notices a big grin on the face of an old woman in the back row. In Achuar culture, women do not sit with the men but have their own special area within the hut. Memory quietly goes to talk to the old woman, who turns out to be Mariano's auntie. She takes Memory outside to show her the plant Mariano is talking about, all the while telling her how men don't know much about this medicine, since it's used strictly by women. When Memory sees the plant, she learns that it's not the root the Achuar use but the leaf. On closer inspection later, Walter discovers that it's not the leaf that has the medicinal quality but an ergot-like **fungus** growing on the topmost leaves of the plant.

THE YOUNG SCIENTIST

Walter

When Walter was 12 his dad asked him what he wanted for his birthday. The Lewis family lived in Victoria, British Columbia, and Walter was fascinated by an uncle who had a plant nursery in the countryside. Walter told his dad he'd like a greenhouse for his birthday, and his father gave him one. It was made of wood and glass and was about three metres long and two metres wide, with planting benches on each long wall. Walter's uncle taught him how to grow roses from cuttings. The next summer Walter began selling his roses in Victoria.

His mom and dad wanted him to become a dentist. Walter went to Victoria College (which later became the University of Victoria) to study toward dentistry, but he took extra botany courses on the side to satisfy his curiosity about plants. After second-year university he announced to his parents that he would become a botanist, not a dentist.

Memory

When Memory was a girl in Vancouver, her father, a physician, took her with him on his house calls. As a teenager she helped in his office. Anything scientific fascinated her and her father encouraged her by helping her understand what he did. She was unsatisfied with the science education she was getting at the small private school she attended and she insisted on going to public school, where she believed she would get a better education. She found her science teachers to be excellent and she always topped the class in science. As a teenager Memory volunteered in the St. John Ambulance Brigade and became a sergeant.

When she took her first **microbiology** course at the University of British Columbia, she remembers thinking, "This is it!"

In 1969 Memory and her co-workers recorded a case of a teenage St. Louis boy dying of strange natural causes, complications from a chlamydia infection that should not have been fatal. Nobody could understand the boy's case history or figure out why he died, so blood specimens were put away and frozen. Twenty years later, when acquired immune deficiency syndrome (AIDS) was characterized, Memory recognized the symptoms and had the boy's frozen blood analyzed. The case is now recognized as the first recorded case of AIDS in the United States.

The Lewises credit many of their discoveries to the way they work as a team. If Walter had been in the jungle on his own, perhaps he never would have discovered this medicine. As a man he would probably not have talked to the women of the tribe, and he would have embarked on a futile search for the active ingredient in the roots of the plant.

The Science

Ethnobotany is the study of plants by obtaining information from people around the world. The Lewises specialize in discovering new drugs extracted from plants used in **folk medicine** by native tribes in South America and other tropical parts of the world.

Three-quarters of all modern drugs come directly or indirectly from plants used in folk medicine. The Lewises are desperately trying to catalogue the wide variety of plants used by tropical rainforest cultures before the forests are chopped down. They have collected thousands of plants and found dozens of traditional medicines. These include a wound-healing tree sap that helps cuts and scrapes heal 30 percent faster. Other plants treat malaria, hepatitis, diarrhea and more. In 2003 Walter Lewis and his colleagues at Washington University in St. Louis submitted an

The hut: The Achuar hut sits in a clearing in the forest. It's about 12 metres long and seven metres wide. Several families live together inside. Unmarried and widowed women live at one end. Meetings are held at the other end around a Snake Stool, where the headman or *apu* sits. Open fires burn on the floor and the smoke goes out a hole in the roof.

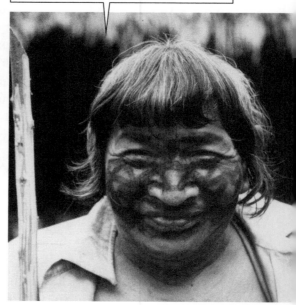

An Achuar elder: Now dead, this wise elder taught the Lewises much about the medicinal plants of the Achuar.

anti-malarial patent based on their collaborative research with Peruvian natives, who also own part of the patent. Meanwhile, Memory Elvin-Lewis collaborated with Peruvian physicians and U.S. researchers on studies demonstrating the value of traditional hepatitis remedies.

The tropical jungles where most of these plants grow are disappearing. At the same time, the people who know how to use these plants are becoming more "Westernized" (steeped in the culture of North America and Western Europe) and are losing their traditional culture and knowledge of the forest. The Lewises are trying to talk with these people before it is too late. The plants they discover may become widely used miracle drugs of the future.

By observing and talking to native people from India, Africa and the Americas, the Lewises have learned how some trees cause allergies. They have been called upon to advise cities in their tree-planting policies. The Lewises have also studied the use of chewing sticks by hundreds of millions of native people around the world instead of toothbrushes. One example is the bark of the neem tree, which, when chewed, provides anti-microbial and anti-inflammatory effects that can reduce gingivitis (gum disease). However, the couple report that neem bark also contains chem-

Gourd with holly leaves: Each morning, before dawn, the Achuar men drink guayus, a very strong, pleasant-tasting **caffeine** drink made from holly leaves. Each man usually drinks about a litre; within 45 minutes he vomits about half of it back up. The vomiting is not caused by the guayus but is a custom of the tribe. When boys reach maturity, they join the men in the morning ritual of drinking and regurgitating guayus. It is considered an honour, and boys look forward for years to this right of passage. The Lewises do not know why the tribe has developed this custom. Perhaps vomiting every morning is a healthy ritual in a jungle environment where many deadly parasites thrive.

Methylergonovine: When Walter Lewis returns from the jungle to his university laboratory, he uses chemical identification techniques to determine the molecular structure of the active ingredients in the **medicinal plants** he brings back. This is a typical diagram of a molecule similar to the active ingredient in the ergot-like fungus the Lewises found growing on a plant used by Achuar women to aid in childbirth.

icals that could cause **cancer**. Memory Elvin-Lewis, commenting on the safety of natural herbal remedies in her 2001 landmark review of herbal medicines in the *Journal of Ethnopharmacology*, says, "The notion that 'natural is safe' has little meaning in reality unless, of course, one puts into the same context the idea that 'pharmaceutically derived' is not always totally beneficial." The Lewises like to point out that naturally occurring medicines can be very beneficial, but they must be treated with the same caution and respect as conventional medicines from commercial drug companies.

The Lewises have achieved their goal as ethnobotanists by cataloguing the medicinal plants of the world in an 800-page book, *Medical Botany: Plants Affecting Human Health*. While they started by observing and recording how indigenous cultures used medicinal plants, eventually their research shifted: they began working with chemists and pharmacologists to develop new medicines from the plants they discovered. "Things have changed," says Walter Lewis. "Everyone is concerned with intellectual property when you collect a plant. If you use native know-how, you have to pay them upfront for the privilege of collecting specimens even during the development phase."

The Lewises now spend the greatest percentage of their time negotiating among native peoples, the university and pharmaceutical companies. They want to get marvellous new drugs to cure diseases such as hepatitis, tuberculosis and malaria, but they also want the native people to be adequately compensated and to retain part ownership of patents and the medicinal knowledge of the plants their tribes have used for centuries. "We invent the chemistry and pharmacology to say precisely what is going on with a medicinal plant," says Dr. Lewis, "but the native people *own* the knowledge of the *medicinal qualities* of their plant." But large drug companies wish to benefit commercially from these new medicines, too. It's a delicate balance and takes a lot of time.

Twenty years ago, Western ethnobotanists like the Lewises could find a remote rainforest tribe, learn its herbal remedies and simply take whatever plant material they wanted back to their laboratories for study. Today, things are different. The potential commercial value of drugs derived from jungle herbal medicines is in the hundreds of billions of dollars. Realizing this, indigenous peoples have formed organizations to protect their wealth of plant knowledge. The Lewises now must arrange their explorations with a Peruvian group called the Confederación de Nacionalidades Amazónicas del Perú (CONAP), which represents 18 Amazonian tribes. They have to negotiate payment for doing research, and they must agree to share any wealth arising from discoveries. The Lewises also want to help protect the tribal knowledge, so they now encode data and keep plant names secret to ensure nobody steals that knowledge.

There are other ethical dilemmas in the rainforest. "If you discover that one tribe has found a cure for some disease, can you ethically tell a neighbouring tribe which plant it is?" asks Dr. Lewis. He will not give out this information, but he will name a contact person in the other tribe.

> *The native people own the knowledge of the medicinal qualities of their plant.*

Careers

So You Want to Be an Ethnobotanist

The Lewises enjoy their work because they are often forced to learn a lot of new things. Bringing a drug out of the rainforest requires many skills. Besides a basic knowledge of biology, medicine and chemistry, the Lewises must be politicians, ethicists and entrepreneurs. There are legal aspects of intellectual property law that must be learned, as well as plant pathology (diseases of plants), **genetic engineering**, plant breeding, pharmacology (the study of drugs), viruses, microbiology and **anthropology**. "You learn to stretch your knowledge in every area," says Dr. Lewis. Because of the many extra things you must learn along the way "it takes you all your life to get where you're going," adds his wife, Dr. Elvin-Lewis. She cautions that there are many 18-hour days and full seven-day work weeks, but she loves the travel and the excitement of living in the jungle with native people. The couple's greatest challenge is finding enough money to bring these very valuable drugs out of the rainforest. "I feel very committed to the wonderful indigenous people we've been privileged to work with, and the trust they have in us so the world can benefit from their knowledge," says Dr. Elvin-Lewis.

Walter Lewis enjoys the fieldwork, too. "It's 'work' in a sense," he says, "but I find it relaxing and enjoyable. I'm fortunate that my *work* is my *play*." (Collecting plants is his hobby.) The things he dislikes about his job are report writing, committee meetings and administration. His advice to young scientists: diversify and explore many avenues. Don't be too narrow in your studies.

Mystery

In the Peruvian jungle, the Achuar have shown the Lewises a plant they use to treat "the frightened people." The Lewises do not know what the Achuar mean by this, but they feel that if this mystery could be solved, a new drug for anxiety or some forms of mental illness might be discovered.

Explore Further

- Memory Elvin-Lewis, "Should We Be Concerned about Herbal Remedies?" *Journal of Ethnopharmacology*, no. 75, 2001.
- Walter Lewis and Memory Elvin-Lewis, *Medical Botany: Plants Affecting Human Health,* John Wiley & Sons, 2003.
- Walter Lewis, et al., "Ritualistic Use of the Holly *Ilex Guayusa* by Amazonian Jivaro Indians," *Journal of Ethnopharmacology*, no. 33, 1991.

Personal web page: dbbs.wustl.edu/RIB/Lewis.html
U.S. National Health Museum online website about ethnobotany:
www.accessexcellence.org/RC/Ethnobotany/page2.html

ACTIVITY

Activity 1

Objective:

To be an ethnobotanist in your own family.

You need:

- Six objects made of wood from around your house or classroom
- A notebook

What to do:

To get a feeling for what it's like to be an ethnobotanist, go around your home or classroom and try to find six objects made of wood. List these in your notebook. Now try to identify what type of wood was used for each object. Where did the wood come from? How was it made into the final product? You can ask your "tribal elders" (your parents or teachers) if they know where the wood came from. Take notes in your notebook. What does the origin of the wood tell you about you, your family or your culture?

Activity 2

Objective:

To be an ethnobotanist by discovering a new kind of food in your own town or city or rural community.

You need:

- A grocery store that sells ethnic foods different from those you normally eat
- A notepad
- A small amount of money

What to do:

Visit an ethnic grocery store. For example, Chinese, Filipino, Mexican, European deli, African, East Asian or Caribbean food shops. Look around until you find an unfamiliar fresh fruit or vegetable, or a can or package containing something that you've never eaten before. Politely ask someone in the store where the fruit, vegetable or food product comes from and find out how to prepare it. Be brave. Most people enjoy talking about food and they will be pleased that you show an interest in their culture. The person you ask can be a customer or the owner or an employee. If the first person you ask is too shy or you can't speak their language, ask someone else. Often customers know more about the food than the employees because they are buying it to prepare food for their families. Be patient, and above all polite, and keep asking until you find someone who will help.

Remember to watch the facial expressions of the people you talk to, as well as people watching. The Lewises have found over and over again that a slight grin or twinkle in the eyes means there's more to the story. It's important to ask more questions when you see something like this or else you might miss an important step in the food's preparation. Ask where does the vegetable grow? How is it used? Keep asking questions and take notes as the person answers your questions. Make sure you write everything down, being sure to get every step involved in the preparation, including any other ingredients involved. Afterwards, you may wish to buy a small amount of the food, take it home, and try preparing it for yourself or your family.

Foods we take for granted today such as corn, potatoes and tomatoes were all "discovered" in just this way. We depend on people from different cultures around the world because the knowledge they have about preparing foods and medicines enriches our lives every day.

Tak Wah Mak

Immunologist and Molecular Biologist
Discovered the T-cell receptor, a key to the human immune system.

His Story

Tak Mak is a very imaginative fellow. When asked to describe his work as an **immunologist**, instead of telling a story about himself he came up with the following tale concerning the life of an imaginary **T-cell**.

Tommy T-Cell is a biodetective. His job is to patrol the human body, investigating suspicious characters. Think of the **cells** in the human body as shops on a city street. Billions and trillions of police detectives like Tommy T-Cell are driving by all the time, looking in all the shop windows for something unusual going on. Each T-cell is trained to find one — and only one — type of criminal. There are several different kinds of T-cells. Tommy is known as a **helper T-cell**, part of the body's **immune system**, but you can think of him as a cop.

As Tommy cruises through blood and tissue he meets a **macrophage**, a specialized cell that's a combination reconnaissance and disposal unit in the body. Macrophages go around collecting bits of your own living and dead cells. They find parts of invading viruses and **bacteria**, dust, pollen and any junk that's floating around. They stick pieces of this garbage on their outside surfaces in special places where detectives like Tommy can see them.

Tommy has unique Y-shaped spikes called receptor sites all over his surface, and they recognize one kind of garbage. (In 1983 Tak Mak discovered these **T-cell receptors**.) Tommy's got about 5,000 receptor sites and each one is exactly the same. No other T-cell has spikes like Tommy's. His are specially designed to collect a tiny bit of protein from a virus that causes colds. Tommy tries his receptors on the macrophage, but nothing happens, so he moves on. The whole thing takes less than a second.

As Tommy floats along, he remembers his days years ago at the body's police academy, the **thymus**, where he learned how to tell foreign invaders from good cells that belong to the body. The T in T-cell is for "thymus," because that's where T-cells come from. The thymus is a fist-sized gland located just above the heart. It's bigger and more active in babies than in adults. In the first years of life, the thymus gives all the T-cell detectives in the body their lifelong assignments.

> **" Don't be afraid to tackle science if you enjoy it. "**
>
> –Tak Mak

PERSONAL INFO

Born
October 4, 1946, China

Residence
Toronto, Ontario

Family Members
Father: Kent Mak
Mother: Shu-tak (Chan)
Spouse: Shirley Suet-Wan Lau, died 1998
Children: Shi-Lan, Shi-Yen

Character
Absent-minded, impulsive, driven. Gentle, never loses temper.

Favourite Music
Mozart's Piano Sonata number 331

Other Interests
Tennis, golf

Titles
Professor of Immunology, University of Toronto; Senior Scientist, Ontario Cancer Institute in Toronto; Director, Campbell Family Institute for Breast Cancer

Office
Campbell Family Institute for Breast Cancer, Toronto

Status
Working

Degrees
Bachelor of science (biochemistry), University of Wisconsin, 1967
Master of science (biophysics), University of Wisconsin, 1968
Doctorate (biochemistry), University of Alberta, 1971

Awards
E. W. R. Steacie Award (National Sciences and Engineering Research Council, Ottawa), 1984
Stacie Prize (Stacie Trust Foundation), 1986
Fellow, Royal Society of Canada, 1986
Canadian Association of Manufacturers of Medical Devices Award, 1988
Emil von Behring Prize (Phillips-Universitat Marburg, West Germany),1988
University of Alberta 75th Anniversary Distinguished Scientist Award, 1989
Gairdner International Award (Gairdner Foundation), 1989
McLaughlin Medal (Royal Society of Canada), 1990
Canadian Foundation for AIDS Research Award, 1991
Cinader Award, 1994
Royal Society of London, 1994
Sloan Prize (General Motors Cancer Foundation), 1994
King Faisal International Prize for Medicine, 1995
Officer, Order of Canada, 2000
Izaak Walton Killam Prize, 2003
Paul Ehrlich and Ludwig Darmstaedter Prize, 2003

Mentors
Professor Howard Temin at the University of Wisconsin.
Ernest McCulloch, director of the Ontario Cancer Institute from 1983 to 1992.
Roland R. Ruekert, director of virology at the University of Wisconsin.

T-cells start out in the thymus as police cadets. They are trained by special macrophages that show new T-cells every possible little bit of garbage that a normal healthy body produces. These bits are called "self." T-cells whose receptors recognize "self" are killed in the thymus before they can leave; if they ever got out, they would become bad cops that attack good cells instead of invaders.

Tommy finally cruises up to a macrophage that shows him a piece of a cold virus. He checks it with his receptors. It's a match. The virus has been in the body for only five minutes, but Tommy leaps into action. First he sends out chemicals that signal regular police officers in the body — **B-cells** — to make **antibodies**. Antibodies are like heat-seeking missiles that zero in on a particular virus and kill it. Tommy, the helper T-cell, also calls in a SWAT team of **killer T-cells** and together they go out in search of the invader. They start

THE YOUNG SCIENTIST

Tak Mak was the son of a successful businessman in southern China. After the Communists took power in 1949, Mak's father moved the family to Hong Kong to escape the turmoil of political revolution. They were very well off and lived in a predominantly white, upper-middle-class district made up mainly of Dutch, Danish, Swedish, Norwegian and British families. They lived next door to the consulates of Norway and Denmark. "It was a rich neighbourhood," says Mak. He was the only Asian kid on his street, but like all the other boys he liked to play marbles in the dirt and kick soccer balls around.

Mak wasn't particularly interested in school, but his mother insisted that he do well and study hard. It helped that at school he was in a very bright group of about 20 kids. Most of them went to universities all over the world.

He was the only Asian kid on his street, but like all the other boys he liked to play marbles in the dirt and kick soccer balls around.

Mak went to the University of Wisconsin in Madison.

In the early 1970s, after he had received his doctorate (PhD) from the University of Alberta, Mak began his research at the Ontario Cancer Institute in Toronto. He is still a senior scientist there today. After his discovery of the T-cell receptor he became a professor at the University of Toronto, and in 1993 he also became director of the Amgen Research Institute in Toronto, which develops, patents and markets transgenic mice — animals that carry immune-system **genes** transferred from human beings. During his years at Amgen, Mak led a team that produced 20 patented molecular discoveries for use in drug development. In 2004 Mak left Amgen to become director of a new Institute for Breast Cancer Research.

dividing rapidly, doubling in number about every six hours. It takes four days before millions of T-cells, B-cells and killer T-cells are mobilized to kill all the virus in the body. Immune-system cells are some of the fastest-dividing cells we have inside us.

One day, Tommy is cruising the body on his usual rounds when he meets a thug in a black leather jacket, an AIDS virus. He decides to check him out with his receptors, but before he can do anything the little creep gets right inside Tommy through a tiny hole near the handle that Tommy uses when he visits macrophages. Viruses don't usually attack T-cells, but AIDS does. That's what makes AIDS so bad. Now that Tommy has the AIDS virus, little bits of AIDS proteins will appear on his surface. This makes him look very bad to other cells in the immune system. Tommy sees a killer T-cell coming and says his prayers: he knows that a killer T-cell is trained to kill anything that looks foreign. The killer T-cell sees that bit of AIDS on Tommy and, without a second thought, kills his boss. That's the end of Tommy.

The tragedy of AIDS is that T-cells are the mastermind detectives of the body's defence system, the ones that organize the other cops. Once AIDS is inside a T-cell, those T-cells look like spies to the rest of the immune system. So the body kills off its best cops, which then makes it harder to fight AIDS and any other infection. Most people with AIDS actually die of a common disease, such as a chest infection that would never kill some-one with a healthy immune system.

The Science

As an immunologist and molecular biologist, Mak examines the structure and function of molecules and cells in the human immune system, which protects the body from microscopic dirt and disease. His immune-system research may lead to cures for many autoimmune diseases in which the body's immune system malfunctions — diseases such as diabetes, multiple sclerosis, rheumatoid arthritis, lupus, myasthenia gravis and others. His current **cancer** research is aimed at finding a cure for breast cancer.

After Mak discovered the genes for the T-cell receptor, he began using this knowledge to create **"knock-out" mice**. These are mice with missing DNA instructions for making just one protein in the immune system. Mak's group was one of the first labs in the world to make knock-out mice and they made about 100 kinds throughout the 1990s.

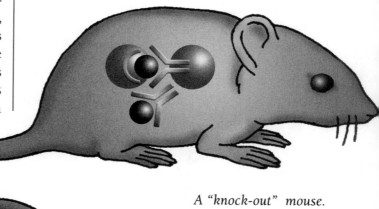

A "knock-out" mouse.

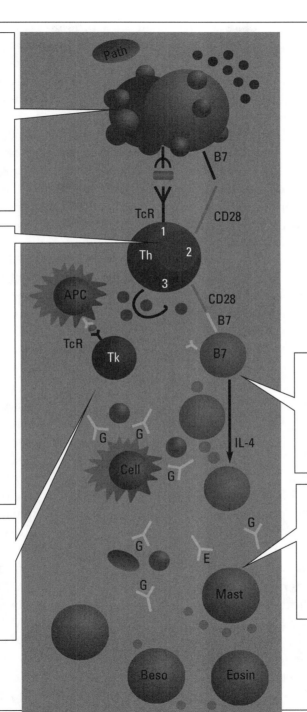

Macrophages are like combination reconnaissance and disposal units. They get bits of molecules from invaders and present them to T-cells for identification. They can also surround and digest dead cells and foreign substances in the blood.

Helper T-cells (Th) are the "masterminds" of the immune system. They use their receptors to identify invaders and send signals to B-Cells (B) and killer T-cells (Tk) to start the attack. Each T-cell receptor recognizes one short piece of a protein molecule, about eight amino acids long. There are trillions of unique T-cells in a healthy person, enough to recognize any foreign molecule that enters the body.

Killer T-cells (Tk) are best at killing viruses. They can recognize a virus and then release a toxin, or poison, that kills it and any others in the vicinity.

B-cells are particularly good at destroying bacteria. They make antibodies (G) that glom onto bacteria and make them easy to kill.

B-cells can also trigger **mast cells** that act as a kind of long-term memory for the immune system, so a defence can be mounted faster the next time the body is attacked.

To Mak, the immune system is like a huge company that's so big and complicated you can't easily tell how it functions. But there is a systematic way to find out. One day you take "John Smith" out of the company building, and see what stops functioning. Maybe the mailroom grinds to a halt. Now you know what John Smith does. Then you put John Smith back and you try the same thing with another person. Eventually you find out how the whole company works. Along with many other researchers around the world, Mak is using a similar process to understand the immune system. They "knock out" certain genes in mice and then they see what part is missing in the immune systems of those mice.

The human immune system is very complicated and this book gives just a simple explanation of one major part.

Because the immune system kills invading cells to protect the body, Mak's research eventually led to the study of how cells die and how cell death is regulated within the body. Scientists had discovered that one way T-cells rid the body of a virus is by inducing virus-infected cells to commit suicide. This process of programmed cell death is called **apoptosis** and is a normal part of life. Damaged cells in living things sometimes need to die to protect the rest of the organism from potential harm. For instance, the thymus "police academy" in the story above kills self-attacking T-cells by apoptosis. (Mak had to learn all about this process of orderly, controlled cell death to better understand T-cells and disease.) In the process of building up

To Mak, the immune system is like a huge company that's so big and complicated you can't easily tell how it functions.

an army of police to attack the intruders, the T-cells make billions of copies of themselves so they can have enough troops to fight. After the battle is over, most of these T-cells also have to "commit suicide"; otherwise, they might upset the balance of different kinds of blood cells in the body. However, too much apoptosis causes cell-loss disorders, and too little results in uncontrolled cell proliferation, as in cancerous tumours. Through much of the 1990s Mak was working on cancer, which is really about cells that won't die.

In 2004 Mak's research took a new direction when he became director of the Campbell Family Institute for Breast Cancer at Toronto's Princess Margaret Hospital. He wants to devote his time to breast cancer, the second-most-common cancer in women (after lung cancer).

According to the U.S. National Cancer Foundation, more than 200,000 American women are diagnosed with breast cancer each year and nearly 40,000 die because of it. In Canada, with its smaller population, an estimated 23,000 women will develop breast cancer this year, and 5,300 will die from it. "It's the number one cause of death for young women," says Mak. "That's a lot of mothers, a lot of children, a lot of daughters, a lot of wives. A lot of reasons to do breast cancer research."

Mak's research now focuses on apoptosis and the many biochemical processes that regulate cell death in cancers. "We found out how complex apoptosis is when we were making knock-out mice, and how some genes are essential for cellular suicide while others are redundant." His team is following many avenues of research; for instance, it has started breeding fruit flies to gain a deeper understanding of fundamental biological systems that may have an impact on human diseases. The **genome** of the fruit fly was completely decoded in 2000, and much of the genetics and **biochemistry** of apoptosis is the same in fruit flies as in humans, making it relatively easy to identify which genes are involved in turning apoptosis on and off. Fruit flies have a much shorter lifespan than mice, so results can be obtained faster since more experiments can be done in a shorter period of time. The goal is to use the technique of knocking out certain genes to identify specific biochemical factors that stop the growth of various kinds of tumours.

Mak is also active in developing what are called targeted therapeutics — special drugs that attack only diseased cells. In 1999 he and his team found a specific growth factor that appears to fuel the growth of Hodgkin's lymphoma, a type of cancer. "Right now the disease is treated with radiation and chemotherapy and patients have a 70- to 80-percent chance of long-term remission, but the treatment is very harsh and often results in a high rate of sterility and secondary tumours." In test tube experiments and in mice, when Mak added a chemical that blocked the fuel supply to Hodgkin's lymphoma cells, the tumour cells stopped growing and died by apoptosis. The growth factor he blocked is not something our bodies absolutely need most of the time, as it functions mainly to fight parasites, so Mak is hopeful that it will stop the disease and yet be mostly free of side effects.

Mystery

Mak believes that in the future scientists will use the immune system to clean out leftover cancer cells after tumours are surgically removed or killed with chemotherapy. He also believes that much better vaccines can be developed for malaria and other diseases that are currently difficult to control. He thinks a cure will be found for juvenile diabetes. But for him the biggest unsolved mystery of all is the way the immune system distinguishes between foreign invaders and "self." He says the thymus is only half the story, because many new **antigens** (or foreign molecules) attack our bodies long after the thymus has finished the bulk of its work training T-cells.

Explore Further

- C. Janeway, "How the Immune System Recognizes Invaders," *Scientific American*, September 1993.
- Pam Walker and Elaine Wood, *The Immune System: Understanding the Human Body*, Lucent Books, 2002.

Personal web page:
medbio.utoronto.ca/faculty/mak.html
U.S. National Institutes of Health website:
www.niaid.nih.gov/final/immun/immun.htm
University of Hartford website:
uhaweb.hartford.edu/BUGL/immune.htm
Wikipedia entry on apoptosis:
en.wikipedia.org/wiki/Apoptosis

ACTIVITY

Objective:

Find out how many unique kinds of T-cells the human genome can create.

You need:

- A calculator

Background:

T-cell receptors consist of two proteins called alpha and beta. All proteins are made of chains of amino acids. Each T-cell receptor's **protein chain** has a bottom part that is constant, like the trunk of a tree (the alpha chain has one kind, the beta has two), and a top part that is divided into major sections: alpha has two sections, called Variable and Joining, and beta has these two and a third section, called Diversity. The huuman genome contains the **genetic code** to make 109 different protein segments for the Variable portion of the alpha chain. Similarly, there are 61 different possible alpha Joining segments. Since the alpha chain has no Diversity segment and only one constant trunk segment, to calculate the number of possible different alpha chains just multiply 109 x 61 x 1 to get 6,649.

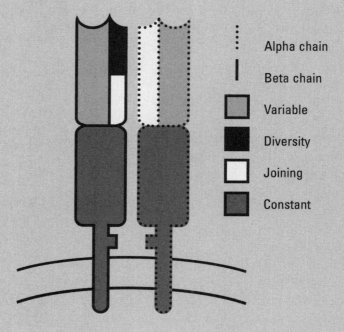

Alpha chain

Beta chain

Variable

Diversity

Joining

Constant

	Variable	Diversity	Joining	Constant
Alpha	109	0	61	1
Beta	64	2	13	2

What to do:

Calculate the total possible number of T-cell receptors that your immune system can make. (Hint: Multiply everything together.) How big is your number? Is it in the millions, billions or trillions? Now add this fact: a special **enzyme** puts a few extra amino acids between the Variable and Diversity chains. These are chosen randomly from our 21 amino acids, so you need to multiply again by 21, three or four times for each chain. Now how many possibilities are there?

John Charles Polanyi

Physical Chemist

Won the 1986 Nobel Prize in chemistry for using chemiluminescence of molecules to explain energy relationships in chemical reactions.

His Story

At about eight o'clock on a Thursday night in 1956, John Polanyi walks into the janitorial closet he calls a laboratory. The young University of Toronto lecturer can't expect much more; he isn't even an assistant professor yet. Polanyi's graduate student, Ken Cashion, who is wearing one of his many short-sleeved Hawaiian shirts, says, "Well, I think we're ready for another run."

"Did you check the seals on the 'Stokes'?" asks Polanyi, glancing at the giant vacuum pump thwapping away in the corner.

"Yes. They're not great, but I think she'll hold for one more experiment," says Cashion.

The fresh-air scent of ozone catches Polanyi's nose as Cashion opens the hydrogen valve and flicks a switch. For this experiment they need hydrogen gas as single atoms. (Hydrogen occurs naturally in pairs of hydrogen atoms.) Ken has scrounged the electrical discharge unit from an old neon sign. By jolting the flow of hydrogen with 6,000 volts of electricity, Polanyi and Cashion break the gas into single hydrogen atoms. Polanyi likes the soft, pinky neon glow that hydrogen makes, but he worries about its explosive power. Some hasty calculations they had made the day before indicated the lab wouldn't blow up, but they hadn't been entirely sure.

As it turned out, the experiment was a success and Polanyi and Cashion recorded something that no one had ever seen before — a tiny amount of light produced by the reaction of hydrogen with chlorine. This light was **chemiluminescence**. Because Polanyi understood the source of the feeble light emissions in his experiment, he was able to predict exactly what kind of energy needed to be applied to make this chemical reaction take place. Over the years he expanded his theories for other reactions, which unexpectedly led to the development of powerful new kinds of chemical lasers. Ultimately that experiment in a broom closet resulted in a Nobel Prize.

> **"The most exciting thing in the twentieth century is science. Young people ask me if this country is serious about science. They aren't thinking about the passport that they will hold, but the country that they must rely on for support and encouragement."**
>
> —John Charles Polanyi

PERSONAL INFO

Born
January 23, 1929, Berlin, Germany

Residence
Toronto, Ontario

Family Members
Father: Michael Polanyi, chemistry professor
Mother: Magda Elizabeth Kemeny
Spouse: Anne "Sue" Ferrar Davidson, piano teacher
Children: Michael, Margaret

Character
Busy, boyish, enthusiastic, helpful

Favourite Music
Tchaikovsky

Other Interests
Skiing, walking, art, literature, poetry, peace activism

Title
Professor of Chemistry

Office
Department of Chemistry, University of Toronto, Toronto, Ontario

Status
Working

Degrees
Bachelor of science, Manchester University, 1949
Master of science, Manchester University, 1950
Doctorate (chemistry), Manchester University, 1952

Awards
Marlow Medal (Faraday Society), 1962
Steacie Prize for Natural Sciences, 1965
Fellow, Royal Society of Canada, 1966
Royal Society of London, 1971
Officer, Order of Canada, 1974

Foreign Member, American Academy of Arts and Sciences, 1976
H. M. Tory Medal (Royal Society of Canada), 1977
Foreign Associate, U.S. National Academy of Sciences, 1978
Companion, Order of Canada, 1979
Wolf Prize, 1982
Nobel Prize in chemistry (Swedish Royal Academy of Sciences), 1986
Member of the Pontifical Academy, Rome, 1986
Royal Society of Edinburgh, 1988
Izaak Walton Killam Memorial Prize, 1988
Royal Medal (Royal Society of London), 1989

Mentor
His father, Michael Polanyi.
E. W. R. Steacie, a Canadian

THE YOUNG SCIENTIST...

When Polanyi was 11 years old his father, who was a chemistry professor at the University of Manchester in England, sent him to Canada so that he would not be hurt when Germany was bombing Britain during World War II. Polanyi stayed with a family in Toronto for three years. He remembers going on a bicycle camping trip and reading the *Count of Monte Cristo* and *War and Peace*. He was not interested in science as much as in sociology and literature.

In school Polanyi thought it was sort of dumb just to follow instructions for a chemistry experiment and get the "right" result. He would always fool around and try to vary things, just to see what would happen. He was very curious. The problem was that he would always get the "wrong" result. This would get him in trouble and his teachers often said he lacked the discipline to learn. He kept at it, however, and eventually became very interested in science. But he likes to tell kids that a lifelong commitment to something need not start out with a love affair.

After the war Polanyi went back to Manchester, where he completed high school and obtained his university education. He returned to Canada after that, first for a job at the National Research Council, where he worked for a while with Gerhard Herzberg (see p. 67), who was studying energy states of molecules. After a stint at Princeton University in New Jersey, Polanyi took a job lecturing at the University of Toronto in 1956.

He was very curious. The problem was that he would always get the "wrong" result.

Throughout his career as a scientist, Polanyi has been very active and outspoken in the Peace Movement. In a 2003 article in the *Globe and Mail* newspaper, he criticized the proposed trillion-dollar U.S. National Missile Defence system, saying "National Missile Defence points the world down the wrong path; it is the path of fortress-building, which, in the 21st century, is hopelessly anachronistic. Unchecked, weapons and counter weapons lead only to the development of further weapons."

According to Polanyi, science teaches a number of lessons concerning peace. First, none of us is in full possession of the truth, but we all work together, groping toward it. Second, for scientists, the pursuit of that truth is to be achieved through reason, not through violence. But he adds, "Of course, we shall always need faith. Reason would hardly suffice to get us out of bed in the morning. We need faith in what the day holds. But faith alone, as we have learnt, is inhuman, crushing all in its path. Reason listens, as well as talks. Of its nature it acknowledges the existence of others, since it triumphs only by persuading others. And that is how science advances. Not by scientific 'proof' ... We do not go to scientific meetings to announce results, but to debate them. We can never be sure. That is a lesson that science has to offer humanity."

The Science

As a physical chemist, John Polanyi studies the physics of chemical reactions — the energy states and the movements of molecules during the moment of reaction. This field of chemistry is called **reaction dynamics**. His work has helped answer the question, how do you get a chemical reaction to go? Do you tickle the molecules, or do you slam them together? It turns out that in some cases tickling works, in others you just have to slam them against each other. As Polanyi says, "The importance of this work is that we have a picture of reacting atoms in the transition state." The transition state of a chemical reaction is the brief period, often only millionths of a second long, when the starting materials have combined together but have not yet completely transformed themselves into the products of the reaction. This knowledge of reaction dynamics has allowed chemists to fine-tune reaction conditions to improve yields in chemical processes.

In one recent series of experiments, Polanyi and his research team worked with the chemical methyl bromide and silicon to learn how to "print" patterns of atoms. They use million-dollar scanning tunnelling microscopes that work at very cold temperatures of minus 223°C. They can manipulate and see individual molecules. Polanyi and his research team are able to weakly attach methyl bromine atoms to an underlying silicon crystal in neat, circular patterns of 12 molecules per circle. Then, by exposing the molecules to ultraviolet light, they have discovered the bromine atoms will form strong chemical bonds with the silicon underneath while the methyl part (CH_3) breaks off and floats away.

Polanyi says, "We can now photoprint molecular-scale patterns permanently onto silicon chips. Could be useful." He is fascinated by the notion that physical spacing of chemical reactions can be controlled like this. "One can dream of a molecular-scale printing press in which the pattern is present in the ink and the press is the light." Potential future applications in the world of nanotechnology and microchip fabrication are likely.

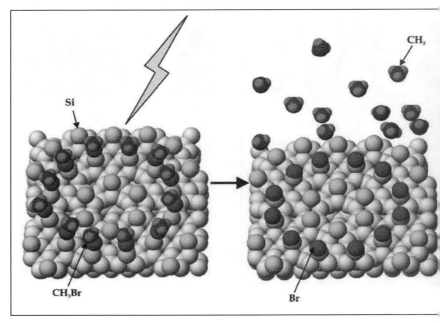

In a two-step process, methyl bromide is first adsorbed weakly to a silicon crystal and exposed to ultraviolet light (left), after which the methyl part breaks off and the bromine forms a strong bond with the silicon in a precisely controlled circular pattern.

The Nobel Prize-winning experiment: A lot of energy is given off when hydrogen and chlorine react to form hydrogen chloride, but nobody knew much about this energy when Polanyi arrived at the University of Toronto in 1956 and decided to study it. Little did he realize that this simple reaction would lead to a Nobel Prize 30 years later.

Chemiluminescence: Polanyi used an **infrared spectrometer** to measure the light energy emitted by the newborn products of the chemical reaction. The product molecules emit a very feeble light called chemiluminescence, which Polanyi recorded. He used this information to distinguish between vibrational and rotational energies in the molecule. His understanding of light emitted by chemical reactions later allowed him to propose vibrational and chemical lasers, the most powerful sources of infrared radiation ever developed.

Transition state: For a brief instant at the moment of reaction, the molecules are in a transition state as they turn into new chemicals. Polanyi's experiments led to a picture of the arrangement of atoms in the transition state. At the time, it was known that molecules had three kinds of motion: spinning or **rotational energy**; buzzing or **vibrational energy**; and the energy of movement from one point to another, or **translational energy**. What was entirely unknown was the relationship between these three types of energy during a chemical reaction. Polanyi's experiments began a new field of chemistry called reaction dynamics, the prediction of the pattern of the motion of molecules in a chemical reaction.

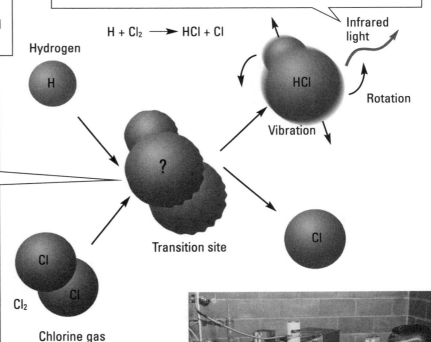

$H + Cl_2 \longrightarrow HCl + Cl$

Hydrogen

H

?

Transition site

Cl

Cl

Cl_2

Chlorine gas

HCl

Vibration

Rotation

Infrared light

The "Lab": Polanyi's graduate student assistant, Ken Cashion, set up the Nobel Prize-winning apparatus and was the first to see the result of the experiment. The two researchers had to "borrow" the spectrometer from other scientists who would have been furious if they had realized how it would be dismantled and modified for the experiment.

Careers

So You Want to Be a Physical Chemist

A few years ago, in a German magazine, Polanyi described his life as a research chemist. "I have had a life in which I have been paid to play. I haven't been paid much, but my toys continue to be the best." However, he went on to point out that the very expensive, fancy scientific instruments he gets to "play with" can be temperamental, and sometimes they don't work at all. "That is worrying, since I have to make new discoveries if I am to be allowed to continue doing science, which is what I love to do," he said. "So you can imagine the delight when finally that wretched machine for looking at molecules works, and I and my students get a glimpse of something nobody has ever seen before. We share for a moment in the relief and wonder that Christopher Columbus must have felt when, just at the moment that all seemed to be lost, a smudge of land appeared on the horizon. At that moment we are united with all the discoverers of history and are proud to call ourselves scientists."

And what is Polanyi's secret for succeeding as a scientist? "Above all, I would say, by wishing to do so," he says. People of many different talents have succeeded in science, but nobody has succeeded who did not passionately want to do so.

Mystery

Polanyi believes that one of the great mysteries is the molecular basis of life. He thinks that in the future we will have devices that operate in the molecular dimension, allowing observations of chemical reactions under much more widely varying conditions than is currently possible. He says, "If, perhaps, you are worried that by the time today's scientists leave the scene and your turn comes there will be nothing left to discover, stop worrying. What we know is surely only a tiny fraction of what remains to be known. At the centre of the atom, in the nucleus of the living cell and at the outer edges of the universe lie new worlds awaiting their discoverer."

Explore Further

• Mark Ladd, *Introduction to Physical Chemistry*, Cambridge University Press, 1998.

Polanyi's personal web page:
www.utoronto.ca/jpolanyi
Physical chemistry on the web:
www.haverford.edu/chem/depaula/pcw.htm

Hubert Reeves

Astrophysicist
World-famous cosmologist and science communicator.

Hubert Reeves looked out the window. The Alps, magnificent and snowcapped, caught his eye as the train rounded a curve on its way from Geneva to Berne, Switzerland. It was October 1970. Beneath the mountains, an autumn patchwork of gold and vermilion framed a winding brook. Reeves briefly wondered if its source was melting snow, and then it came to him, the answer to the puzzle. The stream triggered a memory, a scene from a movie about mountains and cold water: *La Bataille de l'eau lourde* (*The Battle for Heavy Water*). The 1947 French film by Jean Dréville tells the true story of how, near the end of World War II, Allied commandos destroyed a top-secret heavy-water plant in the mountains of Norway. The Nazi invaders were going to use the **heavy water** to make an atom bomb.

Heavy water, **heavy hydrogen** ... Reeves' mind flashed: You extract heavy water from ordinary water at super-cold temperatures and it takes a long time ... That was it! He now felt he could explain the huge discrepancy in recent experimental results about the nature of the solar wind, the huge flux of atomic particles blown into space by the burning sun. He was on his way to Berne to discuss this very problem with his colleague Johannes Geiss, the Swiss physicist who had conducted the experiment. Reeves grabbed a notepad and, as the scenic panorama unfolded outside, he tried to capture his thoughts on paper. His mind still resonated with ideas from the nuclear astro-physics lecture he had just presented at the Geneva observatory. At the same time, he felt he now had a theory that could explain why Geiss had found five times less heavy hydrogen in the solar wind than its natural occurrence on Earth. Theoretically, the sun and Earth originate from the same primordial matter, mostly hydrogen, so physicists were very bothered by this five-fold difference. What caused it?

Hydrogen is the simplest element in the universe. One **proton** in a nucleus orbited by a single **electron**: That's it. However, another kind of natural hydrogen exists, called **deuterium**, or heavy hydrogen. It's heavier because a deuterium

> **" Modern physics allows us to shout 'Long live Freedom!' "**
>
> —Hubert Reeves

PERSONAL INFO

Born
August 13, 1932, Montreal, Quebec

Residence
Paris, France

Family Members
Father: Joseph-Aimé Reeves
Mother: Manon Beaupré
Spouse: Camille Scoffier
Children: Gilles, Nicolas, Benoit, Evelyne
Grandchildren: Five

Character
Congenial, private, charming

Favourite Music
Schubert's String Quintet in C (Second Movement)

Other Interests
Hiking

Title
Associate Professor

Offices
University of Montreal; Observatory of Paris at Meudon

Status
Semi-retired

Degrees
Bachelor of science, University of Montreal, 1953
Master of science, McGill University, 1955
Doctorate, Cornell University, 1960

Awards
Chevalier de la Legion d'Honneur (France), 1986
Grand prix de la francophonie décerné, 1989
Einstein Prize (Einstein Society, Berne), 2001

Mentors
Père Louis Marie, childhood family friend, geneticist and botanist who knew everything in the woods.
Philip Morrison, Cornell physicist who combined culture, science and literature with an enthusiasm for the nature of

nucleus contains a neutron as well as a proton. Deuterium is rare, but chemically it behaves like ordinary hydrogen, so on Earth, as with most of the planet's hydrogen, it exists primarily as water. There are two hydrogen atoms in every water molecule (H_2O). The water molecules in Earth's oceans contain about one heavy hydrogen atom for every 2,000 plain hydrogen atoms.

This so-called heavy water is required in a certain type of nuclear reactor, such as Canada's CANDU (from *Can*adian *d*euterium *u*ranium) reactor, because it slows down fast neutrons, and if these neutrons are not kept in check a terrific nuclear explosion can occur. Heavy-water reactors also produce plutonium, which is a major component of an atom bomb. This is why the Nazis wanted heavy water in 1944.

In 1969, after long negotiations with the U.S.

THE YOUNG SCIENTIST

When Hubert Reeves was six he used to go with his family to visit Père Louis Marie, a friend of Reeves' mother. Père Marie was a Trappist monk who lived at the monastery in Oka, Quebec. A naturalist and geneticist, Père Marie used to let Reeves turn the pages of his fabulous herbarium, a giant book of dried plant specimens. Reeves went for long walks in the woods with the naturalist, who would teach the boy how to identify plants and flowers.

When Reeves was in grade 10 his physics teacher took the class up to the roof to make a special telescope to view sunspots. They had a frame called an **optical bench** that accurately held lenses in precise alignment. With two lenses, a mathematical formula and a few measurements they were able to point the whole thing at the sun to make an image appear on the viewing plane, a sheet of white paper. After some fiddling, a bright, shining disc came into focus on the paper, with a series of black dots clearly visible across the centre of the glowing image.

"To be able to see sunspots was marvellous to me. It was like magic."

"To be able to see sunspots was marvellous to me. It was like magic," says Reeves. He was amazed that a few calculations and a bit of do-it-yourself could make the invisible visible. He imagined the emotion Galileo must have felt when, in 1610, he did something similar to see the moons of Jupiter for the first time. From then on, Reeves was hooked on astronomy and astrophysics.

He went on to study at the University of Montreal and at Cornell University in New York. He worked for several years as a professor at the University of Montreal, but in 1965 he became a top researcher for the National Centre of Scientific Research in Paris, France. He maintains an associate professorship at the University of Montreal and teaches courses there each year. Reeves holds dual Canadian and French citizenship. He is president of the *Ligue ROC pour la préservation de la faune sauvage*, a French organization for the preservation of wild animals.

National Aeronautics and Space Administration (NASA), Johannes Geiss persuaded the Americans to conduct a simple experiment for him. On five of the 15 Apollo rocket trips to the moon, astronauts hoisted flags of aluminum foil and left them out for times varying from 77 minutes on Apollo 11 to 45 hours on Apollo 16. Each foil sheet was retrieved, brought back to Earth and examined by Geiss. With no atmosphere on the moon, Geiss expected it to be the ideal place to "feel" the solar wind. Particles in the solar wind would embed themselves into the aluminum foil flag.

When Geiss analyzed the foil, he found, among other things, that the solar wind consisted of one heavy hydrogen atom for every 10,000 regular hydrogens. Why should this be? If Earth and the sun originated from the same primordial stuff, why would there be five times as much heavy hydrogen on Earth as on the sun?

This was the puzzle Reeves had solved on the train. During the war, in much the same way as it is done today, the Nazis were separating heavy water from ordinary water by subjecting it to near vacuum at temperatures approaching absolute zero, or minus 273 degrees Centigrade — similar to conditions in outer space that favour the formation of heavy water. Current cosmological theory holds that solar systems originate when a **nebula**, a giant interstellar gas cloud, condenses under its own mass to form a hot, burning star at the centre of a rotating disc of particles and gas, from which planets eventually coalesce over millions of years. Reeves made the calculations and determined that the pressure and temperature of the solar disc near Earth's orbit would favour the same chemical reaction used to produce deuterium for the nuclear industry. It's a much slower process in space, but the time scale was right —

about 10 million years, plenty of time to account for the five-times difference.

When Reeves got off the train he said to Geiss, who had come to meet him at the station, "You know your problem with the heavy-hydrogen abundance? I think I've got it figured out."

"You've got a theory! Well, I've got one, too," said Geiss. It turned out that both physicists had come to the same conclusion, but in slightly different ways. More than 30 years after that breakthrough they were awarded the Einstein Prize for their experiment and theory, first published in 1971, that estimates the density of ordinary matter in the universe. The predictions have since been confirmed in many ways and are still remarkably close to current observations.

Reeves likes to remind people that amazing scientific discoveries can come anywhere and at any time. "Going to the movies can help you do physics," he says.

The Science

An astrophysicist is a nuclear physicist who studies thermonuclear reactions in the cores of stars, how stars are born, how all the chemical elements are created within them and how they die. Ultimately, Reeves is trying to discover the origin and fate of free energy in the universe.

He considers the idea of the **big bang** and an expanding universe to be the most important scientific discovery of the 20th century. Before this, scientists from Aristotle to Einstein considered the cosmos to be static and changeless, disconnected from the bustle of life on Earth. Questions about how stellar objects formed were considered meaningless or beyond the scope of science. But now we know the universe has a history, and

When a solar system forms, astrophysicists believe that it starts with a huge rotating nebular cloud of dust. Although nobody knows how such a protoplanetary disc starts or exactly how it works, scientists believe that gravitational forces, possibly caused by shock waves from the collapse of a nearby star or supernova, induce a central star to form from the cloud over tens of millions of years. When enough hydrogen is present, the collective gravity is enough to compress it to the point for nuclear fusion to occur and a star is born. Similarly, planets are thought to condense from the orbiting dust. The cloud probably consists mostly of hydrogen and helium, with carbon and oxygen being secondarily abundant.

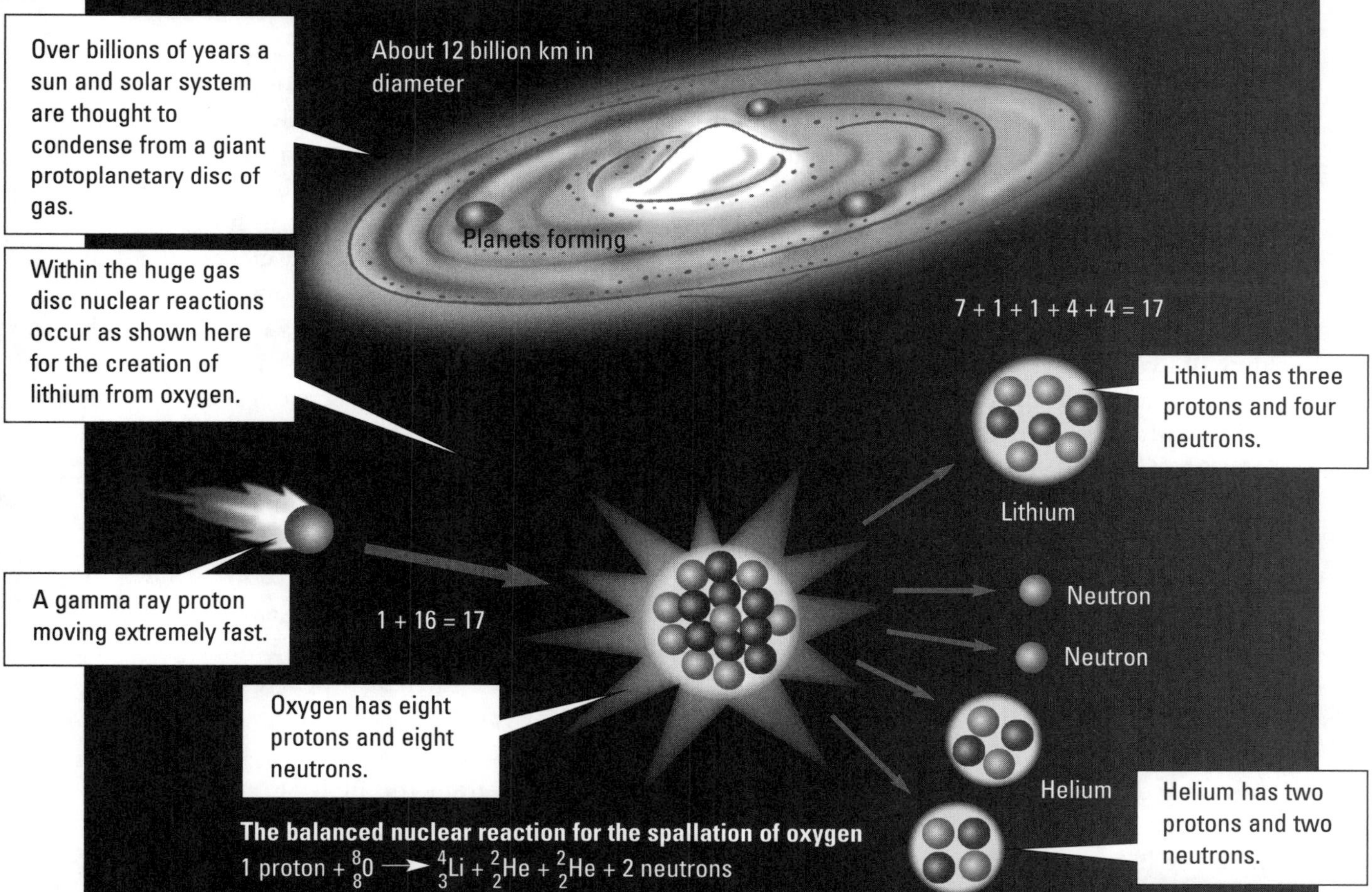

Over billions of years a sun and solar system are thought to condense from a giant protoplanetary disc of gas.

About 12 billion km in diameter

Planets forming

Within the huge gas disc nuclear reactions occur as shown here for the creation of lithium from oxygen.

$7 + 1 + 1 + 4 + 4 = 17$

Lithium has three protons and four neutrons.

Lithium

A gamma ray proton moving extremely fast.

$1 + 16 = 17$

Neutron

Neutron

Oxygen has eight protons and eight neutrons.

Helium

Helium has two protons and two neutrons.

The balanced nuclear reaction for the spallation of oxygen

$1 \text{ proton} + {}^{8}_{8}O \longrightarrow {}^{4}_{3}Li + {}^{2}_{2}He + {}^{2}_{2}He + 2 \text{ neutrons}$

Hubert Reeves has shown how numerous other elements can be created (over long periods of time) by chance collisions of high-energy protons, gamma rays or cosmic rays, with just these few primordial elements. This illustration shows how lithium and helium can be created from oxygen via the process of **spallation** when the oxygen is hit by a very high-energy proton, a cosmic ray.

Reeves considers himself to be a sort of cosmic historian. "I am fundamentally a nuclear physicist," he says, "but the 100 or so chemical elements were formed as a result of nuclear reactions in stars. So my work is about trying to unravel how things went — the history of our origins." He likes to point out that Earth and everything on it, including us, began as stardust.

Besides the famous paper with Geiss about the density of matter, Reeves has helped explain exactly how certain elements can originate from nuclear reactions in space. In particular he has elucidated the origins of the very light elements lithium, beryllium and boron. The formation of such light elements cannot be explained by fusion — the melding of two hydrogen atoms to form helium, for instance. Stars are constantly fusing hydrogen and helium into heavier and heavier elements, and generally this is how nearly everything originated. Lithium, beryllium and boron, however, cannot be made this way. What's more, these three elements are fragile and easily split into other elements. Therefore, they must constantly be under production to account for their currently observed abundance in the universe. Where, then, do they come from and how are they made? The answer is a process called **spallation**.

While he has published many scientific books and papers on the subject of spallation of the elements and other aspects of astrophysics, Reeves is best known, particularly in the French-speaking world, for his many popular books and TV shows on **cosmology** and astronomy. He is the French version of the popular American astrophysicist

Carl Sagan, who wrote books and had a TV show before he died in 1996. Reeves is also an active environmentalist, and in that capacity he can be compared to the Canadian biologist David Suzuki.

As a scientist who focuses on origins, Reeves is sometimes challenged by those who feel the currently accepted **big bang theory** is a myth, equivalent to creation stories found in religious books like the Bible. Reeves never uses the word "creation" when he talks about the origin of the universe or the formation of galaxies and stars. He won't even use "creation" to describe the big bang. "Creation in the philosophical sense means starting from nothing," he says, whereas in science you can never create something from nothing; you always start with something you assume to be there. So where does the big bang start from? No one knows. Reeves says, "I like to think of the big bang as a horizon: the horizon of our knowledge. That's as far as we go, and beyond this we don't know." It does not mean that nothing exists over the horizon. The big bang is where it's at right now, but scientific knowledge progresses and the horizon moves with it as we find out more about our origins.

The stories from the Bible, Koran and other religious books are meant to teach lessons on how to live. For them it doesn't really matter if the world was made in seven days or fifteen billion years. Religious books impart wisdom about living with each other. Reeves says, "These are stories related to the very important human desire that life must have a meaning. If life has no meaning, you die. You cannot live." Their prime

He likes to point out that Earth and everything on it, including us, began as stardust.

role, according to Reeves, is to teach morality, relations with our ancestors and how to live. Science offers something else.

Reeves grew up Roman Catholic. He doesn't feel the Bible should be taken literally as a book of science. "Science is robust," he says. "I have some basis to defend myself when I make statements in scientific papers. It's not just something that I invent — a story that comes out of my mind and tomorrow I can make up another story." The strength of science, he believes, is that if you ask why we believe in the big bang, scientists can point to a number of observations, physical measurements, that confirm the scenario of the big bang. But what's even more important is an essential feature of science called *prediction*. A scientific "story" is not good enough if it just explains what we have seen. It must also go out on a limb and predict something new, something never before seen. Then a new experiment is devised to test that prediction and new observations are made. If they are in agreement with what was expected, that strengthens the theory.

As an example, Reeves points to a series of experiments designed to settle the problem of solar neutrinos. **Neutrinos** are particles with no electric charge and, scientists believed at the time, no mass. Hence they are very hard to detect, because they pass through all matter with little or no interaction. Three kinds of neutrinos are known to exist. The sun emits a type called electron neutrinos. Previous experiments had found a third fewer electron neutrinos coming from the sun than predicted based on how astrophysicists think the sun burns. This was the solar neutrino problem. Reeves says, "Either we don't know the sun well enough, or we don't know the neutrino."

As it turned out, it was the neutrino. After almost 10 years of preparation, an experiment was conducted deep in an abandoned mine in Sudbury, Ontario, to detect solar neutrinos with much greater sensitivity than ever before. (The detector is located two kilometres below Earth's surface to shield it from cosmic rays that would give false positive readings.) Researchers made an amazing discovery: solar neutrinos change type on their way from the sun to Earth. "Neutrinos can evolve into other forms, just like Pokemon characters," says Reeves. The sun emits electron neutrinos, but by the time they reach Earth they transform into **tau** or **muon** neutrinos. To accomplish this they have to change the way they vibrate, and to do that they must have mass — not much, only about a millionth the mass of an electron. Reeves says, "So the experiment tells us our solar burning model is okay, but we learned something new about neutrinos and physicists must now incorporate these new ideas into their theories."

Experiments are always being conducted to learn more about our origins. In September 2004, NASA's *Genesis* space mission returned a relatively large sample of the solar wind to Earth, after two years of collecting while sitting 1.5 million kilometres away from our planet and facing the sun. It's like having a piece of the sun here on Earth. Scientists believe these samples will tell us what the original primordial solar nebula disc consisted of five billion years ago. Unfortunately, the Genesis return module's parachute failed to open and it crashed into the Utah desert at about 300 kilometres per hour. The sample-collection system was bent and cracked but still intact. Despite this mishap, scientists expect to learn more about the origin of our solar system from this experiment.

Careers

So You Want to Be an Astrophysicist

At first it may appear that all of physics is based on mathematical equations, and indeed it was this theoretical basis that fascinated the young Hubert Reeves. Just by thinking, by calculating, he was amazed how accurately scientists could predict the positions of stars, planets, atoms and much more. But later he realized there was more going on. Something else must come before number and theory. That missing factor is observation. "You always need to start with an observation," says Reeves. "Mathematics alone can do nothing about knowing the real world. It cannot even tell you what is the number of dimensions you feel." First comes the observation, he says, then the theory. Ultimately, the theory allows us to do calculations that lead to more observations that confirm or improve the theory. It was this "dialogue" between what we see and what we think that fascinated Reeves, and he feels it should be the driving force behind any career in science.

Typical physics careers include specialties in electronics, communications, aerospace, remote sensing, biophysics, nuclear, optical, plasma or solid state physics, astrophysics and cosmology. Some physicists focus mostly on experiments, while others just do theory.

Mystery

Only about 5 percent of the universe is made of known matter; 25 percent is dark matter; 70 percent is made of dark energy, a repulsive force that operates over very long intergalactic distances. We don't know anything about dark matter or dark energy. In other words, we don't know what 95 percent of the universe is made of.

Explore Further

- Hubert Reeves, et al., *La plus belle histoire du monde* (published in English as *Origins: Speculations on the Cosmos, Earth and Mankind*), Editions du Seuil, 2004.
- J. Geiss and H. Reeves, 1972, Astr. Ap. 18, 126.
- H. Reeves, W. A. Fowler and F. Hoyle, *Nature* (London),1970, pp. 226, 727.

NASA website about the solar wind experiment:
nssdc.gsfc.nasa.gov/database/MasterCatalog?sc=1971-008C&ex=3
NASA Genesis Mission:
www.nasa.gov/mission_pages/genesis/main/index.html
How to make a telescope:
www.funsci.com/fun3_en/lens/lens.htm
Spallation of O_2: www.macalester.edu/astronomy/people/mattc/LIBEB.htm

William Ricker

Fisheries Biologist

Inventor of "the Ricker Curve" for describing fish population dynamics.

His Story

Standing on a thin ledge of rock, just below **Hell's Gate** rapids on the **Fraser River** in British Columbia, William Ricker dips his net into the eddy at his feet. He brings up a big **sockeye** salmon for tagging. This one is fresh and strong, not like the tired ones who are having trouble with the rapids. Again and again the weak ones find their way into his net. From a pocket, Ricker pulls out two little red and white metal discs and a five-centimetre pin. He wipes his brow and waves to his partner, who is tagging fish a few metres away. The sun is hot. A steady, hot wind blows up the narrow canyon. There is no road down to where they are, only a steep trail.

Ricker is 30. It is the summer of 1938, the first time he has worked on the big river, and he's enjoying himself. It's also the first year of the Canadian Salmon Commission's study of Fraser sockeye. At the time, nobody really knew how or why salmon returned after years in the sea to mate and lay eggs in the very same creek where they were born.

While his partner holds down the lively fish, Ricker uses a pair of pliers to attach the bright tag through its body, just below the dorsal fin. Then he throws the wild sockeye back into the water to fight its way up the gorge through the roaring rapids. The team of four men catches and tags up to 20 fish per hour, several thousand in all — enough to accomplish the goal of the study, which is to find what fraction of the fish go to each of a dozen or so **spawning grounds** to mate and lay eggs at different seasons. Spawning grounds are the shallow creek beds where female salmon lay eggs, which male salmon then fertilize. Other fisheries scientists in those regions are on the lookout for the salmon and are making estimates of the numbers on each spawning ground.

By examining tags and counting fish, Ricker and his team are able, for the first time, to get an accurate picture of the Fraser River sockeye's migration pattern.

> **" Try and arrange your work so that you're doing something that you're interested in. "**
>
> –William Ricker

PERSONAL INFO

Born
August 11, 1908, Waterdown, Ontario

Died
September 8, 2001, Nanaimo, British Columbia

Family Members
Father: Harry Edwin Ricker
Mother: Rebecca Rouse
Spouse: Marion Caldwell
Children: Four sons
Grandchildren: Three

Character
Generous, modest, self-effacing, quiet

Favourite Music
Bach's Brandenburg Concertos, Handel, Mozart

Other Interests
Plants, birds, geology, insect classification, bass viol, Canadian history, languages, archaeology, trains

Title
Retired Chief Scientist, Fisheries Research Board of Canada

Office
Pacific Biological Station, Fisheries and Oceans Canada, Nanaimo, B.C.

Status
Deceased

Degrees
Bachelor of arts, University of Toronto, 1930
Master of arts, University of Toronto, 1931
Doctorate, University of Toronto, 1936

Awards
Fellow, Royal Society of Canada, 1956
Gold Medal (Professional Institute of Public Service of Canada), 1966
Award of Excellence (American Fisheries Society), 1969

Flavelle Medal (Royal Society of Canada), 1970
Fry Medal (Canadian Society of Zoologists), 1983
Order of Canada, 1986
Eminent Ecologist Award (Ecological Society of America), 1990

Mentors
Professors Dymond, Walker, Coventry and Harkness, University of Toronto.
W. A. Clemens and R. E. Foerster, Pacific Biological Station.
F. I. Baranov, for his 1918 monograph about fish.
R. A. Fisher, for his book *The Genetical Theory of Natural Selection.*

THE YOUNG SCIENTIST

When he was 11 years old, William Ricker began studying his dad's star charts. His father was the science teacher at North Bay Normal School in North Bay, which is on Lake Nipissing in Ontario. Eventually Ricker could name all the constellations and the brightest stars. All through high school, in the springtime he would get up most mornings at five o'clock. For three hours before breakfast he would ride his bike into the woods or along the shore of Lake Nipissing, looking for birds. While he was at university, he used to get summer jobs at the Ontario Fisheries Research Laboratory, mainly working on trout in the Great Lakes.

After a job studying salmon life history and enhancement at Cultus Lake, British Columbia, he became a professor of zoology at Indiana State University in Terre Haute, where from 1939 to 1950 he taught about birds and fish. Then he went back to Canada to work as editor of publications for the Fisheries Research Board of Canada in Ottawa, Ontario. In 1964 he moved to Nanaimo to become chief scientist of the Fisheries Research Board of Canada. From his retirement in 1973 until his death in 2001, he continued to work on a voluntary basis on the history of Fraser River salmon fisheries and on other projects.

During his life Ricker identified 90 new species of stoneflies, a major source of food for fish. He wrote a Russian/English dictionary of fisheries terms and was fluent in Russian. Toward the end of his life, he was working on a history book about early travel on the Fraser River canyon. He also had a keen interest in Sir Arthur Conan Doyle's fictional detective Sherlock Holmes and even wrote a Sherlock Holmes mystery that was published in a Canadian Holmes anthology. As a railway buff he had an encyclopedic knowledge of North American routes of the past. Ricker was an accomplished musician and played bass viol in the Nanaimo Symphony Orchestra. He was interested in folk music of many types and often sang old cowboy songs, serenading his family around the fire on camping trips.

Curiously, Ricker was not a good fisherman, though he loved to fish and spent countless hours trolling the waters around Nanaimo and up and down the coastline of Vancouver Island — rarely catching anything.

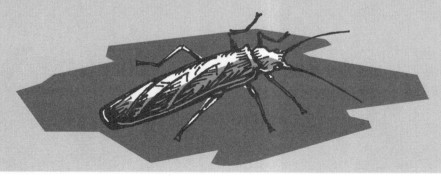

The Science

Fisheries biology is the study of fish habitat and population. Knowing the number of **spawners** in a given year is crucial for predicting how many fish will be available for future harvest. Ricker knew salmon runs like some baseball fans know World Series statistics. He had kept track of the Canadian Salmon Commission's estimates of the Fraser River sockeye ever since 1938.

Each year different numbers of salmon return to spawn, depending on the species. The five salmon species in British Columbia go through different cycles. For example, the big Fraser sockeye run of 2001 was the same "line" or "cycle" as the record run of 1913, which was around 100 million fish. For sockeye, such huge numbers occur only every four years. Other years are one-tenth as numerous or even less.

Ricker was the first scientist to suggest several possible reasons for the cyclic variation in returning salmon stocks. Biologists are still collecting evidence to determine the correct explanation. The Fraser sockeye are on a four-year cycle possibly because most of the fish mature at four years of age. Farther north, age five is also common. **Pink salmon** have a

The W. E. Ricker, a 58-metre Canada Coast Guard research ship, is named for Bill Ricker.

two-year life cycle. For **coho** it's usually three years, while **chinook** or "spring" salmon return at any age from two to seven years. Chinook are the largest and most powerful of all salmon. In fact, the largest salmon ever caught in the world was a chinook weighing in at over 57 kilograms.

Ricker is famous for his mathematical model of **fish population dynamics**, now called the Ricker Curve, which he first described in a book he wrote in the 1950s on the computation of fish population statistics. Today that book is known

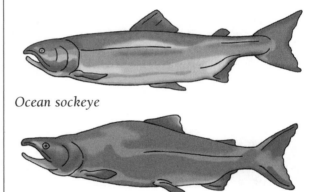

Ocean sockeye

Spawning sockeye salmon.

throughout the world as the "**Green Book**."

Ricker retired just before the age of personal computers, and he never used one. According to his son, Eric, his father was a man who had little interest in things that changed established, well-functioning habits. He never had a dishwasher, for example. Ricker used to tell a story about the time he uncovered some serious computer calculation errors with a few quick moves on his trusty old slide rule.

The Ricker Curve is still used all over the world to determine average maximum catches for regional fisheries. Each curve represents a different type of fish population. This is what governments use to decide how many days commercial fishers can be allowed to fish for salmon or cod, so that there are enough fish left to reproduce more than their current numbers the next year.

1 **Line of natural replacement**: Along this line, spawners (adult fish that lay eggs or fertilize them) are replaced by an equal number of progeny (fish that grow up to be adults).

2 Natural equilibrium: At this point, spawners equal progeny. If there were no commercial fishery, this is where the fish population would tend to stay. In nature, fish don't go much beyond this level because they get too crowded. Spawning beds get messed up and many eggs die.

3 For a fish species that followed Ricker Curve A, if commercial fishers were allowed to catch 20 percent of the mature spawners the fish population would be at this point. There would be fewer progeny, but enough to sustain the catch — a 20 percent surplus.

4 Salmon are interesting because their Ricker Curve looks more like this. At this point, at the top of the curve you have reduced the population to 40 percent of the natural equilibrium by fishing, but some fish, such as salmon, produce many more mature progeny when their spawning grounds are less crowded.

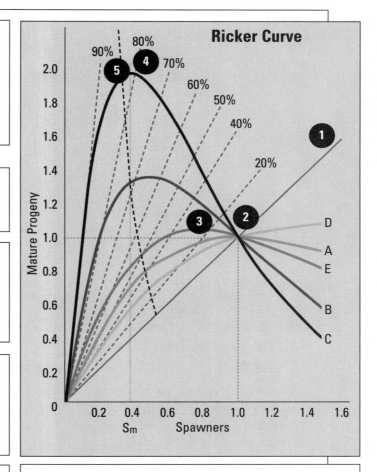

5 The point of **maximum sustainable catch** on any Ricker Curve is shown by the curving dotted line ("S_m" shows the maximum point for salmon). Note that it's actually a bit to the left of the peak of a curve. This is because the distance between the curve and the natural replacement line is the greatest at this point. Anywhere to the left of this line, you are overfishing and will reduce the next generation's harvest.

ACTIVITY

Objective:

To tell the difference between many different varieties of fish.

You need:

- A book with pictures and descriptions of local fish. Try cod, trout or salmon, but any fish will do.
- A trip to a big fish market or your favourite fishing spot

What to do:

At the market:
Take your book to the fish market and try to find the distinguishing feature of each type of trout, salmon or cod that is available. Write down their proper Latin names. See if you can find any fish that are mislabelled in the market.

If you go fishing: Try to identify everything you catch. Keep track of the size and number of fish you get. Write down the depth, water temperature and time of day. Keeping records like this is not only scientific, it will help you catch more fish, because you'll be able to check your records and know where and how to catch them the next time you go to a particular spot.

Careers

So You Want to Be a Fisheries Biologist

Ricker felt that anyone planning a career in science should be sure to choose a subject that is of great personal interest. Some aspects of scientific work can be boring, consisting of very repetitive experiments or endless data collection. Only a keen interest in the subject will make the tedium of the day-to-day work tolerable.

Explore Further

- David R. Montgomery, *King of Fish: The Thousand-Year Run of Salmon*, Westview Press, 2003.
- William Ricker, *Computation and Interpretation of Biological Statistics of Fish Populations*, Bulletin of the Fisheries Research Board of Canada no. 191, 1975. (This is "the Green Book.")

Pacific Fisheries Management Council: www.pcouncil.org/
Alaska Salmon website: cybersalmon.fws.gov/

Michael Smith

Biochemist and Molecular Biologist

Won the Nobel Prize in chemistry in 1993 for discovering site-directed mutagenesis: that is, how to make a genetic mutation precisely at any spot in a DNA molecule.

His Story

Michael Smith arrives in his office wearing his usual shabby old sweater and trousers that long ago should have been sent to a charity like the Salvation Army. You would never guess that just a few days before he had been awarded half a million dollars, his share of the 1993 Nobel Prize in chemistry. Smith passes by a wall of shallow shelves jammed full of medals, awards and plaques for prizes he has won. The office is modestly furnished, with a cluttered, lived-in look. A beautiful picture window looks out onto the treed University of British Columbia campus with the Coast Mountains in the distance. Smith picks up the telegram from Sweden to take another look at the Nobel announcement.

"Darlene?" he calls out the door to his administrator, Darlene Crowe, who is sitting at her desk.

"Yes, Mike," she calls back, cheerily. Everyone's in a good mood because of the prize.

"If you ever see my behaviour start to change and I get a swelled head with all this attention, I want you to give me a good, swift kick," says Smith.

Crowe remembers only one occasion on which she had to "kick" him. Mostly, he behaved himself. Smith relied heavily on people like Crowe. "He was a bit like the rabbit in *Alice in Wonderland,*" she says fondly of her boss, who like the rabbit often ran late. Smith rewarded his co-workers generously. He took 12 colleagues to Stockholm with him, mostly graduate students and research assistants, all expenses paid, to share in the glory of the Nobel awards ceremony.

Smith didn't keep the Nobel Prize money. He gave half of it to researchers working on the genetics of schizophrenia, a widespread mental disorder for which research money is scarce. The other half he shared between Science World BC and the Society for Canadian Women in Science and Technology.

Certainly Smith could afford it. He had made a small fortune in 1988 when he sold his share of Zymogenetics Incorporated, a Seattle-based **biotechnology** company that he co-founded in 1981. Even before he won the Nobel Prize, his

> **In research you really have to love and be committed to your work because things have more of a chance of going wrong than right. But when things go right, there is nothing more exciting.**
>
> —Michael Smith

PERSONAL INFO

Born
April 26, 1932, Blackpool, England

Died
October 4, 2000, Vancouver, British Columbia

Family Members
Father: Rowland Smith
Mother: Mary Agnes Armstead
Children: Tom, Ian, Wendy

Character
Shy, caring, busy, focused, generous. He was also a procrastinator.

Favourite Music
Sibelius' Second Symphony (Second Movement)

Other Interests
Philanthropy, Scouts, camping, hiking, sailing, skiing, reading *New Yorker* magazine and the *Guardian* newspaper.

Title
University Killam Professor, Peter Wall Distinguished Professor of Biotechnology

Office
Faculty of Medicine, University of British Columbia

Status
Deceased

Degrees
Bachelor of science (honours, chemistry), University of Manchester, 1953
Doctorate (chemistry), University of Manchester, 1956

Awards
Jacob Biely Faculty Research Prize, (University of British Columbia), 1977
Fellow, Royal Society of Canada, 1981
Boehringer Mannheim Prize (Canadian Biochemical Society), 1981
Gold Medal (Science Council of British Columbia), 1984
Fellow, Royal Society of London, 1986
Gairdner Foundation International Award, 1986
Killam Research Prize, UBC, 1986
Award of Excellence (Genetics Society of Canada), 1988
G. Malcolm Brown Award (Canadian Federation of Biological Societies), 1989
Flavelle Medal (Royal Society of Canada), 1992
Nobel Prize in chemistry (Swedish Royal Academy of Sciences), 1993
Manning Award, 1995
Laureate, Canadian Medical Hall of Fame

Mentor
Har Gobind Khorana, Nobel Prize-winning chemist who taught him the organic chemistry of biological molecules that make up DNA.

THE YOUNG SCIENTIST

Michael Smith was born into a working-class family in Blackpool, England. He was seven when World War II broke out. Though his family lived in northern England and was quite far away from London, he does remember one time when his mom and dad were not home and German bombs fell on either side of their house, barely missing him and his brother, Robin.

In those days, English working-class children had to take an exam called the Eleven-Plus when they were 11 to see if they would go on to a private school or continue in the public school system, where they would learn a trade and finish at age 16. Smith did very well in his Eleven-Plus and was offered a scholarship to a local private school called Arnold School, but he didn't want to go, because the students there were considered snobs and he thought his friends would make fun of him. His mother insisted that he go.

His time there was not a happy period. He lost most of his old friends. He had homework to do every night and they didn't. He did not like the food. He was not very good at sports, which were very important in English private schools. He had few friends. His schoolmates teased him because of his big front teeth. He was sent to a dentist to see about his overbite and, fortunately, the dentist happened to introduce him to the world of Boy Scouts, where he made friends and learned about camping.

Smith did not go to a prestigious English university, but he did get into the honours chemistry program at Manchester University. He hoped to earn all As, but alas, he was a B student. He was very disappointed, but he still won a state scholarship and managed to complete his doctorate.

Smith wanted to do post-doctoral research on the west coast of the United States and he wrote to many universities, but was rejected by all. Then in 1956 he heard of a young scientist in Vancouver, Gobind Khorana, who had a position available for a biochemist. This was not the chemistry in which Smith had been trained, but he went to Canada anyway. It turned out to be a very good decision, because in Khorana's lab, Smith began learning the chemistry that would lead to his Nobel Prize. Khorana himself received a Nobel Prize in 1968.

In 1961 Smith took a job as chemist at the Fisheries Research Board of Canada laboratory in Vancouver and published many papers about crabs, salmon and marine molluscs, but he managed to sustain his research in DNA chemistry with grants he obtained on his own, outside his fisheries-related work. The lab was located on the UBC campus and, because he was collaborating so much with professors in **biochemistry** and medicine, in 1966 he was appointed a UBC professor of biochemistry in the Faculty of Medicine, where he worked until his death.

genetic engineering techniques were used by Zymogenetics to develop a strain of yeast implanted with the human gene for insulin. With the drug company Novo-Nordisk, Zymogenetics commercialized a process that used yeast to produce human insulin.

The original idea for his award-winning discovery, **site-directed mutagenesis**, came to Smith while talking with an American scientist named Clyde Hutchison over coffee in an English research institute. Every seven years, university professors get one year off, with pay, to travel anywhere in the world to do research; the break is called a sabbatical. It was 1976 and Smith was spending a sabbatical year in Fred Sanger's lab, part of the famous institute in Cambridge, England, where DNA was first explained by James Watson and Francis Crick. Smith was there to learn how to sequence genes — how to determine the order of the thousands of links that make up a chain of DNA.

He was in the cafeteria explaining to Hutchison how he was making short chains of **nucleotides** — the chain links in DNA — for use in the separation and purification of DNA fragments. His technique was based on the natural affinity of one DNA chain to link up with its mirror image. It didn't take much of a leap to realize that the same method might be used to induce **mutations** — new qualities or traits in offspring not found in their parents — but it meant changing directions again, and not for the first time. It took Smith and his team several more years to perfect the method. At first it didn't work at all, but he kept at it. Eventually the technique became so well known and useful that it ended up winning the Nobel Prize.

Smith didn't become successful by accident. He was a very hard worker, some say a workaholic. Things were not always easy for him. When he submitted his first article on site-directed mutagenesis for publication in *Cell*, a leading academic journal, it was rejected; the editors said it

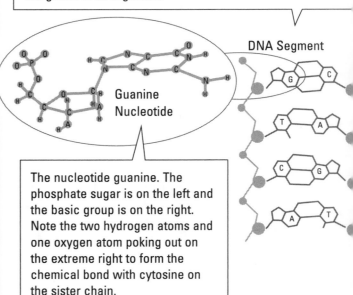

A small portion of a long DNA molecule showing the backbone (in light grey) made of **deoxyribose**, a type of sugar. The backbone sugar segments are all the same, but they can have one of four different basic "connectors" — adenine, thymine, cytosine and guanine (A, T, C and G in the figure) — that couple with complementary connectors on a second sugar chain. An A on one side always matches up with a T on the other. Similarly, C always matches up with G. These couplings are called **base pairs**. A DNA strand is made up of two chains, one a mirror image of the other (that is, if one side's sequence goes ATCG, then the other side will be TAGC). In real DNA the chain could continue up for millions of base pairs and down for thousands more. The sugar elements (A, T, G and C) are known as nucleotides and their sequence is what makes up the genes in an organism.

DNA Segment

Guanine Nucleotide

The nucleotide guanine. The phosphate sugar is on the left and the basic group is on the right. Note the two hydrogen atoms and one oxygen atom poking out on the extreme right to form the chemical bond with cytosine on the sister chain.

was not of general interest. But Smith never stopped working on it. Above all, he was always prepared to do what he called "follow-your-nose research" — repeatedly changing directions to explore new ideas even if it meant learning entirely different processes and techniques.

The Science

Molecular biology is the study of biological systems at the level of individual chemicals and molecules. Michael Smith was an expert on the chemistry of DNA — the molecule that makes up

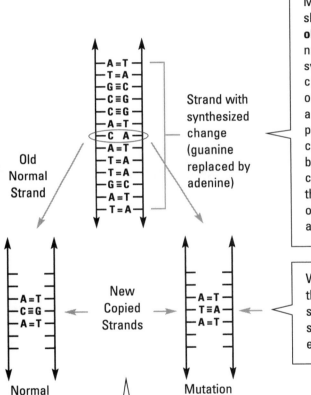

Old Normal Strand

Strand with synthesized change (guanine replaced by adenine)

New Copied Strands

Normal

Mutation

Michael Smith's idea for which he won the Nobel Prize was to slip a synthetic stretch of nucleotides — called an **oligonucleotide** — into one DNA chain. **"Synthetic"** means the nucleotide was created in a test tube, not by nature. The synthetic segment is added to normal DNA using standard chemicals for breaking and reforming DNA chains. But there is one thing wrong with this synthetic oligonucleotide: it has an adenine where there should be a guanine. This is done on purpose to create a mutation. (Remember, A normally combines with T, and G goes with C.) The four nucleotides below and above the adenine act as a kind of address that causes this stretch of DNA to match up to the correct place on the other DNA strand. (In humans, it turns out that you need only 17 nucleotides to define a unique match somewhere among the three billion nucleotides of the entire genome.)

With Smith's technique, geneticists can **mutate** a gene in three ways: substitution, deletion and addition. Precise substitution of one or more nucleotides in a DNA sequence is shown here. Scientists can also delete nucleotides or add extra nucleotides to the sequence.

When this new altered DNA is put back into an organism, say a bacterium, and it divides in the normal process of growth and reproduction, one half of the DNA will recombine normally and will produce a correct copy of the original gene — a normal bacterium. The other side with the synthetic oligonucleotide will create a mutation, because a thymine is sitting where there should be a cytosine. The resulting mutant bacterium might have some new appearance or function that it never had before.

genes, the instructions required to create every part of an organism. DNA is a large molecule that is like a twisting chain. Actually it is two chains twisted together. Smith worked on **genomics**, the sequencing of the DNA of an organism to understand how it works.

Smith won fame and fortune by developing a new way to create mutations in living organisms. Plant and animal breeders rely on naturally occurring beneficial mutations that result in improved plants and animals. Conversely, unwanted natural mutations can cause diseases such as **cystic fibrosis** or sickle-cell anemia. Smith found a way to create a specific mutation by precisely changing any particular part of the DNA in an organism. This has allowed countless researchers around the world to develop special **bacteria**, plants and animals with new qualities or abilities that either do not occur naturally or would take years and years of trial and error in breeding to achieve. With further research, his technique might even be used to correct mutations that cause disease.

Before Smith's technique of site-directed mutagenesis, there was no way to create specific mutations. Geneticists had to expose a bunch of organisms to radiation or chemicals that would result in all sorts of mutants, then select the one they wanted. It was all by chance, and it could take a long time to get exactly the right mutation.

Careers

So You Want to Be a Biochemist

As in any career in which you are investigating the unknown all the time, scientific research often leads to a lot of disappointments. Things go wrong. Smith said, "For kids who have been very bright all the way through school, all the way through undergraduate university, and almost aced all their classes, sometimes getting into research is very traumatic for them, because it doesn't matter how bright they are, chances are, any experiment they do is not going to work the first time." For brilliant young people used to succeeding, it can be very upsetting. Yet the only way to be successful in research is to do experiments, have them go wrong, and then do another experiment, and then another one. So anyone planning a career in scientific research ought to be commited to long-term goals. "Even though you'll have disappointment in the short term, ultimately discovering new things is so exciting, it's worth putting up with that for the long-term excitement and pleasure of discovering something new about the biological or the chemical or the physical world in which we live," said Smith.

However, as a biochemist he wanted to do more than just discover new things. "I wanted to do something that was useful experimentally to other people," he said. Certainly, his technique of site-directed mutagenesis is one of the more useful contributions ever made to the field of biochemistry and genetics. It is used daily by tens of thousands of researchers worldwide.

ACTIVITY

Objective:

To design your own oligonucleotide and see if it's part of a real gene.

You need:

- Pen and paper
- A computer connected to the internet

What to do:

Using the four basic nucleotides of the DNA chain (A, C, G, T) make up a DNA chain by randomly choosing about 20 or 30 units. AACTGCTTCGGATATCGCAGC, for example. Now take the chain you made and point your web browser to www.ncbi.nlm.nih.gov/BLAST. At the web site, look for the heading "Nucleotide," and click on "Nucleotide-nucleotide BLAST (blastn)" which takes you to a page where you type your sequence into the big "Search" box at the top of the screen. This is where you put in AACTGCTTCGGATATCGCAGC, or whatever you chose for your sequence. Don't change any settings on the page. Just click the "BLAST" button. A new page will come up and you click the "Format" button, again without changing any settings. A new window opens and in a minute or two an automated system will show you the probable gene matches for your made-up oligonucleotide, if there are any. Be patient: it may take a few minutes if the BLAST computers are busy.

If you get a match, you will see one or more possible candidates for your sequence. The BLAST result contains a lot of information, such as the number of nucleotides that matched, the names of organisms where the sequence has been found, the surrounding sequence of nucleotides, the scientists who first decoded it, and much more. By clicking on items on this report you will come to pages that give much more detail about the organism whose genetic code matches your sequence. Sometimes your sequence matches a gene that codes for a particular protein.

Did you get a match? The string AACTGCTTCGGATATCGCAGC turns out to match a protein that occurs in a type of bacteria called *Bradyrhizobium japonicum* that lives on the roots of plants. It also matches the gene in a fungus for an enzyme that breaks down cellulose. What gene, protein or creature does your sequence match? If your sequence was not part of any known gene, try some other sequence until you find one.

Mystery

In a 1996 interview, Smith predicted a change in the way people do biological research. He was right. With the completion of the human genome project in 2003, the total sequence of the DNA in all the genes for a human being — the human genome — is known. Genomes have now been completely decoded for many plants and animals. Those genes have the code or "recipe" for the tens of thousands of proteins that make up people, plants, insects or other animals. As time goes by, geneticists are amassing more and more genetic information detailing what the genome encodes. According to Smith, the hard part will be discovering which part of the genome does what, picking out what is crucial, and learning how to recognize the most important bits of DNA.

Explore Further

- Eric Damer, *No Ordinary Mike: Michael Smith, Nobel Laureate*, Ronsdale, 2004.
- Gina Smith, *The Genomics Age: How DNA Technology Is Transforming the Way We Live and Who We Are*, AMACOM, 2004.
- Donald Voet and Judith G. Voet, *Biochemistry, The Expression and Transmission of Genetic Information*, Wiley, 2004.
- James D. Watson, *The Double Helix: A Personal Account of the Discovery of the Structure of DNA*, Touchstone, 2001.

U.S. Centre for Biotechnology Information: www.ncbi.nlm.nih.gov/

U.S. Department of Energy Human Genome Project: doegenomes.org/

Louis Taillefer

Physicist
World expert on superconductivity.

His Story

In French, *taille* means "cut" and *fer* is "iron," so Louis Taillefer's name literally means "cut iron." One evening at Cambridge University in England, working in the famous Cavendish physics laboratory, Taillefer was making an alloy with special magnetic properties for his doctoral research. He had to melt a combination of platinum and iron in a high-tech furnace and then, with great patience, carefully draw it into a shiny, crystalline sample. Before beginning the melt, he needed to cut the precise amount of metal from a small rod. So there he was, sitting in the basement lab at night, slowly cutting this little piece of metal, and he suddenly broke out laughing: "Wow! This must surely be my vocation. I'm cutting iron, at last!"

Another time in the Cavendish lab, Taillefer was all alone. It was the week before Christmas 1985 and everyone else had left for the holidays. The room smelled of hot vacuum-pump oil. Taillefer first checked to make sure he was wearing no rings on his fingers. Then he removed any metal objects from his pockets, otherwise they might be heated by accident. The one-tonne induction furnace he was about to use could heat metal by sending out intense radio waves, so rings could get hot enough to burn. He cranked up the power to 100 kilowatts and the room buzzed with a steady 500-kilohertz hum. He moved a little water-cooled 10-centimetre copper crucible containing elemental uranium and platinum into position in the centre of the furnace coils under very high vacuum. Taillefer watched as the materials sputtered and melted together. The radio frequency emitted by the coils induced the **electrons** in the uranium and platinum to move so fast that they created enough heat to melt the metals into an alloy, called uranium platinide (UPt_3). Now it was time to "zone it." Taillefer slowly pulled the crucible out of the molten zone in such a way that the metal would solidify into a small ingot made of several perfect crystals. He was especially good

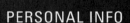 *Follow your intuition. In my own experience, this has always paid off.*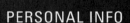

—Louis Taillefer

PERSONAL INFO

Born
October 28, 1959, Montreal, Quebec

Residence
Lennoxville, Quebec

Family Members
Father: Laurent Taillefer
Mother: Andrée Lepage
Spouse: Louise Brisson, architect
Children: Raphaël, Charlotte

Character
Open-minded, happy, optimistic

Favourite Music
Jacques Brel, Gilles Vigneault

Other Interests
Developing community "Waldorf
school," cross-country skiing

Office
Physics Department, University of
Sherbrooke

Status
Working

Degrees
Bachelor of science (physics),
McGill University, 1982
Doctorate (physics), Cambridge
University, 1986

Awards
Herzberg Medal (Canadian
Association of Physicists), 1998

Brockhouse Medal (Canadian
Association of Physicists), 2003
Prix Marie-Victorin, Government of
Quebec, 2003

Mentors
Gil Lonzarich, Cambridge University
professor who taught high
standards and confidence,
urging students to push the
limits.
Claude Côté, farmer, who showed
that you can do anything or
make anything, that there are no
limits if you trust your abilities.

at making ultra-pure compounds.

Purity is essential for this type of research because **superconductivity** and **magnetism** depend on it. Materials become superconductors when electrons spontaneously decide to pair together. Once paired, the electrons can move through the material effortlessly, transporting electricity perfectly with no resistance. Impurities can sometimes break up these pairs, causing problems in experiments. Superconductivity is a particular phase of a material, as, for example, when water is turning to ice. Many materials turn to superconductors at extremely low temperatures.

Taillefer was particularly excited because a brand new piece of equipment had just arrived, a special kind of refrigerator that could cool things down to near absolute zero, minus 273 degrees Centigrade, which is the coldest temperature in the universe. The new dilution refrigerator could freeze things to about 10 millikelvin, ten-thousandths of a degree above the point beyond which no further temperature drop is possible, absolute zero. Professor Mike Pepper had just bought the fridge and nobody had used it, so Taillefer wanted to run its first experiment. , But for various reasons he had to wait a couple of months until spring break and it turned out that his was the second experiment with the fridge, but the first one that worked.

Before running his experiment, he had to go upstairs to a second-floor lab to prepare the sample. It was a low-temperature materials-characterization lab filled with electronics and **cryogenic** equipment for working with materials near absolute zero. Big vacuum-insulated Dewar flasks of super-cooled liquid helium and liquid nitrogen sat next to various microscopes, detectors and other instruments. Taillefer was excited as he placed the tiny rod of uranium platinide under a microscope. But he turned away for a moment and it rolled off the edge, shattering into about 25 little pieces all over the floor. Oddly, this turned out to be a lucky accident.

Taillefer wore surgical gloves to collect the shards and selected one for his experiment. He and his research team had access to the new fridge only 10 percent of the time, so he was anxious to try it as soon as possible. "At the time I was *maniaque,* as we say in French Canadian," says Taillefer. He set up a special tiny coil of copper wire he had wound by hand under a microscope — 5,000 turns of 11-micron wire. The sample of uranium platinide was placed in the middle of the coil inside the refrigeration chamber. A powerful superconducting electromagnet swept a varying magnetic field over the sample as it was cooled to near absolute zero. Taillefer watched the pen of a chart recorder displaying voltage changes from the small copper pick-up coil around the sample. If the pen squiggled in a certain way (with **sinusoidal oscillations**) it would directly show quantization of electron energy coming from the circular motion of electrons in the metal sample. "It's like the electrons are talking to us," says Taillefer. "Boy, did we watch that pen."

The experiment worked the first time, a rare occurrence in experimental science. Taillefer was attempting to measure the mass of electrons in a new class of materials called heavy electron

"It's like the electrons are talking to us. Boy, did we watch that pen."

THE YOUNG SCIENTIST

When Louis Taillefer was 16, he was a top student at his high school in Montreal but he was bored in class. Around that time he became friends with a farmer named Claude Côté. Taillefer's father had a hobby farm near Valcourt, Quebec, and Côté's farm was next door. Taillefer would see Côté working in the fields and would talk to him over the fence. "I became fascinated with farming," says Taillefer. He asked his parents if he could quit school to become a farmer and work for Claude. His mom said, "Do what your heart tells you to do. If it means stopping school to be a farmer, then do it."

When Taillefer showed up on Côté's farm, Côté asked him to plow a field. Taillefer had limited experience driving a tractor. He was a city boy from Montreal. "I'd never even seen a cow up close," he says. But Côté showed him the basics — start in the middle of the field, don't cut too deep, don't drive too fast — and said, "Go." Taillefer spent days and days plowing fields. He was in heaven.

To Taillefer, Côté at 26 was a real-life example of a guy with no limits. Côté did everything himself. He was his own veterinarian, animal breeder and mechanic. He trained his own horses. Later he would go on to design and build a horse carriage and a house from scratch, cutting the trees and milling all the lumber. "He really taught me to have confidence in myself," says Taillefer.

Sitting on that tractor proudly plowing fields, Taillefer felt good. But one day the engine started making noises and he drove the tractor back to the barn. He felt awful. He thought he had wrecked it, but Côté didn't get upset at all. He just hauled the tractor to his garage, pulled out the engine, went to a scrapyard, got another crankshaft and popped it in.

"For Claude, everything was possible," says Taillefer. "He showed me that a person can do anything."

After a year on the farm Taillefer began to miss school, so he returned to Montreal to finish high school. At that point, he had no idea what he wanted to do at university. He was thinking of majoring in theatre, as it was his main interest in high school. Though he is French-speaking, Taillefer decided to go to McGill, an English university in Montreal, because he had won an entrance award to study mining engineering there. His mom said, "Bien, au moins t'appren-

dras l'anglais." ("Well, at least you will learn English.")

Even when he finished at the top of his class and won (together with his identical twin brother, Eric) the Anne Molson Gold Medal for top student in math or physics at McGill, Taillefer was not sure a life in physics was right for him, but he went to graduate school because that's what everyone did. He was registered for Harvard University in Cambridge, Massachusetts, but won a Commonwealth scholarship to go to Cambridge University in England, for one year. "I took the opportunity because I had never been to Europe," says Taillefer. At Cambridge he started working on a project, but after eight months he could not see the relevance of the work and was on the verge of dropping out. Fortunately, his supervisor, Gil Lonzarich, gave him a fascinating new project: a search for a theory of magnetism, something Professor Lonzarich had been working on himself in his spare time. Taillefer rapidly became absorbed with this new work and eventually called Harvard to say he would not be attending.

Magnetism was fascinating to Taillefer. While magnets are all around us, much of the physics of magnetism remains to be explained. Based on his doctoral research, Taillefer wrote a paper in 1985 presenting a theory that accounted for the so-called **critical temperature** of magnets — the point at which magnetism disappears in a heated metal. It was Taillefer's first publication and is still one of the most highly cited papers on the topic.

metals, a potential superconductor of a new kind, in which extraordinarily strong electron interactions caused an electron mass increase, but nobody knew by how much. Seeing the quantized oscillation would provide a direct measure of that mass. The Cambridge group was competing with other teams in Europe and United States who also were trying to see these effects. Everyone was (and still is) trying to understand what is going on inside heavy electron metals like uranium platinide, so there was a race to get the results.

As it turned out, the piece of metal that Taillefer chose from the shattered rod had a particular **crystalline orientation** — the atoms making up the atomic crystalline structure of the metal — that lined up perfectly within the magnetic field. When Taillefer saw the first good series of oscillations coming out of the plotter, he ran to the classroom where his supervisor, Gil Lonzarich, was speaking, burst into the lecture hall and yelled, "We've got oscillations!"

At least three lucky events were involved: the uranium platinide that Taillefer made was of uncommon purity; the new fridge was available; and Taillefer, by chance, had placed the crystal in the apparatus with ideal orientation. It would be 10 years before another lab would duplicate Taillefer's results from that lucky spring of 1986. A few months later, Taillefer graduated with a doctorate (PhD) from Cambridge University.

The Science

Louis Taillefer is a materials scientist, a physicist who specializes in the behaviour of electrons in matter. He considers himself a modern-day alchemist — medieval chemists who worked at turning ordinary metals into gold or silver —

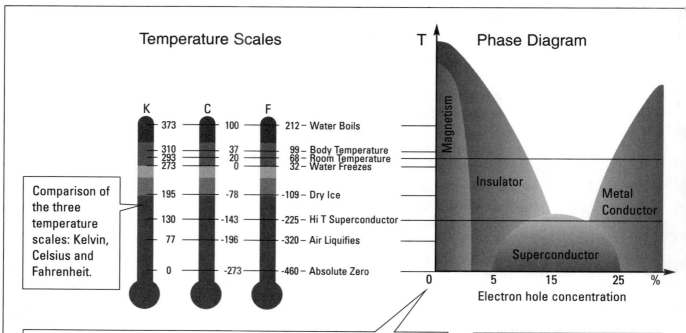

Temperature Scales

K	C	F	
373	100	212	Water Boils
310	37	99	Body Temperature
293	20	68	Room Temperature
273	0	32	Water Freezes
195	-78	-109	Dry Ice
130	-143	-225	Hi T Superconductor
77	-196	-320	Air Liquifies
0	-273	-460	Absolute Zero

Comparison of the three temperature scales: Kelvin, Celsius and Fahrenheit.

Phase Diagram

Magnetism

Insulator

Metal Conductor

Superconductor

0   5   15   25   %

Electron hole concentration

Superconductivity is a phase of matter. This graph shows where phase changes occur in high-temperature copper-oxide superconductors, depending on the temperature (in Kelvin) and the number of electrons in its crystal structure. (Holes are the places left when atoms in the surrounding crystal matrix pull electrons away. Holes are like electrons, because they can move around and carry charge in conductors or superconductors.) Superconductivity occurs in the half-circle region at the bottom, when the material has from 5 to 25 percent holes and the temperature is below about 130K. At low-electron hole concentrations, the material becomes an insulator, while at high concentration it is a conventional metal — a good electrical and heat conductor. Remarkably, by changing electron concentration only 5 percent, the material goes from a perfect insulator (incapable of transporting any electricity) to the strongest known superconductor (a perfect conductor of electricity).

The superconducting material $YBa_2Cu_3O_7$, yttrium-barium-copper oxide, is part of the mineral family called "Perovskites." This brittle ceramic material was one of the first high-temperature superconductors discovered, in 1987. Superconductivity occurs in the copper-oxide planes (speckled grey balls) as a result of electron interactions that are not entirely understood, but could involve the formation of Cooper pairs. Yttrium (black ball in centre), Barium (large, dark grey).

$YBa_2Cu_3O_7$ Crystal Superconductor

Electrons have spin, which makes them into tiny little magnets. They also carry a negative charge. As charges repel, so do electrons normally strongly repel each other. However, in special circumstances they may be drawn to each other to form so-called Cooper pairs. This occurs when the surrounding crystal matrix, made of positively charged atoms, is locally deformed by the passage of a single electron, which in turn attracts a second electron in its wake. Think of the way two people can roll toward each other on a waterbed; it works something like that. In general, a Cooper pair of electrons "join" in such a way that their total spin is cancelled out (that is, the spin of one points up and the other points down, cancelling each other.) Because of this, a Cooper pair behaves like a single particle with zero spin and mass twice that of a single electron. But Cooper pairs do not behave independently of each other like single electrons in a normal metal conductor. They form a single coherent quantum state, which means that instead of having random behaviour, they all act in exactly the same way. In this sense, superconductivity is a large **macroscopic quantum phenomenon.**

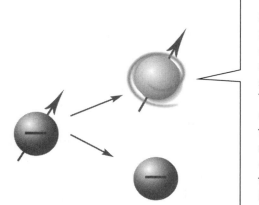

Electrons have two major features, charge and spin. Charge is responsible for the phenomenon of electricity — when electron charge flows, an electric current is created. Spin is responsible for magnetism — when all the electron spins in a material line up in the same direction, the material becomes a magnet. Scientists like Taillefer find new properties of materials as they discover how electron spin and charge behave in different materials. One new theory suggests that in high-temperature superconductors, electrons may lose their usual integrity, so that spin and charge are no longer carried together. If such spin/charge separation indeed occurs, then the fundamental particles in materials are no longer electrons but can be thought of as of two smaller particles, "chargeons" and "spinons." In his research, Louis Taillefer is observing unusual phenomena that may be caused by such spin/charge separation.

because his research involves cooking up materials that have never been made before. He uses super-powerful furnaces in which metals and ceramics are melted by electric arcs (the same as a lightning bolt), intense radio waves or focused beams of super-hot light. Elements of unequalled purity are combined in new and precise ways. The ultimate goal: a superconductor, a material in which electrons can move happily with no resistance at all.

Many materials can be superconductors, but only at extremely low temperatures. Scientists have known for about 100 years that superconductivity can occur in aluminum, lead, mercury, tin and other metals, but it only happens below -250°C. This is near absolute zero, which is a temperature of -273°C (-460°F). Materials scientists use the Kelvin temperature scale, which uses the same units as Celsius but places "zero" at absolute zero, not as we register it in the Celsius or Fahrenheit scales. Nothing can be colder than absolute zero, which technically means the absolute lack of entropy, a physical property of matter sometimes called thermal agitation or disorder — the need for atoms to jiggle around. Think of it this way: when liquid water turns to ice, it loses entropy. The water molecules that were zooming around all over the place in the liquid are now locked into a solid crystal and they can't move as much. They are also colder. By lowering the temperature, the water went through a phase change, from liquid phase to solid phase. It's the same material, but a different physical phase of matter, hard and solid instead of a soft, flowing liquid.

"The ultimate goal: a superconductor, a material in which electrons can move happily with no resistance at all."

The same thing happens with superconductivity. It's just another phase change. When some metals are cooled down to near absolute zero, around one to 10°K, they become superconductors. This temperature at which they change phase to superconductors is called the critical point. So, for instance, aluminum becomes superconducting at 1.2°K and mercury at 4.1°K. Pretty cold.

In 1986, superconductivity got hotter. Two Swiss physicists working at IBM Labs in Zurich, Karl Alexander Müller and J. Georg Bednorz, discovered that a certain type of copper oxide became a superconductor at temperatures around 40°K — quite a lot warmer than ever before. Within a year, scientists around the world began creating similar materials and raised the temperature of superconductivity to 93°K. It took the world of science by storm. Müller and Bednorz won the 1987 Nobel Prize for their discovery. Today the "warmest" superconductor works at about 133°K.

Liquid nitrogen has a temperature of 77°K and is cheaper than milk, so we can now easily create an environment where superconductivity works. Before this, superconductors had to be cooled with liquid helium, which costs about the same as whisky (30 times more than liquid nitrogen) and does not last very long.

The new so-called **high-temperature superconductors** (HTS) have led to new applications such as ultra-high-performance radio frequency filters for use in cellphone network base stations or high-current electricity transmission. In the summer of 2001 three 400-foot HTS cables were installed in Detroit, Michigan, capable of delivering 100 megawatts of power. Superconductors are also appearing in high-speed "maglev" (magnetic levitation) trains in Japan, Germany and Singapore. These trains have no wheels and ride on a frictionless magnetic "cushion." Future HTS applications include ultra-fast computers capable of operating at petaflop speeds, much cheaper and smaller scanners for medical imaging, ultra-efficient electrical generators and new electric motors twice as efficient as and half the size of conventional motors.

The mathematical explanation of superconductivity was worked out in 1957 and is called BCS **theory**, after the three American scientists who discovered it: John Bardeen, Leon Cooper and Robert Schrieffer. In a normal conductor, flowing electrons collide with crystal impurities that slow them down and cause electrical resistance. In a superconductor this does not happen because the electrons pair up and form a coherent quantum state, making it impossible to deflect the motion of one pair without involving all the others. So collisions have no impact and there is no resistance. While BCS **theory** works for conventional superconductors, it does not explain the behaviour of the new high-temperature superconductors. Taillefer thinks the mechanism is a purely electronic interaction, possibly involving the magnetic spin of the electrons.

His work demonstrates a classic strength of the scientific technique: Scientists invent theories that predict and explain the behaviour of the physical world. However, they keep testing and retesting these theories, especially under extreme conditions, to see where they break down. In this way they discover newer and better theories that reveal the essential qualities of nature. Taillefer's most recent experiments question a basic theory explaining why good electrical conductors are also good heat conductors. He showed that under certain conditions (extreme cold and pressure), a type of copper-oxide superconductor appears to conduct electricity and heat differently. Experiments like Taillefer's inspire new, improved theories to explain more of the physical world.

Once a current gets going in a superconductor, it can be made to flow forever in a circular loop. This is the closest we come to perpetual motion in nature. Superconducting coils can become powerful lightweight electromagnets. Mounted on a Shanghai maglev train, with conventional magnets or electromagnets in the guideway, the train floats on magnetic fields, moving with no friction except air resistance. Such maglev trains cruise at 580 kilometres per hour. The train shown does not use high-temperature superconductors. It works with conventional superconductors requiring liquid helium, which is very expensive.

Careers

So You Want to Be a Physicist

It was pure chance that Louis Taillefer became a physicist. He simply accepted a scholarship to study mining engineering at McGill University. "If some other place had given me an award in biology, I would have gone there," he says. At McGill he soon switched to geophysics, but he enjoyed the fundamental science so much that he ultimately graduated with an honours degree in pure physics. Taillefer likes to tell young people, "Go in some direction, but don't feel you need to be stuck there. Go with your intuition and change, readjust to what interests you. Feel free to switch to subjects where you feel more at home."

As a graduate student, Taillefer's quest for more relevant research brought out Gil Lonzarich's passion for theoretical work on magnetism. This in turn inspired the young Taillefer to discover something essential in the natural world. Now that Taillefer himself supervises graduate students, he finds it to be the most satisfying part of his job as a university professor for the same reason. Seeing students find their own path is a wonderful feeling for him, and the only way this happens is if he gives them the freedom to do so. "The key point is that people must go where they feel their inspiration," says Taillefer. "I give my students the freedom to develop as independent scientists but also to follow their destiny as individuals."

Typical physics careers include specialties in electronics, communications, aerospace, remote sensing, biophysics, nuclear, optical, plasma or solid state physics, astrophysics and cosmology. Some physicists concentrate on experiments, while others prefer theory alone.

Mystery

Is room-temperature superconductivity possible? So far, scientists have created materials that are superconductors at $133°K$, which is still $-140°C$ — mighty cold. Taillefer wonders if we will ever find a material that is a superconductor at room temperature ($293°K$). Other big questions in materials science: What makes some materials magnetic, and others not? And why does heat destroy the magnetic properties of some materials more rapidly than others?

Explore Further

- Jean Matricon, Georges Waysand (translator) and Charles Glashausser, *The Cold Wars: A History of Superconductivity*, Rutgers University Press, 2003.
- Michael Tinkham, *Introduction to Superconductivity*, second edition, Dover Books, 2004.

Explanation of maglev trains:
travel.howstuffworks.com/maglev-train.htm
Some of Taillefer's research findings:
www.nserc.ca/news/features/taillefer_e.htm

ACTIVITY

Objective:

To determine which of a variety of materials best conducts heat.

You need:

- Various kinds of materials to test. Each one should be long enough to stick out of a pot of water. Examples are: wooden, plastic or metal spoons; brass, steel, magnesium, silver, copper or aluminum rods, bars, wires or tubes.
- Pot of boiling water
- Thermometer
- Masking tape
- Clock or stopwatch

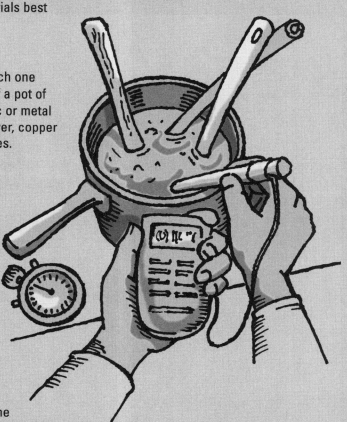

What to do:

Boil some water in a large pot. For a quick test, place in the hot water three items, such as a plastic spoon, a glass rod and a metal rod. Wait a minute, then feel the parts that are sticking out of the water. Which one is getting hot fastest?

For a more detailed experiment, fasten the thermometer sensor tip to one end of the material with masking tape. Check the clock and write down the time. Put the other end of the item into the boiling water. Every 15 seconds, write down the temperature of the thermometer. Do this for at least three different materials, preferably more. Graph your results on a chart that plots temperature versus time. Which materials conduct heat best?

> **Knowing science can enrich your life. Basically, science is a foundation for genuine common sense.**
>
> —Lap-Chee Tsui

PERSONAL INFO

Born
December 21, 1950, Shanghai, China

Residence
Hong Kong, China

Family Members
Father: Jing-Lue
Mother: Hui-Ching (Wang) Hsue
Spouse: Lan Fong Ng
Children: Eugene, Felix

Character
Shy, positive. Laughs a lot.

Favourite Music
Puccini's opera *Turandot*, end of act 1

Other Interests
Travelling, food, basketball, drawing

Title
Vice-Chancellor of the University of Hong Kong

Office
University of Hong Kong, China

Status
Working

Degrees
Bachelor of science (biology), Chinese University of Hong Kong, 1972

M.Phil. (biology), Chinese University of Hong Kong, 1974
Doctorate (biological sciences), University of Pittsburgh, 1979

Awards
Paul di Sant'Agnese Distinguished Scientific Achievement Award (Cystic Fibrosis Foundation, U.S.A., 1989
Gold Medal of Honour (Pharmaceutical Manufacturers Association of Canada), 1989
Fellow, Royal Society of Canada, 1990
Award of Excellence (Genetic Society of Canada), 1990
Officer, Order of Canada, 1991
Cresson Medal (Franklin Institute), 1992
Distinguished Scientist Award (Canadian Society of Clinical Investigators), 1992
Sarstedt Research Prize, 1993
XII Sanremo International Award for Genetic Research, 1993

J. P. Lecocq Prize (Academie des Sciences, Institut de France), 1994
Canadian Medical Association Medal of Honour, 1996
Fellow, World Innovation Foundation, 2000
Foreign Associate, U.S. National Academy of Sciences, 2004

Mentor
K. K. Mark, who taught him how to concentrate on a single thing and to be good at it;
Roger Hendricks, who taught him how to encourage independent thinking in students;
Manuel Buchwald, who taught him how to be critical and look at the broad perspective;
and Han Chang, an older friend of his family who taught him how to be flexible, and to understand the American way of thinking.

Lap-Chee Tsui

Molecular Geneticist
Found the gene that causes cystic fibrosis.

His Story

Richard Rozmahel passes time by reading the bulletin board hanging above the wheezing printer attached to the DNA sequencer. There's an advertisement from a company selling genetic research chemicals. They're offering a free T-shirt sporting the words: ULTRA PURE HUMAN BEING. At the bottom of the ad he reads, "Send six peel-off seals from any GIBCO BRL Enzymes and receive an I MAKE MY LIVING MANIPULATING DNA briefcase free."

Ain't it the truth, thinks Rozmahel to himself as he pulls yet another variation of the same tedious experiment from the printer. He looks at the printout absently as he makes his way back to his desk in the corner of the crowded genetics lab. People and equipment take up every possible space. Shelves groan with bottles, dishes and jars. He passes a friend staring into a microscope. A big humming refrigerator juts out into the passageway. Another student wears gloves while she puts hundreds of precisely measured portions of various liquids into tiny test tubes.

Rozmahel stops suddenly, just before he gets to his desk. Something is unusual about this printout. There it is: a three-base-pair deletion — a type of genetic mutation in a sequence of DNA. DNA molecules are long chains of instructions for making proteins, which themselves are long chains of connected molecules called amino acids.

Each DNA instruction comes in a three-piece unit called a three-base pair, and each one stands for a particular **amino acid** needed in the construction of a protein. To Rozmahel, this three-base-pair deletion is as if one bead had vanished from a precious necklace. A mutation such as this might cause something as simple as a change in eye colour or as complex as a deadly disease.

Instead of sitting down at his desk, Rozmahel rushes to show his supervisor, Dr. Tsui (pronounced "Choy"). It's almost six o'clock and most people have left for the night, but Lap-Chee Tsui is still working.

Tsui's office is small. When Rozmahel arrives, Tsui is hunched over the desk, poring over some other experimental results. The shelves are loaded with books. Piles of paper cover every horizontal surface. Rozmahel looks at the shabby green rug while he waits.

"What is it, Richard?" asks Tsui, with a smile.

"I'm pretty sure I've found a three-base-pair deletion. Look here." He indicates the two DNA sequences, one from a healthy person's genes and one from a person with **cystic fibrosis** (CF) — a fatal disease that kills about one out of every 2,000 Canadians, mostly children. Cystic fibrosis is the most common genetic disease among Caucasians. Kids who have cystic fibrosis are born with it. Half of them will die before they are 25 and few will make it past 30. It affects all the parts of the body that secrete mucus; places like the lungs, the stomach, the nose and mouth. The mucus of kids with cystic fibrosis is so thick that sometimes they cannot breathe.

Tsui looks at the printout and says, "This is very good, Richard. Now show me that it's real." Tsui doesn't seem excited at all, but he knows this

THE YOUNG SCIENTIST...

Lap-Chee Tsui grew up in Dai Goon Yuen, a little village on the Kowloon side of Hong Kong near the Kai Tak airport. He would hang out with a group of kids, mostly boys, and they would go exploring in ponds, catching tadpoles and fish to do simple experiments.

One favourite project was to go to the market and buy silkworms. They would bring home the silkworms and feed them with leaves picked off the mulberry tree in the neighbour's yard. Tsui remembers one day when he and his friends picked almost all the leaves off the tree and the furious neighbour came out and chased the kids away.

As a boy Tsui dreamed of being an architect, and he still draws all his own diagrams and slides. He did not take up genetics until after he obtained his doctorate. He was more interested in studying the nature of diseases.

After Tsui earned his bachelor's and

As a boy Tsui dreamed of being an architect, and he still draws all his own diagrams and slides.

master's degrees from the Chinese University of Hong Kong, he went to study at the University of Pittsburgh in the United States. Hong Kong in those days was still a British dependency and Tsui was familiar with Western ways as practised by the British, but learning to adapt to the American way of doing things was challenging. He says, "It's like if you go to play basketball, but all your life you've only played soccer, it takes a while to learn not to kick the ball."

The first job Tsui got after receiving his doctorate was in Tennessee, at Oak Ridge National Laboratory. After spending about a year there, he took a position in the Department of Genetics at the Hospital for Sick Children in Toronto, Ontario, where he worked for 20 years and made his great discoveries. In 2002 Tsui returned to Hong Kong, where he became vice-chancellor of the University of Hong Kong.

is a solid clue, a major hint that they have found what they are looking for: the gene for cystic fibrosis, the cause of that terrible disease. But he has had false hopes before, so he is not going to celebrate until they check this out carefully. Maybe the difference between the two gene sequences is just a normal variation between individuals. If you take any two healthy people and compare 1,000 DNA bases, you have a good chance of finding the same thing Rozmahel had just found. There are plenty of little variations between individuals.

But Tsui remembers that day — May 9, 1989 — as the day they discovered the gene for cystic fibrosis.

He and his team spent the next five months making sure that their discovery was real, doing tests over and over to see whether the results would be the same. They identified a "signature" pattern of DNA on either side of the base-pair deletion, and using that as a marker they compared 100 healthy people's genes with the identical DNA sequence from 100 cystic fibrosis patients. By September 1989 they were sure they had the cystic fibrosis gene.

Thanks to Tsui, scientists have a better idea of how cystic fibrosis works.

The Science

Molecular geneticists try to understand the structure and function of genes. Lap-Chee Tsui is particularly interested in the gene for cystic fibrosis and other genes on human chromosome number 7. **Chromosomes** are threadlike strands found in the nuclei of animal and plant cells that carry hereditary information about the organism in DNA molecules.

After Tsui found the CF gene in 1989, he had to figure out exactly what that gene did. Over the years, he and his team have discovered that the DNA sequence with the mutation was part of the instructions for making a special protein called CFTR (Cystic Fibrosis Transmembrane conductance Regulator), a part of the cell membrane in certain special **epithelial** (surface) cells that generate mucus. These special cells might line the airways of the nose and lungs or the stomach wall.

The CFTR protein regulates a channel through the cell wall for **chloride ions**, which, through a process called **osmosis**, adjusts the "wateriness" of fluids secreted by the cell. Proteins are made of long chains of amino acids. The CFTR protein has 1,480 amino acids. Kids with cystic fibrosis are missing one single amino acid in their CFTR. Because of this, their mucus ends up being too thick and all sorts of things become difficult for them. Thanks to Tsui's research, scientists have a much better idea of how the disease works. We can now easily predict when a couple will produce a child with cystic fibrosis. With increased understanding, scientists may also be able to devise improved treatments for children born with the disease.

Why do one in 25 Caucasians carry the mutation for CF? Tsui thinks that people who carry it may also have linked beneficial mutations that might, for instance, give them more resistance to diarrhea-like diseases. It's not uncommon in nature to find the "good" linked with the "bad."

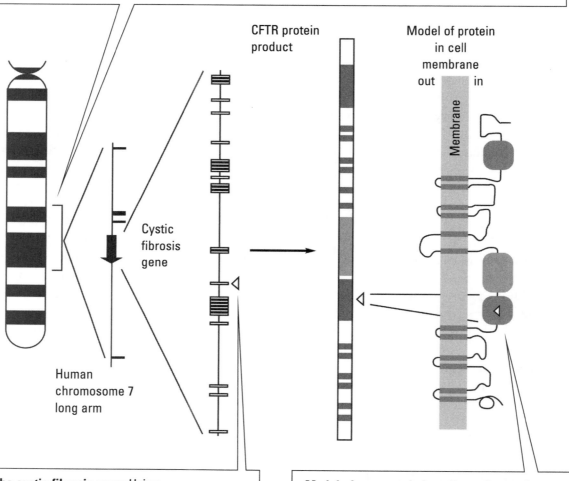

Human chromosome 7: The cystic fibrosis gene sits on the long arm of chromosome 7. One out of every 25 people in the Caucasian population carries the genetic mutation for CF in this gene. Chromosome 7 has 150 million base pairs or units of DNA.

CFTR protein product

Model of protein in cell membrane
out   in

Membrane

Cystic fibrosis gene

Human chromosome 7 long arm

The cystic fibrosis gene: Using microbiological techniques, Tsui first localized the CF gene product to a region of the chromosome. The region has 230,000 DNA base pairs that spell out a series of 1,480 amino acids that curl up to make the Cystic Fibrosis Transmembrane conductance Regulator (CFTR) protein. The little triangle shows the location of the three-base-pair deletion mutation that Tsui and his team discovered.

Model of CFTR protein in cell membrane: A normal gene makes CFTR that regulates the passage of chloride ions and hence the secretion of mucus in epithelial (surface) cells lining the gut, lungs and so on. One missing amino acid at this spot causes the majority of cases of CF. The remainder are caused by more than 1,200 other kinds of mutations of the CFTR gene, each accounting for a small percentage of cases.

Careers

So You Want to Be a Geneticist

Lap-Chee Tsui encourages people to consider a career in the "life sciences." In addition to the typical jobs of technician or university researcher and professor, new opportunities are emerging as biotech company managers, or even biotechnology investment bankers. "As genomic biology is the key discipline that underlies all research in life sciences and medicine, a biology graduate does not have to be limited to jobs in the bio field," says Tsui. There are many non-university research institutes, as well as biotechnology and pharmaceutical companies. After high school, it takes from 11 to 15 years of training to reach the level of an independent research biologist like Tsui. His advice to aspiring geneticists: "Cultivate your curiosity, persistence and passion."

Tsui normally works about 10 to 16 hours a day. "I feel great if I can manage to get experiments to give results more or less as predicted to support my original hyptheses," he says. But he gets even more excited when his experiments give results that are totally unexpected. The most exciting part of his work is when he can interpret unexpected data and uncover something new.

A wide spectrum of jobs is available to individuals with genetics training. Plant and animal breeders, medical specialists, pharmaceutical workers and government regulators are just a few possibilities.

Mystery

The genes of a monkey and a human are almost identical, varying by only about 2 percent. How can such a small difference result in such different animals? Why do humans develop into humans and monkeys into monkeys? It has to do with the way an organism controls which genetic instructions are read from its DNA. This control system is called "the regulation of gene expression" and is still very poorly understood. Tsui likens the situation with monkeys and humans to two orchestras, each having exactly the same instruments and the same music to play: they can sound entirely different if they have different conductors. The greatest mystery to Tsui is identifying and characterizing the "conductor" in the human genetic system.

Explore Further:

* Frank DeFord, *Alex: The Life of a Child*, Rutledge Hill Press, 1997.
* David M. Orenstein, *Cystic Fibrosis: A Guide for Patient and Family*, Lippincott Williams & Wilkins, third edition, 2003.

Websites on cystic fibrosis:
Mayo Clinic: www.mayoclinic.com/invoke.cfm?id=DS00287
Medline Plus: www.nlm.nih.gov/medlineplus/cysticfibrosis.html

ACTIVITY

Objective:

To identify your own **blood type** based on your parents' blood types. (Note: if you cannot find out both your parents' blood types, just pick two of the four possible blood types and do the activity for fun.) You will also learn the difference between your blood genotype and phenotype.

You need:

- Your mom's blood type (A, B, AB, or O)
- Your dad's blood type (A, B, AB, or O)

What to do:

Knowing that you get one chromosome from your mom and one from your dad, can you figure out what your possible blood type is? Those two chromosomes make up your genotype for blood type — the genetic information you carry that defines your blood type. But the genotype still does not tell you what your blood type is, because that information can be expressed in a couple of ways. Your phenotype is the actual observed blood type you have; in other words the expression of the genotype in you. People whose phenotype is blood type A can have either two A chromosomes (genotype = AA), or one A and one O chromosome (genotype = AO). Similarly, people with type B blood have chromosomes in the form of BB or BO. Type AB people have one A and one B chromosome (AB) and type O people must have two O chromosomes (OO). So, for example, if a person with a genotype AA is the mother and the father has the BO genotype, there are two chances for an AB child and two chances for an AO child.

Try to figure out what blood type you (and any brothers or sisters) probably have.

Blood Type	A	B	AB	O
Possible Blood Chromosomes	AA or AO	BB or BO	AB	OO

Possible blood chromosomes for children from AA-type mother and BO-type father:

	A	A
B	AB	AB
O	AO	AO

Which means the couple has a 50/50 chance of having either AB-type children or AO-type children. Use the same sort of reasoning to figure out your own family's combinations. (NOTE: The ABO blood-type system is somewhat more complex than this, due to several rare genetic variations that can cause varying results, but for 99.999 percent of the population this experiment should work.)

Endel Tulving

Cognitive Psychologist

World authority on human memory function. His theory of how memory works is one of the leading scientific concepts in memory research.

His Story

It is 1963. Endel Tulving is standing at the blackboard before a fourth-year cognitive-psychology class at the University of Toronto. He's teaching eight students. The classroom is on the fourth floor of the new Sidney Smith Building in a long, unfriendly classroom with no windows. There's a smell of fresh paint. The blackboard stretches the length of one wall. Everyone is sitting around a big table. Tulving is telling students that memory consists of two important parts, that laying down memories and retrieving them are separate functions.

"Just because a person cannot recall a word seen only a minute ago does not mean that the word is not in memory," he says.

A student asks, "Do you have any evidence for this?"

Tulving says, "But this should be self-evident."

Nevertheless, he notes the doubtful expression on the student's face.

They break for coffee and Tulving goes to his office around the corner. Deep in thought and troubled by the situation in the classroom, he thinks he has time to prepare a simple experiment to demonstrate his point to the students. When he returns to class, he tells everyone to concentrate and listen carefully while he calls out 20 familiar but unrelated words: "Yellow," "rifle," "desk," "violin" and so on. When he is finished, he asks the students to write down as many words as they can remember. Most can get about eight or 10. When they have completed their lists, he picks up the skeptical student's paper and notices that she did not remember the word "yellow." He says, "Wasn't there a colour on the list?" Instantly the student says, "Yellow!" Tulving repeats this for the other missed words, with the same result. Finally, the student who thought that once something was in memory it could always be recalled reluctantly admits, "Perhaps you have a point."

Tulving explains to the class, "You see my point: for someone to know something it is, of course, necessary to have that knowledge in memory, but that presence in memory alone is not enough. Something else is needed, something that makes the stored knowledge accessible."

Everyone has experienced the frustration during a test of knowing the answer to a question but not

❝ *Don't listen to authorities. Find out what the problem is, get the facts, and make up your own mind. Use the scientific method to work things out. Experiment. Trust your feelings and try out various things.* **❞**

—Endel Tulving

PERSONAL INFO

Born
May 26, 1927, Estonia

Residence
Toronto, Ontario

Family Members
Father: Juhan Tulving
Mother: Linda
Spouse: Ruth Mikkelsaar
Children: Elo Ann, Linda

Character
Creative, impatient, positive, optimistic

Favourite Music
Dvorak's New World Symphony (opening movement), anything by Sibelius

Other Interests
Walking (sometimes with golf clubs), chess, history and sociology of science

Office
Rotman Research Institute, Baycrest Centre, North York, Ontario

Status
Semi-retired

Degrees
Bachelor of arts (honours, psychology), University of Toronto, 1953
Master of arts (psychology), University of Toronto, 1954
Doctorate (experimental psychology), Harvard University, 1957

Awards
Fellow, Center for Advanced Study in Behavioural Sciences, Stanford, California, 1972
Senior Research Fellowship (National Research Council), 1964-65
Izaak Walton Killam Memorial Scholarship (Canada Council), 1976
Howard Crosby Warren Medal (Society of Experimental Psychologists), 1982

Distinguished Scientific Achievement Award (American Psychology Association, 1983
Foreign Honorary Member, (American Academy of Arts and Sciences), 1986
Guggenheim Fellowship, 1987
Foreign Associate, U.S. National Academy of Sciences, 1988
William James Fellow (American Psychological Society), 1990
Foreign Member (Royal Swedish Academy of Sciences), 1991
Fellow, Royal Society of London, 1992
Killam Prize (Canada Council), 1994
Gold Medal Award for Lifetime Achievement (American Psychological Foundation), 1994
Foreign Member, Academia Europaea, 1996
McGovern Award (American Association for the Advancement of Science), 1996
Foreign Member, Estonian Academy of Sciences, 2002

THE YOUNG SCIENTIST

Tulving grew up in the town of Tartu in Estonia, a small country on the Baltic Sea in northeastern Europe. Tartu was famous for its old university, built in 1632. The townspeople knew all the professors, and everyone from the university, including students, was treated with great respect. Tulving was the son of a judge and as a child he went to a private boy's school called Hugo Treffner's Gümnasium. He was a good student, always first in his class, but he was not very interested in school. He thought subjects like history, literature and science were totally boring.

Instead, Tulving loved all kinds of sports — skating, skiing, basketball, volleyball, and most of all, track and field. He dreamed of becoming a decathlon champion and he built a primitive but usable track at the family farm where he spent his summers. His friends were fascinated by crystal radios, which were the great new invention of the day, but Tulving was not interested. He was concentrating on running 100 metres in under 12 seconds or throwing the discus farther than he had ever done before.

As a teenager Tulving was not interested in becoming a scientist. Subjects such as physics, chemistry, zoology and botany were dull to him because he had the impression that everything in these fields was already known. But he would wonder, When did time begin? What was there before time? Where does the universe end? What is beyond the end? Is extrasensory perception (ESP) possible? To him, these were the big unanswered questions and therefore worthwhile.

When Tulving was 17, World War II was coming to an end and the Soviet Union's Red Army entered Estonia. Because of this he was separated from his parents and had to leave Estonia for Germany, where he finished school. Tulving would not see his parents again for 20 years. In his last year of school in Germany he studied psychology and liked it right away because of the many mysteries surrounding the brain and behaviour. He decided to become a psychologist.

After graduation, he taught in a German school for war orphans, worked as a translator and interpreter for the American army and spent one year as a medical student at Heidelberg University.

Tulving came to Canada in 1949, married his wife in 1950 and worked toward a master of arts (MA) degree at the University of Toronto, studying psychology. He then went to Harvard University in Cambridge, Massachusetts, where he researched human vision for his doctorate in experimental psychology.

In 1956 he returned to the University of Toronto as a lecturer. He wanted to continue his vision research, but the university had no equipment or experimental apparatus for that kind of work. He had never taken a single course on memory in all his years at university, but he decided to try memory research since it required no fancy equipment. He started with nothing more than a pencil and a stack of index cards, picking up the necessary background information by reading.

being able to produce it, no matter how hard one tries. The knowledge is not missing. What is lacking is an access route to the information.

The Science

Cognitive psychologists study the human mind. "Cognitive" comes from the Latin verb *cognoscere*, to know, so cognitive psychologists study how people know things — how we see, hear, acquire information, remember, believe, understand, speak, think, solve problems, make decisions and much more. As a memory researcher, Tulving explores how people learn and know facts, and how they remember their experiences. Knowing and remembering are very important facets of mind, and for Tulving the human mind is by far the biggest and most complex unsolved mystery in the universe.

Sometimes people wonder what a "mind" is. Tulving believes only a life can have a mind. To him a rock cannot have a mind. But does a virus or a blade of grass have a mind? He defines the occurrence of mind in living organisms as a point in evolution when a living thing does something without expressing any overt behaviour. For instance, when you are remembering something, you are doing something, but your body is not outwardly doing anything. Tulving points out that different species have different minds. A bee can remember the location of a flower by using its bee mind. A human remembers a flower's location in a different way, with a different type of mind.

In the early 1960s, guided by others who had gone before him, Tulving devised experiments to study the way people learn words and organize them in their own minds — so-called subjective organization.

Tulving wondered why subjective organization helps people learn and retain verbal information. He assumed that organized information in memory is more readily accessible than unorganized information; that better "access routes" to it must exist. He made a distinction between two kinds of learned information in memory, one that is "available" and another, more organized form, that is "accessible," if not immediately available. In 1966 Tulving and his research assistant, Zena Pearlstone, published the results of a large experiment involving more than 900 high school students. It was based on the 1963 classroom demonstration described above. The experiment showed how *storage* of information could be distinguished from *retrieval* of information and how studies could isolate and capture the two components. This paved the way for further work that culminated in one of Tulving's best-known discoveries: the "encoding specificity principle," the relation between storage and retrieval necessary for the remembering of an event.

Tulving is best known for his concept of **episodic memory**. Again guided by earlier work of others, in 1972 he proposed a basic distinction between two kinds of memory. He called one episodic and the other **semantic memory**. At the time, psychologists believed there was only one kind of long-term memory, so Tulving's idea of two separate memory systems was not accepted at first. According to Tulving, episodic memory is used to recall events we have personally experienced or witnessed, while semantic memory taps into mental stores of general facts and knowledge. Thus, episodic memory is more about remembering, and semantic memory is more about knowing.

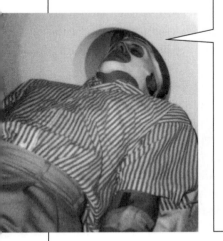

One method Tulving has used to understand human memory is called **functional neuroimaging**, a way of seeing inside a living, functioning brain without hurting it. A **positron emission tomograph** (PET) is a brain-scanning instrument that shows which parts of a brain are functioning during the scan. PET shows where sugar, the body's energy source, is being used up fastest in the brain. Neurologists believe that increased brain activity requires increased sugar consumption at the site of the activity. A person having a PET scan is injected with a special kind of **radioactive sugar tracer** during the procedure. By looking at PET scan maps of the brain, scientists can tell which parts of the brain were functioning during the scan. The procedure can be done while a person is learning something, or while the same person recalls what they have learned. Glowing sections of the brains below show active, functioning regions.

A PET scan subject is fitted with a plastic face mask to minimize head movement. For a typical session, usually six to 10 single scans are done, spaced about 10 minutes apart. Each scan lasts about two minutes, during which the subject is engaged in a particular mental activity. The cognitive activity begins at the beginning of the two-minute period, shortly after the subject receives the injection. The tracer reaches the brain in about eight seconds and then the actual scanning begins, lasting 40 to 60 seconds.

Encoding Brain: Tulving's experiments show that when people are trying to "encode" words in memory (learning), the frontal and temporal cortex in the left hemisphere "lights up" with activity, but the right hemisphere encoding left does not.

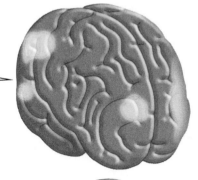

Retrieving Brain: When people "recall" previously learned material, the right frontal cortex comes very much alive retrieval right. The left hemisphere is active in retrieval, too, but to a smaller extent than the right.

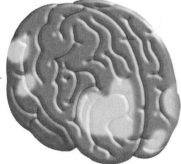

According to Tulving's theory, we use semantic memory to know that the Eiffel Tower is a famous landmark in Paris, and that Paris is the capital of France, but we use episodic memory to remember a trip we took to Paris to visit the Eiffel Tower and any events that occurred there. Other psychologists do not agree. They maintain that knowing about the Eiffel Tower being in Paris and remembering one's trip to Paris rely on one and the same kind of memory. The only difference, they say, is the information the memory contains.

Tulving also believes that animals do not have episodic memory, not even higher primates such as chimpanzees and gorillas. To him, they have only semantic memory. They always live for the moment, lacking the human ability to travel back and forth in time in their mind. That is, they cannot *remember* what they did yesterday or imagine what they will do tomorrow. This capacity for mental time travel seems to be unique to humans. Animals do not have this capacity, nor do some people who have suffered a certain type of brain damage.

Psychologists have done experiments on brain-damaged people with no episodic memory and have found that some can learn new facts, if rather slowly. However, such people cannot recall how, when or where they learned these facts. They have no memory of taking the lessons. One fellow for many weeks went to Tulving's clinic, where he was taught certain facts and phrases such as, "Sun's rays soften asphalt." At the end of the course he was given a test and he did quite well.

According to Tulving, animals like his cat have no episodic memory, so while they may know many things, they do not remember past experiences the way we do. They just know about them.

(Drawing by Ruth Tulving)

When asked what the rays softened, he would say "asphalt." But when he was asked to describe how he learned these things he had no recollection of the lessons and had no idea how he knew all the material.

Tulving extends his theory to children less than four years old. They learn quickly using their semantic memory abilities, but they cannot imagine the past or think of a future time in their own minds. According to Tulving, so far there is no objective evidence that animals or young children have episodic memory. Tulving goes even farther. He believes that some perfectly intelligent and healthy people also lack the ability to remember personal experiences. These people have no episodic memory; they know but do not remember. Such people have not yet been identified, but Tulving predicts they soon will be.

Tulving believes one could use a PET **scanner** to tell whether a person is using episodic memory, remembering an event such as a wedding, or semantic memory, recalling what a wedding ceremony means. In other words, it is now possible to "read people's minds," though in a very limited way. Reading minds is one of the dreams of cognitive science and now, thanks to functional neuroimaging, it seems much more possible than only a short time ago. In this respect, **cognitive psychology** and other branches of brain science have made great progress. As Tulving says, "Progress: knowing more about nature now than we did before is what the game called science is all about."

Careers

So You Want to Be a Psychologist

Most psychologists are employed in practical settings — hospitals, schools, businesses, governments and the military. Many are not engaged in scientific research, which is carried out in universities and research institutions. **Behavioural psychologists** are interested in how people, and animals, behave in different situations, and why they do what they do. Behavioural psychologists do not pay much attention to the "mind" of their subjects, the inner thoughts or feelings related to behaviour. Many behaviours can be understood without knowing exactly what is going on in the brain. Counselling psychologists pay more attention to the minds of their clients, helping people cope with difficult feelings arising from life's hard events such as lost love, death, insecurity and depression.

Psychologists can expect to earn an average of from $35,000 to $100,000 per year. Endel Tulving says, "When it comes to jobs, people naturally try to make rational decisions. They ask: 'Why should I do this or that? How much will a job pay?' But life usually doesn't work like that." And he is glad it does not, because it's not the best approach to choosing a career. A better method is to experiment (in your mind, if necessary) to find a job that seems interesting to begin with and keeps your interest over time. "And if you are doing a job, and find something more interesting, change the job. In your life you will find people who inspire you. Emulate them, says Tulving." As a final piece of advice he adds, "The more you learn and know in the area of your work, the more interesting your jobs and projects become."

There are many jobs in psychology, including career, emotional, marital and youth counsellors; clinical, experimental, behavioural-modification, child, cognitive, developmental, educational, engineering or industrial psychologist; neuropsychologist; and organizational, military, social, sport and vocational psychologist.

Mystery

Human memory is still a big mystery to Tulving. For instance, how do we travel back into our own personal past using only our minds?

Explore Further

- Endel Tulving, "Episodic Memory: From Mind to Brain," *Annual Review of Psychology*, 2002.
- Endel Tulving and Fergus I. M. Craik, *The Oxford Handbook Of Memory*, Oxford University Press, 2000.

McGill University website on how memory works:
www.thebrain.mcgill.ca/flash/a/a_07/a_07_p/a_07_p_tra/a_07_p_tra.htm

ACTIVITY

Objective:

To show that retrieving information from memory is separate from laying down memories.

You need:

- A friend to listen, remember and answer questions for a few minutes
- A watch with a second hand

Ask a friend to name all the months of the year and time the response (most people can do this in about eight seconds). Now ask the person to name the months in alphabetical order (almost no one can do this correctly in less than two minutes). Both questions ask people to use their memory to retrieve something from their mind that they already know. Why do you think one way is faster than the other?

You can also conduct the experiment that Tulving tried with his class in 1963. Here is a list of some category-word pairs.

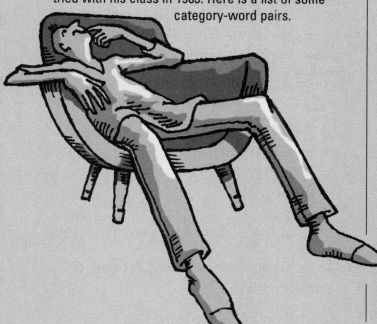

Category	Word
a metal	silver
a precious stone	pearl
a relative	niece
a bird	canary
type of reading material	journal
a military title	major
a colour	violet
a four-footed animal	mouse
an article of furniture	dresser
a part of the human body	finger
a fruit	cherry
a weapon	cannon
a type of dwelling	mansion
an alcoholic beverage	brandy
a crime	kidnapping
an occupation	plumber
a sport	lacrosse
an article of clothing	sweater
a musical instrument	saxophone
an insect	wasp

Ask your friend to listen carefully as you slowly read out each category and the corresponding word. Take two or three seconds to read each category-word pair. Tell your friend that after he or she has heard all the words, you are going to ask him or her to recall all the words, not the categories. Categories are there just to help give a good mental fix on each word. When you have finished, ask your friend to write down all the words he or she can remember. It does not matter if some words are not written down, but do not help or give any hints. After your friend has finished, check the list and note which ones were not remembered. Look in the table and say the category words as hints for the words missed. Can your friend now remember the words that he or she forgot? Was the now-remembered, supposedly forgotten word in memory or not? What does this experiment tell us about forgetting? When someone says that he or she has forgotten a name or a word or a fact, what does it really mean?

Irene Ayako Uchida

Cytogeneticist
World-famous Down syndrome researcher.

Her Story

Irene Uchida has been asked to join the morning hospital rounds at Children's Hospital in Winnipeg, Manitoba. It's around 1960. She's talking about patients who have the symptoms of **trisomy** of chromosome 18 — that is, three number 18 **chromosomes** instead of the normal two. A doctor named Jack Sinclair raises his hand and says, "Hey, I think we have one on the fourth floor."

He takes her up to the ward right away. They get a blood sample from the patient and add some anti-clotting agent. Uchida immediately goes to work to identify the chromosomes. Diagnosing trisomy by actually looking at a patient's chromosomes is something very new, and it has never been done by anybody in Winnipeg — or even in Canada.

She takes the blood to the cytology lab, a place in the hospital for examining cells. The lab has the vinegary smell of acetic acid. Low tables by the windows have lots of microscopes, with technicians in white lab coats seated at most of them. Along the opposite wall, a few people are preparing samples and slides.

First Uchida lets the red blood cells settle in the vial, then she takes the white blood cells off the top with a pipette, a long glass tube that is used to suck up small amounts of liquid. She transfers them to a small glass container containing a medium in which they grow and multiply for three days, inside an **incubator**. Then she takes out the liquid and **centrifuges** it down. A centrifuge is a device that spins test tubes around super-fast to force all the heavy stuff to the bottom, leaving lighter cells and liquid at the top. She "fixes" the cells with **acetic acid solution**, and drops them onto a **glass slide** so that the cells break and spill out their chromosomes. She stains the material on the slide with a dye, puts it under the microscope and looks for the chromosomes — long, twisty, banded strands of protein and DNA. She finally does find three number 18 chromosomes instead of the normal two, confirming the **diagnosis**. This cytogenetic analysis is a first for Winnipeg and Canada.

> **❝ Do your best no matter what you do, even if it's a menial job. ❞**
>
> —Irene Uchida

PERSONAL INFO

Born
April 8, 1917, Vancouver, British Columbia

Residence
Burlington, Ontario

Family Members
Father: Sentaro
Mother: Shizuko

Character
Hard worker, feisty, jovial, gracious

Favourite Music
Beethoven's Violin Concerto

Other Interests
Violin, piano, art, photography

Titles
Emeritus Professor, Departments of Pediatrics and Pathology, McMaster University; Director of

Office
Department of Pediatrics, McMaster University, Hamilton, Ontario

Status
Retired

Degrees
Bachelor of arts, University of Toronto, 1946
Doctorate, University of Toronto, 1951

Awards
Ramsay Wright Scholar (University of Toronto), 1947
Woman of the Century (National Council of Jewish Women), 1967

Manitoba Annual Queen Elizabeth II Lectures Canadian Pediatric Society, first invited speaker, Children's Hospital, Winnipeg, 1967
Named one of 25 Outstanding Women, International Women's Year, Ontario, 1975
Named among 1,000 Canadian Women of Note 1867-1967, Media Club of Canada and Women's Press Club of Toronto, 1983
Officer, Order of Canada, 1993

Mentor
Curt Stern, geneticist, and Bruce Chown, blood-group specialist

THE YOUNG SCIENTIST

At the University of British Columbia (UBC) Irene Uchida was a member of the Japanese Students Club and a reporter for a weekly Japanese-Canadian newspaper. During World War II she was active in the group Japanese Canadian Citizens for Democracy. Because Canada was at war with Japan and feared an invasion, it was a period of great anxiety for the 23,000 people of Japanese heritage who were uprooted from their homes on the West Coast by an order-in-council of the federal government in 1942 and had their possessions and properties seized.

Uchida was forced to stop her education at UBC and leave her home in Vancouver. She and her family were taken to an internment camp at Christina Lake in British Columbia's Kootenay region, where she became principal of the largest internment-camp school, at nearby Lemon Creek. She became known for her creative ideas. Two years later she was allowed to continue her education at the University of Toronto, graduating in 1946 with a bachelor of arts. She planned to take up social work, but one of her professors persuaded her to enter the field of genetics.

In 1951 Uchida received her doctorate in zoology and began her career as a research associate at the Hospital for Sick Children in Toronto. Her work in genetics focused on the study of twins, children with **congenital** heart diseases and those with a variety of other anomalies such as **Down syndrome**.

In 1959, while working with Drosophila (fruit fly) chromosomes at the University of Wisconsin, Uchida turned her attention to human chromosomes. When scientists in France discovered that Down syndrome patients had an extra chromosome (47 instead of 46), she decided to try to learn the cause of the extra chromosome. She continued her research in Winnipeg when she was appointed director of the Department of Medical Genetics at Children's Hospital there, in 1960. In her first study of human chromosomes, Uchida found that there appeared to be an association between pregnant women who received X-rays and the occurrence of Down syndrome in their babies.

In 1969, with a Medical Research Council grant, she went as a visiting scientist to the University of London and to Harwell, England, to study a technique for analyzing the chromosomes of mouse eggs.

After returning to Canada, Uchida continued her research on the effects of radiation on humans and mice at the McMaster University Medical Centre in Hamilton, Ontario, as well as carrying out her teaching duties as a professor. She also initiated a Genetic Counselling Program at the McMaster Medical Centre. As director of the Cytogenetics Laboratory in Oshawa, Ontario, her responsibilities included the diagnosis of chromosome differences in patients with congenital abnormalities, developmental disabilities and other genetic conditions. In addition, Uchida helped diagnose irregularities in the chromosomes of **fetuses**. She has been invited to speak in many countries and is a member of various provincial, national and international scientific organizations.

The Science

Cytogenetics is the study of chromosomes in cells. It concentrates on the behaviour and identification of chromosomes. By knowing the state of the chromosomes and especially the genes within them, scientists can now predict many genetic disorders. Uchida was the first person to bring this technique to Canada. One of the many practical applications of cytogenetics is the ability to

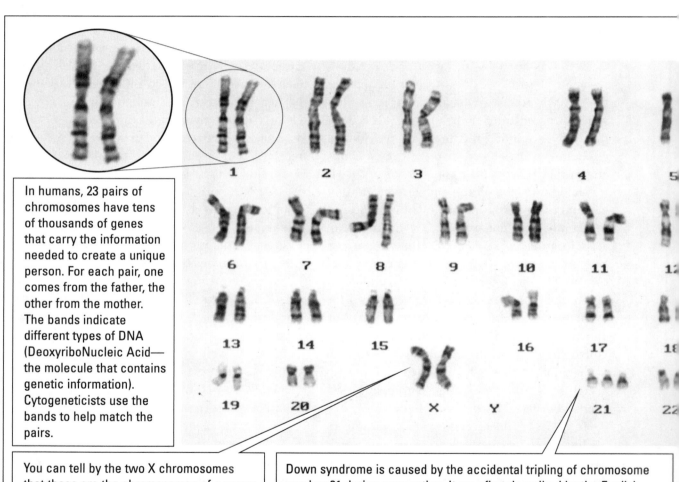

In humans, 23 pairs of chromosomes have tens of thousands of genes that carry the information needed to create a unique person. For each pair, one comes from the father, the other from the mother. The bands indicate different types of DNA (DeoxyriboNucleic Acid—the molecule that contains genetic information). Cytogeneticists use the bands to help match the pairs.

You can tell by the two X chromosomes that these are the chromosomes of a young woman. Males have one X and one Y chromosome.

Down syndrome is caused by the accidental tripling of chromosome number 21 during conception. It was first described by the English physician John Langdon Down in 1866. Other genetic diseases are caused by tripling of chromosomes number 13 or 18. The tripling is called trisomy. People with trisomy of chromosomes 13 or 18 usually die as fetuses, and are miscarried. Those who are born alive do not usually live more than a year. The incidence of Down syndrome is related to the age of the pregnant woman. Women under 30 have a 1 in 1,200 chance of having a Down syndrome baby. By age 35 the chance is about 1 in 500 and by age 45 about 1 in 25.

diagnose genetic diseases in fetuses, thus preparing many pregnant mothers and their spouses for the birth of an abnormal child, or giving them the choice of terminating the pregnancy.

Melanie Laird has Down syndrome. She loves sports of all kinds and, among other things, studies Butokukan karate and is working towards a purple belt. People with Down syndrome are not as different as you might think. According to Uchida, who has known hundreds of them, "They are often very happy and affectionate." Yet like everyone else, they have unique personalities with strengths, weaknesses, interests, dreams and ideas. New education and training programs are helping Down syndrome people live happy productive lives. Unfortunately, because of health problems arising from their genetic disorder, only a few live beyond their mid fifties.

184

ACTIVITY

Objective:

To be a gene detective and uncover the clues to see if a set of chromosomes indicates Down syndrome.

You need:

- Photocopier
- Scissors

Background:

A typical chromosome set is like the one shown here. A complete set of chromosomes like this is called a **chromosome spread**, or **karyotype**.

What to do:

Photocopy the graphic above on a good-quality photocopier, or go to the web and download a PDF file of the image at www.science.ca, then cut out the chromosomes with scissors. Now try to sort them into pairs by carefully looking at the patterns of banding on each chromosome and the lengths of the two arms on each chromosome. See if you can discover whether this person has Down syndrome or some other form of trisomy.

Mystery

Uchida believes geneticists may be able to find out how to deactivate one of the chromosomes in an individual with trisomy. This happens naturally during the embryonic development of all women — one of their X chromosomes is always deactivated. If geneticists can find a technique to deactivate certain chromosomes such as the extra ones at numbers 21, 13 or 18, the related genetic conditions may be cured at an early embryonic stage.

Explore Further

- Jason Kingsley and Mitchell Levitz, *Count Us In: Growing Up with Down Syndrome*, Harvest/HBJ Books, 1994.

Library and Archives Canada website about Uchida:
www.collectionscanada.ca/women/h12-415-e.html
Down syndrome web page:
www.nas.com/downsyn/

Glossary

EACH SCIENCE HAS ITS OWN LANGUAGE of special words. This glossary is an alphabetical list of many of the special words used throughout the profiles in this book.

A

Abelian fields — A field of numbers (e.g. the Rational numbers) that allows two symmetrical operations (such as a+b = b+a) to be applied on numbers in the field in any order and the outcome is independent of the order.

Acetic acid solution (CH_3COOH) — The simplest carboxylic acid dissolved in water. The major component of vinegar.

Activity budget — An accounting of the time spent on various activities by a focal animal under observation in an anthropology experiment.

AIDS (Acquired Immune Deficiency Syndrome) — A severe immunological disorder caused by the retrovirus HIV. People with AIDS have weakened immune systems and their bodies cannot fight disease. AIDS victims usually end up dying of infectious diseases. AIDS is transmitted primarily sexually, or by exposure to blood or blood products from an infected individual.

Algebraic Numbers — The set of all numbers that form the solution of polynomials (algebraic equations). E.g. the value of x in: $x^2 - 2 = 0$.

Allergenic — A substance such as pollen that causes an allergy, an abnormally sensitive reaction characterized by sneezing, itching, or rashes on the skin.

Amazon — The world's second longest river, which begins in Peru and empties into the Atlantic ocean in Brazil. It carries more water than any other river in the world and traverses the world's largest rainforest, which bears the same name.

Amino acid — A type of organic molecule found in living things. It has an amino (NH_3) group on one end, and a carboxylic acid (COOH) group on the other. Amino acids are linked together by enzymes to form proteins, the essential building blocks of all living things.

Angstrom — A unit of length equal to 10^{-10} meters or 0.1 nanometers (a nanometre is a billionth of a metre).

Anthropology — The study of humankind through evolution, culture, and social structures.

Antibody (antibodies) — An immune system protein which gloms onto bacteria thereby inactivating them or their toxins, making them easier to kill by other immune system molecules.

Antigens — A substance that is foreign to the human body and stimulates an immune response. Some antigens are toxins, bacteria, foreign cells, dust, dirt, chemicals, and pollen.

Aphasia — A speech disorder that occurs when people's brains are damaged by some kind of accident or disease. For instance, a person with aphasia might be able to tell you everything about oranges and even write the word orange, but for some strange reason would not be able to say "orange." There are many different kinds of aphasia.

Arthritis — A disease involving inflammation of the joints and connective tissues.

Atmosphere — The gas layer surrounding a planet. On earth it's the air and everything that goes with it, like clouds, rain, and storms.

Atmospheric turbulence — Eddies and winds caused by pockets of air of different pressures and temperatures.

Atom (atoms) — The smallest part of an element that can exist. Atoms consist of a nucleus of protons and neutrons surrounded by a cloud of electrons.

Autoimmune diseases — Any of a number of diseases caused by a malfunctioning of the immune system. Allergies are a common example.

B

Bacterium (bacteria) — Single-cell organisms that can cause disease in plants and animals.

Balmer lines — Characteristic dark lines on a spectrogram. Named after the Swiss high school teacher who first described them mathematically in 1885.

Base pair — A pair of nitrogenous bases linked by hydrogen bonds connecting the complementary strands of the DNA molecule. The base Adenine always pairs with Thymine, and the base Guanine always pairs with Cytosine.

Base pair deletion — A mutation that arises as a result of the deletion of one base pair in a DNA chain.

B-cells — A type of white blood cell; part of the human immune system. When stimulated, they produce antibodies that kill specific antigens.

BCS Theory — A quantum theory of electron interaction explaining superconductivity at the microscopic level. The theory was proposed in 1957 by John Bardeen and his graduate assistants Leon Cooper and John Schreiffer.

Behavioural psychologist — A scientist who studies how brains work in order to understand how people differ from each other.

Benzoporphyrin derivative — A complex ring-shaped nitrogen-containing molecule that is soluble in fat and is the basis for photodynamic therapies to treat cancer and certain types of eye disease.

Bering Sea — A northward extension of the Pacific Ocean between Siberia and Alaska.

Bertrand Russell — The great English philosopher and educator who lived from 1872 to 1970. His most famous book, *Principia Mathematica*, demonstrated that mathematics could be explained by the rules of formal logic. He won the

Nobel Prize for Literature in 1950. He was a pacifist and was jailed twice for his activities on behalf of peace and nuclear disarmament.

Big bang theory — Currently accepted by most cosmologists, this theory about the origin of the universe says that about 12-14 billion years ago, all matter in the universe was created in an instant in one tremendously hot explosion originating from nothing.

Biochemistry — The study of chemical compounds and reactions occurring in living organisms.

Biology — The study of living things.

Biotechnology — The use of microorganisms such as bacteria or yeast to produce commercial products such as drugs, foods, and so on. Also for the treatment of wastes and oil spills.

Black hole theory — The concept of a region of space that has so much mass concentrated in it that nothing can escape its gravitational pull, including light. Hence the name "black hole."

Blood type (blood group) — The classification of human blood based on its immunological qualities. Persons must receive blood transfusions of their own blood group or they will have an adverse immune response. Blood type is passed on genetically from parents to their children.

Borneo — A tropical island in the western Pacific Ocean; the third largest island in the world. The country of Brunei is on the northwest coast while the rest of the island is divided between Indonesia and Malaysia. Biruté Galdikas lives and works in the Indonesian part of Borneo.

Botanist — A person who specializes in botany, the study of plants.

C

Caecilians — legless, tailless tropical worm-like amphibians of the order *Cymnophiona*.

Caffeine — A bitter white alkaloid most often found in tea or coffee and used as a minor stimulant.

Cancer — A disease that happens when certain cells

in the body begin growing in an uncontrolled manner to create a tumour that upsets the function of one or more parts of the body.

Cassava root — The root of a tropical shrub. It has large tubers that are eaten as a staple food after leaching and drying to remove cyanide.

Carbon dioxide (CO_2) — A gas that is the main product of burning, including the combustion of fossil fuels like oil, gas and coal.

Catalysis — A process that speeds up chemical reactions by the introduction of a molecule or atom (catalyst) that promotes the chemical reaction but is not consumed by it.

Catalytic RNA — A special kind of RNA that acts like an enzyme. First discovered by Sid Altman.

CCD (Charge Coupled Device) — An integrated circuit containing an array of linked, or coupled, capacitors on a microchip. Under the control of an external circuit, each capacitor can transfer its electric charge to one or another of its neighbours.

Cell (cells) — The smallest structural unit of an organism that is capable of independent functioning. A simple cell consists of a nucleus and cytoplasm, and is enclosed by a cell wall.

Cell assemblies — Brain structures also known as Hebb synapses — collections of nerve cell connections involving more than one input and able to retain activity even after stimulus ceases. They are thought to be a possible basis for learning and memory.

Centrifuge — An apparatus consisting of a device that can spin test tubes around at very high speed. Used to separate contained materials or to precipitate out by gravity the solids suspended in a liquid.

Chemical — A substance with a distinct molecular composition that is produced or used in a chemical process or reaction.

Chemical reaction — A change or transformation in which a chemical decomposes, combines with other chemicals or shares atoms or groups of atoms with other chemicals.

Chemiluminescence — The feeble emission of light from colliding molecules during a chemical reaction.

Chemistry — The science of the composition, structure, properties, and reactions of matter, especially atomic and molecular systems.

Chicha drink — A sour-tasting beverage made by native women in the Peruvian jungle. They chew a kind of tapioca root and spit it into a huge bowl, then let it stand for a while to ferment.

Chinook — A type of salmon native to the Pacific Northwest. Also known as spring salmon.

Chloride ion — The negatively charged ion of the element chlorine. Usually found in aqueous solution.

Chromosome spread — Also known as a karyotype, a set of chromosomes that has been fixed and spread out on a glass slide for analysis.

Chromosome band — The characteristic banding of chromosomes helps cytogeneticists identify them. Banding is caused by different types of DNA and associated proteins.

Chromosomes — Threadlike strands found in the nuclei of animal and plant cells. Chromosomes are made of DNA molecules and associated proteins and they carry hereditary information.

Classical geometer — A mathematician who studies classic geometrical structures such as points, lines, angles, surfaces and solids.

CMOS (complementary metal oxide semiconductor) — one of the most popular types of integrated circuits including microprocessors, RAM, and other low power microchips.

Cognition — The mental processes of knowing.

Cognitive psychology — A branch of psychology dealing with how the brain processes information, especially concerning perception, memory, knowing, awareness, reasoning, judgment and learning.

Cognitive functions — How brains process

information, especially with regard to perception, memory, knowing, awareness, reasoning, judgment and learning.

Coho — A type of salmon native to the Pacific Northwest. Also known as silver salmon.

Collimate — To line up, as in a parallel beam of radiation.

Complex number — A number that has a real part and an imaginary part. The imaginary part is something like the square root of a negative number that by ordinary logic is impossible.

Conjecture — A statement that, although suspected to be generally true, has not been proven.

Congenital — Some trait or condition that is present at birth.

Coordinates — A means of specifying a point's location in space with numbers. For instance, on a two-dimensional plane, two numbers are needed, one to show how far to the right or left and one to show how far forward or backwards the point is from some other location on the plane.

Cosmology — A branch of physics concerned with the origins of the universe, its history, structure and dynamics.

Critical temperature — In magnetic metals, the point at which magnetism disappears as temperature increases.

Cryogenic — Having to do with extremely cold temperatures approaching absolute zero (below about -150°C or -244°F).

Crystal structures — The regular pattern of atoms or molecules in a solid crystalline substance.

Crystalline orientation — The three dimensional alignment of a crystal structure.

Culture — The socially transmitted behaviour patterns, arts, beliefs, and knowledge as an expression of a particular community, period, class, or population.

Cystic fibrosis (CF) — A fatal disease that kills about one out of every 2000 Canadians, mostly children. Cystic fibrosis is the most common genetic disease among Caucasian people.

Cytogenetics — The study of chromosomes in cells. It concentrates on the behaviour and identification of chromosomes.

D

Data collection — Recording observations from experiments for later analysis.

Deoxyribose — A type of sugar ($C_5H_{10}O_4$) that is a constituent of DNA.

Deuterium — An isotope of hydrogen containing a proton, a neutron and an electron. (Ordinary hydrogen has only one proton and one electron.)

Diagnosis — The act or process of identifying the nature and cause of a disease or injury through evaluation of patient history, examination, and review of laboratory test data.

Dimension — A mathematical concept concerning how many numbers you need to specify uniquely a point in space. On a flat surface you need two numbers. It's called a two-dimensional space. We live in 3D or three-dimensional space where you need three numbers to tell exactly where you are.

Dimensional analogy — The process of stretching geometrical shapes into higher dimensions.

DNA (*deoxyribonucleic acid*) — The molecule that encodes the genetic information that tells cells how to function and grow.

Down syndrome — A congenital disease caused by the accidental tripling of chromosome number 21 during conception. Affected people have mild to moderate mental retardation, short stature, and flat facial features.

E

Ecology — The study of natural systems of plants and animals through the experimental analysis of their distribution and abundance.

Electron — A subatomic particle with a unit of negative electric charge. A constituent of all atoms that are composed of one or more electrons orbiting the atom's nucleus in a sort of electron cloud.

Electrophoresis — A standard laboratory technique for separating chemical compounds. A few drops of a material in solution are placed onto a glass plate on which there is a thin layer of gel, and the plate is then exposed to a strong electric field. This causes the various compounds to move different distances through the gel over a period of time, thereby separating them.

Element — A substance composed of atoms all having the same number of protons in their nuclei. Elements cannot be reduced to simpler substances by chemical means. There are about 110 known elements, of which 94 occur in nature.

Elliptic curves — An area of algebraic geometry dealing with curves satisfying equations like $y^2 = x^3 + Ax + B$.

Emeritus — Retired but retaining an honorary title the same as the one held before retirement. Usually applied to university professors.

Encoding a memory — The recording or laying down of a memory in the brain.

Energy — The capacity of a physical system to do work.

Enzyme — A protein that promotes chemical reactions in living organisms through catalysis.

Episodic memory — The memory of events an individual has personally experienced, including time, place, and the associated emotions. Can be thought of as "stories" like episodes from a TV series.

Epithelial — A type of cell that forms the membranous covering of most internal and external surfaces of the body and its internal organs. For instance, skin cells are epithelial cells. Other epithelial cells in the nose and mouth and other parts of the body secrete mucus.

Ethnobotanist — A person who practices ethnobotany, the study of plants by obtaining information from people around the world.

Event horizon — The point of no return for matter or light falling into a black hole. At this distance from the singularity at the centre of the black hole, gravity is so strong that nothing can escape. To an outside observer, the event horizon appears as the surface of the black hole.

F

Fence or Krebs Effect — The population explosion and crash that results from fencing in an area where rodents live in the wild.

Ferment — The energy-producing process used by some microorganisms to break down sugar molecules, often (but not only) resulting in the products of ethyl alcohol and carbon dioxide.

Fetus (fetuses) — The unborn young still developing in the womb.

Fibre optics — The science or technology of light transmission through very fine flexible glass or plastic fibres.

Fisheries biologist — A biologist who studies fish habitat and population.

Fish population dynamics — The rise and fall of fish populations as a result of natural effects and fishing.

Focal animal — An animal subject that is the focus of the research in an anthropology experiment.

Folk medicine — Traditional medicine as practised by non-professional healers, generally using natural and especially herbal remedies made from local plant materials.

Fossil — The remains of an organism of a past geologic age, such as a skeleton or leaf imprint, embedded and preserved in the earth's crust.

Fourth dimension — We experience the world in three dimensions, but it is possible to imagine a world with four or more dimensions. The fourth dimension could be time or maybe it's where ghosts come from.

Fraser River — A major river in British Columbia. It begins in the Rocky Mountains and drains into the Straight of Georgia near Vancouver.

Free radical — A transition molecule created briefly

in a chemical reaction through which molecules come together and transform themselves into something new. Free radicals last only for the length of time it takes for their constituent atoms to rearrange themselves with other molecules into new molecules — a few millionths of a second.

Functional Neuroimaging — The use of brain imaging technology, such as a PET scanner, to measure an aspect of brain function, usually to link activity in certain brain areas to specific mental functions such as reading or remembering.

Fungus — Plant-like organisms that lack chlorophyll. They include yeasts, moulds, smuts and mushrooms.

G

Gene — A hereditary unit that occupies a specific place on a chromosome and determines a particular characteristic of an organism.

Genetic code — The sequence of nucleotides in a DNA molecule that specifies the amino acid sequence in the synthesis of proteins. Each amino acid is coded by three nucleotides. For instance, glutamic acid is coded by the sequence Guanine, Adenine, Adenine.

Genetic engineering — Using molecular biological techniques to alter the genes in organisms so that they produce or express certain substances or qualities that are desirable or commercially valuable.

Genetics — A branch of biology concerned with genes and heredity and how inherited characteristics are transmitted among similar or related organisms.

Genome — The complete set of genes for an individual organism.

Genomics — The sequencing of the DNA of an organism to understand how it works.

Geometer — A person who studies geometry.

Geometry — A branch of mathematics that deals with points, lines, angles, surfaces and solids.

Geophysical — Having to do with the physics of the earth, including oceans, land and atmosphere. Represented by the sciences of oceanography, seismology, and meteorology, respectively.

Glass slide — A small flat piece of glass used for mounting samples to be viewed under a microscope.

Global warming — The idea that coal, oil and gas burning might cause a large enough increase in carbon dioxide in the atmosphere over the next 100 years to cause a "greenhouse effect," whereby carbon dioxide in the atmosphere traps infrared radiation and warms the planet by a few degrees centigrade.

Green Book — A book written by William Ricker in the 1950s and updated in the 1970s. It presents a mathematical system for the computation of fish population statistics. The Green Book is still used to determine allowable catches for fisheries in many countries, including Canada.

Greenhouse effect — The process whereby increasing carbon dioxide in the atmosphere traps infrared radiation and warms the planet by a few degrees centigrade, potentially allowing the polar ice caps to melt and cause great flooding all over the planet.

H

Haemoglobin — The iron-containing pigment (in red blood cells) that carries oxygen to cells.

Heavy hydrogen — An isotope of hydrogen containing a proton, one neutron and an electron. (Ordinary hydrogen has only one proton and one electron.) Also called Deuterium.

Heavy water — Water molecules each have two hydrogen atoms (H_2O). When the hydrogen atoms are heavy hydrogen (see above), the water is called "heavy water."

Hell's Gate Falls — A deep gorge with rapids and waterfalls in the Fraser River Canyon between Hope and Lytton, British Columbia.

Helper T-cell — A special T-cell that activates other cells in the immune system to mount a defensive response against invading antigens in the body.

Hexagonal — Having six sides.

High-temperature superconductor (HTS) — Any material that demonstrates superconductivity — electrical conduction with zero resistance — at or above the temperature of liquid nitrogen (196°C).

Hormone — A chemical messenger from one cell (or group of cells) to another. All multicellular organisms including plants produce hormones.

Hydrogen (H_2) — A colourless, very flammable gas. The lightest of all gases and the most abundant element in the universe.

Hypercube — The four-dimensional version of a cube. A four-dimensional hypercube is analagous to a three-dimensional cube. Also known as a tesseract.

Hyperdimensional geometry — Geometry that goes beyond the three dimensions of ordinary space.

I

Immune system — The system of organs and cells that is concerned with protecting us from invading organisms or molecules such as germs, dirt, viruses and bacteria.

Immunologist — A person who studies immunology, a branch of medicine or biology concerned with the structure and function of the immune system.

Incubator — An apparatus or a chamber for maintaining living organisms in an environment that encourages growth.

Infrared light — Invisible electromagnetic radiation of a wavelength longer than visible red light, but shorter than microwave radiation.

Infrared spectrometer — A device used to measure emission or absorption of infrared light.

Inner horizon — In a black hole, the point beyond which you cannot see out.

Integers — All the positive natural numbers (1, 2, 3, …), the negative natural numbers (-1, -2, -3, …) and the number zero.

Ion — An atom or molecule with a positive or negative electric charge caused by gaining or losing one or more electrons.

Irrational numbers — Any real numbers that cannot be written as fractions. Their expansion never ends and never enters a periodic pattern. E.g. pi = 3.14159265358979323846264338327950288419 7 … and on to infinity.

K

Kaleidoscope — An instrument that uses mirrors and bits of glass to create an endlessly changing pattern of repeating reflections.

Kantian doom — The idea that we are doomed because even though we know that something is bad for us, we do it because everyone else is doing it. Immanuel Kant was a German philosopher who in the last half of the 1700s wrote a lot about the meaning of existence and morality. Kant's supreme principle of morality is called the categorical imperative and is a test of the morality or quality of our behaviour. In simple terms, Kant tells us to ask ourselves before we do something: what would happen if everyone acted like this?

Karyotype — A spread of chromosomes on a glass slide, often photographed, sorted and analyzed.

Killer T-cells — A special large T-cell that attacks and kills invading target cells bearing specific antigens.

Knock-out mice — Mice with missing genetic instructions for making just one protein.

L

Lemming — A small thickset rodent that lives in the North and is known for periodic devastating population crashes in which almost all the lemmings die.

Light-year — The distance that light travels in one year, or 9.46 trillion kilometres.

Line of natural replacement — In the Ricker Curve, a line that represents spawners (adult fish who lay eggs or fertilize them) being replaced by an equal number of progeny (fish who grow up to be adults).

Lipoproteins — Complex protein molecules that carry fatty material in blood. For instance, lipoproteins are responsible for carrying cholesterol to various parts of the body.

Live-animal trap — A little cage that traps animals without harming them so that animal ecologists can measure and tag the animals for experimental study.

Lynx — A type of wildcat that lives in northern North America and Eurasia. They are identified by their tufted ears and black- tipped tails.

M

Macrophage — A specialized cell that's part of the immune system. Like a garbage truck in the body, macrophages go around collecting bits of living and dead cells and other material to present them to T-Cells for identification.

Macroscopic quantum phenomenon – Normally quantum mechanics explains the behaviour of things at microscopic scales on the order of atoms and molecules. There are a few cases, however, when large scale, or macroscopic quantum effects arise. One of these is high temperature superconductivity.

Macular degeneration — A medical condition where the light sensing cells in the macula (a part of the retina used for discerning fine detail) malfunction and eventually stop working. It is the main cause of blindness in the USA for people over the age of fifty.

Magnetism – A force of nature exhibited by both magnets and electric currents, characterized by fields of force.

Maser (Microwave Amplification by Stimulated Emission of Radiation) — Like a laser but radiating microwaves instead of light. Giant distant masers can be seen from the earth in far away galaxies.

Mast cells — Cells in the body that release substances in response to a disease or injury and can help the body repair itself.

Maximum sustainable catch — The point on a Ricker Curve that shows the maximum number of fish you can catch to sustain the stock of fish for future years.

Medicinal plant — A wild plant that can be the source of a drug or medicine. For instance, willow bark was the original source of the drug aspirin.

Metaphysical — Of or relating to metaphysics, a division of philosophy that is concerned with the fundamental nature of reality and existence.

Meteorologist — A person who studies the atmosphere and in particular, weather.

Meteorology — The study of the earth's atmosphere and weather.

Methane (CH_4) — An odourless colorless flammable gas, the main constituent of natural gas.

Methylene (CH_2) — A hydrocarbon molecule consisting of a carbon atom with two hydrogen atoms, one on either side. Methylene has two free electrons, making it a very reactive free radical.

Microbiology — A branch of biology that deals with living things on a microscopic scale.

Microsaur – Literally "little reptile" that lived 360 – 300 million years ago, a possible ancestor of the dinosaurs. However, we now know they were not reptiles. They were amphibians characterized by small size and a salamander or snake-like body.

Models — Mathematical representations of systems – like the atmosphere or the nucleus of an atom – that account for their properties and may be used to study or predict their characteristics.

Modular forms – A very complicated mathematical object involving groups of imaginary numbers that result in amazing symmetrical patterns.

Molecule (molecules) — The smallest particle of a substance that retains the properties of the substance and is composed of one or more atoms.

Molecular — Having to do with molecules.

Molecular biology — Biology on the molecular level;

the physics and chemistry of molecules in biological systems.

Molecular ions — A group of atoms with a net electric charge caused by gaining or losing one or more electrons.

Molecular geneticist — A person who studies genetics at the molecular level — in particular, the molecules of DNA and associated compounds.

Multiple sclerosis — A chronic degenerative disease of the central nervous system in which patches of the protective myelin sheath around nerves are lost. The cause is unknown and symptoms include disturbances of vision, speech, balance, and coordination. There is no cure, but some drugs can reduce its severity.

Muon — An elementary subatomic particle carrying a negative charge like an electron, but 200 times bigger than an electron and with a very short existence (a few microseconds) before decaying into an electron, a neutrino and an antineutrino.

Mutagenesis — The formation or development of a mutation.

Mutate — The process of mutation whereby an organism changes in character or quality as a result of a change in its DNA.

Mutation — A change of the DNA within a gene of an organism that results in the creation of a new character or quality not found in the parents of the organism.

N

Nanometre — A billionth of a metre, or 10^{-9} metres.

Natural numbers — The numbers 1, 2, 3, … etc.

N-dimensional — Having up to n dimensions, as in 1-dimension, 2-dimension, 3-dimension, and so on. Up to any number (n) of dimensions.

Nebula — Interstellar dust or gas visible as luminous patches or areas of darkness in outer space.

Nervous system — The brain, spinal cord, nerves and related tissues in a person or animal.

Neuropsychological tests — Tests that uncover relationships between the brain and mental functions such as language, memory and perception.

Neutrino — A subatomic particle with zero charge, near zero mass, and spin of one-half. Neutrinos come in three varieties — electron neutrino, muon neutrino, and tau neutrino. They can change from one type to another as they travel through space. When first proposed in the 1930s, neutrinos were thought to have no mass, but now scientists believe they do have mass.

Neutron — An uncharged elementary particle that has a mass similar to a proton. Protons and neutrons are present in the nucleus of all atoms (except hydrogen which only has one proton and no neutrons).

Nuclear physics — The physics of atomic nuclei and their interactions, with particular reference to the generation of nuclear energy.

Nucleotides — The basic chain link of a DNA or RNA chain composed of a backbone, phosphate sugar part, and a purine or pyrimidine base linking part. The four nucleotides Adenine, Thymine, Cytosine and Guanine are the building blocks of the genetic code.

Number field — The totality of all numbers and expressions that can be constructed from an algebraic number by repeated additions, subtractions, multiplications, and divisions. Examples are the set of all Real numbers or all Rational numbers (fractions).

Number theory — One of the oldest branches of pure mathematics, and one of the largest, concerning questions about numbers, usually meaning whole numbers or Rational numbers (integers and fractions).

O

Oligonucleotide — A short chain of nucleotides.

Ophthalmology — The branch of medicine that deals with the diseases of the eye and their treatment.

Optical Bench — A long, rigid base with a linear scale upon which are mounted light sources, lenses, mirrors and screens for image formation. Used to conduct experiments with light, e.g. to design telescopes or cameras.

Orangutans — Great apes that live in the tropical rainforests of Borneo (Indonesia).

Osmosis — The tendency of fluids to diffuse through a permeable membrane until the concentration of the fluid is the same on both sides of the membrane.

Ova — A female reproductive germ cell, or egg.

Ozone (O_3) — A form of oxygen gas that has a slight blue colour. Formed by the exposure of air or oxygen to ultraviolet radiation or an electrical discharge. It is unstable, poisonous, powerfully bleaching and smells like the air around a lightning storm.

Ozone holes — Gaps in the upper atmosphere that appear seasonally over the north and south polar ice caps. They are probably caused by the presence of chlorofluorocarbons released into the atmosphere. Chlorofluorocarbons are synthetic gasses used in refrigeration and as propellants in spray cans. Under the influence of ultraviolet radiation, they react with air to destroy ozone in the upper atmosphere, something that seems to be happening above the earth's poles.

P

Paleontology — The study of ancient plants and animals from fossil remains.

PET scanner — A machine that shows what parts of your brain are especially active while you are doing or thinking something. PET stands for Positron Emission Tomography.

Philosopher — A person who studies philosophy, the search for a general understanding of meaning, values, beliefs and existence.

Photodynamic therapy — Treating disease with drugs that are activated by light.

Photofrin — A first-generation photodynamic drug developed by QLT PhotoTherapeutics Inc. in Vancouver, British Columbia.

Photosensitive — Something that is sensitive to light. Upon being exposed to light, it changes or reacts in some way.

Physical anthropologist — A person who studies the physical evolution of the human species.

Physical chemist — A person who studies the physics of chemical reactions and compounds.

Physics — The study of the laws that determine the structure of the universe and all the matter and energy within it.

Pi or π — A mathematical constant that is roughly 3.14159… and represents the ratio between the radius and circumference of a circle. Pi is a transcendental number, which means it keeps on going and the digits never end or repeat in a pattern.

Pink Salmon — A Pacific salmon also known as humpback salmon.

Pollen — Fine powder-like material produced by the anthers of seed plants.

Polygon — A plane figure with a number of sides, such as a square (4) or a hexagon (6).

Polyhedron — A solid bounded by polygonal faces, such as a tetrahedron (4 triangular faces) or a cube (4 square faces).

Polytope — Higher dimensional versions of a hypercube.

Population explosion — The rapid geometric expansion of a biological population of animals (including people).

Population crash — The sudden fall of a biological population due to natural causes.

Precursor-RNA — An intermediate form of RNA that is one of at least six kinds of RNA involved in the process of transcribing the genetic code from DNA to make protein molecules.

Prism — A transparent body usually made of glass in a triangular shape and used for separating white light or other electromagnetic radiation into a spectrum.

Protein (chain, or molecule) — A large complex organic molecule composed of one or more chains of amino acids. Proteins are fundamental components of all living cells and include many substances such as enzymes, hormones, antibodies and cell wall structures.

Proton — An elementary particle that is stable, has a positive charge and can be found in the nuclei of all atoms.

Psoriasis — A noncontagious skin disease characterized by recurring reddish patches covered with silvery scales.

Psychological subject — A person who participates in a psychological experiment usually involving some test of perception, memory, behaviour or other cognitive function.

Psychology — The science that studies behaviour and thinking.

Pythagorean theorem — A theorem in geometry that states, given a right triangle, the sum of the squares of the lengths of the legs is equal to the square of the length of the hypotenuse.

Q

Quantum mechanics — A mathematical system of describing the behaviour of very small particles such as atoms and molecules. Quantum mechanics cannot describe precisely where a particle will be. Rather it expresses the probability of the particle's being someplace at a particular time.

Quantum theory — A relatively modern theory of physics, which is based on the idea that certain properties such as energy occur in discrete amounts or quanta.

R

Radiation — Energy travelling in the form of electromagnetic waves or particles — for example, light or neutrons or X-rays.

Radioactive nuclear pile — The core of a nuclear reactor in which a controlled fission reaction takes place. A source of neutrons.

Rainforest — The tropical jungle that girdles the earth at equatorial latitudes and typically has rainfall greater than 2.5 metres per year. Temperate rainforests also exist in the North American Pacific Northwest, Chile, and New Zealand.

Rational numbers — The set of all real integers and fractions. "Rational" comes from the word "ratio" because any rational number can always be written as the ratio of two numbers, i.e. fractions.

Reaction dynamics — A field of chemistry concerned with the motions and energies of molecules during the course of a chemical reaction.

Relativity — A mathematical system of mechanics developed by Einstein in the early 1900s. It is based on the idea of describing the motion of a body in a manner that is independent of the motion of any observer who may be studying the body. In other words, no absolute frame of reference exists.

Retrieving a memory — The process by which the brain recalls memories, which it has previously encoded.

Rhombus — A rhombus is a squashed square. It has sides of equal length.

Ricker Curve — A mathematical model of fish population dynamics developed by William Ricker and used to determine allowable fish catches worldwide.

RNA (ribonucleic acid) — A molecule that is part of the biological system in a cell that decodes instructions in DNA.

Rotational energy — The energy in a particle, atom or molecule arising from its spin.

S

Salamander — Small lizard-like amphibians of the order *Caudata*, having porous scaleless skin and four, often weak or rudimentary legs. Most salamanders are amphibian, spending their adult life on land in damp places, but returning to the water to breed.

Sample group — A randomly selected group of subjects for an experiment. It could be people, rabbits, bacteria, genes, rocks or anything. The important thing is that they are chosen to represent the typical variability found in the total population from which the sample group is chosen.

SAT (Scholastic Aptitude Tests) — National university-entry level exams taken by high school students wishing to study in universities in the United States.

Semantic memory — The memory of meanings, understandings, and other knowledge — in contrast to episodic memory.

Simulation — An imitation or a representation of one system by another, as in a computer model of the weather.

Singularity — An infinitely massive point in space.

Sinusoidal oscillations — A simple repeating wave pattern.

Site-directed mutagenesis — A technique developed by Michael Smith that allows geneticists to make a genetic mutation precisely at any spot in a DNA molecule.

Snowshoe hare — A medium-sized rabbit with large furry feet that lives throughout the northern latitudes. The snowshoe hare's fur is brown in summer and white in winter.

Social behaviour — The relationships and behaviours among individuals in a community of animals.

Sockeye — A type of salmon native to the Pacific Northwest, characterized by very bright red oily flesh.

Solar mass — An astrophysical unit that is the mass of our sun (Sol). A solar mass is about 330,000 times the mass of the earth.

Solid state physics — The study of the physical properties of solids such as crystals, rocks, gems, and so on.

Spallation — In nuclear physics, the process through which a heavy nucleus emits a large number of nucleons as a result of being hit by a high-energy proton or cosmic ray.

Spawners — Mature adult mating fish.

Spawning grounds — The shallow creek beds where female salmon lay eggs that male salmon then fertilize.

Spectrogram — The photograph of a spectrum that is obtained with a spectrograph.

Spectrograph — A device that is a spectrometer with a camera mounted on the eyepiece so that you can take photographs of spectra (see definition of spectrum below).

Spectrometer — A device that measures the angle, wavelength or energy of light or other type of radiation.

Spectroscopy — The study of radiant energy emitted or absorbed by a burning chemical.

Spectrum (spectra) — The distribution of radiant energy emitted or absorbed by a substance, as in a rainbow.

Spherical harmonic expansion — A computational technique developed by Roger Daley for atmospheric simulation models of weather patterns.

Structural brachiators — Animals that swing from branches with their arms, like monkeys and orangutans.

Superconductivity — A property or phase of some materials at very cold temperatures in which the material's electrical resistance drops to zero, and they acquire the ability to carry electric current with no loss of energy whatsoever.

Superstring theory — The idea of describing the building blocks of matter with tiny line-like strings instead of point-like particles and waves.

Synthetic — Something produced in a laboratory. Not naturally occurring.

T

T-cell — A principal type of white blood cell that is responsible for identifying foreign antigens in the body and activating other immune cells to attack the antigens.

T-cell receptor — A protein structure on the surface of a T-cell that is a specific match for one of trillions of possible eight-amino-acid protein chain particles derived from invading viruses and other foreign material in a body.

Test tube — Small glass tubes with one sealed end. Used by chemists and biologists to conduct small experiments.

Thymus — A small glandular organ behind the breastbone; part of the immune system responsible for T-cell development.

Toxin — A poison, usually a protein, produced by living cells and capable of causing disease or killing other cells.

Tracer atoms — Radioactive isotopes of atoms that have been substituted for normal atoms in biological molecules so that the molecules will become mildly radioactive and detectable by various experimental methods.

Transcendental numbers — In mathematics, any irrational number that is not an algebraic number. Such numbers have endlessly expanding values that never repeat such as π (3.14159…) and e (2.718282…).

Translational energy — The energy in a chemical reaction arising from the motion of atoms or molecules from point A to point B.

Triple-axis neutron spectroscope — The spectroscope developed by Bert Brockhouse for which he won the Nobel Prize in 1994.

Trisomy — The tripling of a chromosome during conception. Trisomy results in genetic conditions such as Down syndrome.

t-RNA (transfer-RNA) — One of a group of RNA molecules involved in the transcription of the genetic code from DNA into protein molecules.

V

Velocity — The rate of change of an object's position over time.

Verteporfin — The pharmaceutical name for the photosensitive compound benzoporphyrin derivative used in the treatment of certain eye diseases.

Vertex — A point in a geometrical shape that is at the end of a line or is the intersection of two or more lines — for instance, the corner of a cube or a square.

Vibrational energy — The energy arising from the in and out stretching of chemical bonds in a molecule .

Virus — A simple submicroscopic parasite that causes disease in animals and plants. Viruses consist of just RNA or DNA within a protein coat. They can only replicate inside a host cell, so they are not considered to be living things.

Vole — A rodent much like a mouse but with shorter legs and a heavier body.

W

Wavelength — The distance between one peak of a wave of light, heat, or other energy and the next peak. A measure of the colour or energy of radiation or light. Long wavelengths are red and of low energy. Short wavelengths are blue and beyond. The shorter the wavelength, the higher the energy content of the wave.

Weather satellite — A satellite orbiting the earth and collecting information about the atmosphere with various cameras and sensors that can be used to predict the weather.

Weather forecaster — A person who predicts the weather based on historical and present conditions.

Wildlife biologist — A scientist who studies animals in the wild.

Wormhole — A theorized rift in the space-time continuum; the rift leads to a parallel universe.

XYZ

X and Y chromosomes — The chromosomes associated with male and female characteristics. Females have two X chromosomes, while males have one X and one Y chromosome.

X-ray — A powerful form of radiation similar to visible light, but with a shorter wavelength. X-rays can pass through solids and act on photographic film as light does.

Zoology — The study of animals.

Index